Moustafa El-Guindy was born in Egypt on August 10, 1943. He grew up in Cairo; since youth, his passion for literature has been overwhelming, and he was deeply influenced by the great writers of Egypt like Taha Hussein and Najib Mahfouz (Nobel Prize 1988). Later in 1961, he joined the University of Cairo, getting his degree as a biochemist in June 1965. During this time, he started to publish his articles and poems in Egypt. In 1969, he moved to Brazil, where he worked as a university professor. Now, he lives in the beautiful city of Murrieta, CA, USA.

Moustafa published many literary works, articles, poems and books in Egypt, Brazil and the United States.

Moustafa El-Guindy

TEARS ON THE EUPHRATES

AUSTIN MACAULEY PUBLISHERS™

LONDON * CAMBRIDGE * NEW YORK * SHARJAH

This is a work of fiction. Names, characters, businesses, places, events, locales, and incidents are either the products of the author's imagination or used in a fictitious manner. Any resemblance to actual persons, living or dead, or actual events is purely coincidental.

A CIP catalogue record for this title is available from the British Library.

ISBN 9781035834334 (Paperback)
ISBN 9781035834341 (Hardback)
ISBN 9781035834365 (ePub e-book)
ISBN 9781035834358 (Audiobook)

www.austinmacauley.co.uk

First Published 2024
Austin Macauley Publishers Ltd®
1 Canada Square
Canary Wharf
London
E14 5AA

Chapter 1

Pike Place Market is one of the most appealing attractions of the beautiful city of Seattle. Overlooking the Elliott Bay Waterfront on Puget Sound, the fascinating long and old building that extends from Pike Street northwest to Virginia Street is the most popular tourist destination in the city and the 33rd most visited tourist attraction in the world. The building, inaugurated on 17 August 1907, is the destination of thousands of visitors every day, especially on the weekends. The colourful fruits, vegetables, and flowers on sale in the booths add beauty and an air of liveliness to the place. Across the street, many stores, shops, bars, and restaurants make the site the perfect destination for the whole day, and that was where Omar and Rania chose to spend Saturday 9 May 1981, with their children.

Omar Assad El-Dahany was an Iraqi doctor who graduated from the University of Baghdad Medical School. After getting his Ph.D. from the University of Cairo, his mentor in Egypt, Professor Mahmoud Abdel-Akher, encouraged him to pursue his research at the University of Washington as a senior fellow. After two years of hard work, Omar concluded his work at the university and was awarded the last two weeks of his two years stay in USA to enjoy America before leaving the country. Omar and Rania, his wife, decided to start their vacation by visiting their favourite spot in the city, the Pike Place Market. They arrived about ten o'clock in the morning; Omar left the car at a parking lot on Stewart Street and then he and his wife walked to the market with their children, Khaled, three years and six months old and Dina, who had just turned two years old. It was Saturday, and the market was crowded, looking like the whole population of Seattle decided to do the same thing on the same day. However, that was the way the Al-Dahany liked the market, full of life, people, and joy.

The family started, as always, by the Pike Place Fish Market, where they enjoyed watching the workers calling the clients in a very artistic way as they tossed the fish, customers had purchased, among themselves.

On this day, a few minutes later, Omar told Rania that he needed to go to the bathroom and moved in the direction of the restrooms. Rania, who was carrying Dina and was distracted by the surrounding people, did not notice that Khaled had followed his father. Omar also wasn't aware that Khaled was behind him, so when he turned left and entered the restroom, he didn't notice that the boy continued walking in the direction of the lower post alley entrance until the end of the building. Suddenly, Khaled found himself out of the building, in the street, alone and began crying and calling for his father.

"Dady baba, Dady Omar, where are you?"

Quickly, several adults gathered around, and some started to call 911, while others tried to comfort the frightened child.

At that moment, a man came from inside the market and embraced the child, saying, "Calm down, I will take you to your father. He is waiting for you, just stop crying." Then he turned to the people, saying, "It is okay, he is safe now."

The onlookers, relieved, dispersed, and no one noticed that the man carrying Khaled disappeared into the crowd.

When Omar returned from the bathroom, he found Rania dashing about the market's aisles, shouting "Khaled! Khaled! Where are you?" Minutes after Omar had left, she realized that her son wasn't near her and panicked, jerking her head about rapidly and swerving around in every direction yelling his name. Many people put them self to help her looking for the kid in the stores, some went up others went down guessing that the kid might have gone there, but they found nothing. When Rania saw Omar, she threw herself upon him, crying, "Khaled is not here, I don't know where he has gone. When I looked, he wasn't here anymore."

Abruptly jolted by his wife's agony, Omar started running in all directions inside and outside the market. Many volunteers joined him to help look, yelling Khaled's name and asking everyone, but the child had disappeared into thin air. Noticing a police car stationed on the other side of the street, Omar rushed over begging "Please, officer, my son, my son, officer. Khaled officer, please help me." He was extremely agitated and unable to connect his words.

"My son, my son is gone, I can't see my son, the market officer, my son, Khaled." One of the officers got out of the car and hugged Omar, trying to calm him down.

"Please, sir, calm down and tell me what happened? How can I help you?" The officer asked.

Omar answered crying, "My son, I lost my son, disappear in the market, please officer, my son."

The officer questioned, "How old is your son?"

"Three years old, he is a small kid, Khaled, my son Khaled, where are you, son?"

When the police officer understood that a child in this age had disappeared, he turned to his partner warning. "Emergency, three years old child missing, ask for support."

The police officer rushed with Omar into the market to join the search while his partner was passing the alert to the dispatcher.

"Three years old kid missing in Pike Place Market, asking for support, unit 32 to dispatcher."

Time passed and it became clear that the child was no longer in the market or anywhere nearby. After two hours of exhaustive searching, the officers and the others who joined them later, approached Omar and one of them said in a wounded voice, "Sir, I am really sorry, but there is nothing we can do here. We should go to the station now to make a missing person's report for the child in order to start a wider and more effective search."

In the station, Omar and Rania were devastated. Rania felt unwell, and the police had to call an ambulance to take her to the emergency room. Meanwhile, Omar, with great difficulty, was filing a missing child report. The officers in the station did their best to help him, and they brought warm milk for the baby and a female officer offered to take care of her. They promised to make every effort to find the boy. They immediately released the information with Khaled's photo and a description of his clothes and physical characteristics. They also released the news to the media asking the public for help. Almost at the end of the day, the police received a call from the hospital. "Mrs Rania had been medicated; she will be transported by ambulance to her home."

Receiving this message, the police officer advised Omar, "There is no reason to stay here anymore, it is better to rush home to take care of your wife, one officer will drive your car home."

At the same time his parents were frantically searching for him, Khaled was crying desperately in the cab of an 18-wheeler truck, driven by the man who had taken him from the market. Donald McCoolen drove on Interstate I-5 as fast as he could without attracting attention, heading for his home in Everett, thirty miles north of Seattle. McCoolen, who was forty years old, had been married for seven years, and his wife Verona was in despair at their failure to have a child. Three years after they married, they consulted a doctor and tried a couple of fertility treatments without success. Lately, they have been contacting local and foreign adoption agencies in search of a child. When he saw the lost boy in the market, he didn't hesitate; he had grabbed him saying that he would take care of him and rushed to his truck that was parked close by on Western Avenue and hurried through the downtown streets to reach the freeway before the police arrived on the scene. When, minutes later, the child started crying, calling for his father and mother, McCoolen tried to calm the boy, telling him that they were going to the boy's home where his parents would be waiting for them. About half an hour later, the truck took the exit to Hewitt Avenue in Everett heading to the McCoolens' home. Arriving home, Donald drove the truck into his yard and stopped as close to his back door as he could. Stepping into the yard to meet her husband, Verona was stunned to see Donald carrying a small sleeping child in his arms.

"Donald, what is this? Whose child is this?" Verona asked, clutching her fist against her neck.

"Shh, not so loud," Donald said, "just calm down. Come inside and I'll tell you everything." In the house, he placed the boy on the sofa, taking care not to wake the boy up, then turned to his wife and said, "I found this kid lost in the marketplace, and I snatched him, telling the people that I would return him to his family and drove directly here."

Her eyes going wide, Verona said, "What do you intend to do? How are we going to explain this? How the hell can you be sure that the police won't find out about us?"

"Don't worry, no one in the place will remember my face, and I fled the scene before the police arrived. There's no reason for anyone to suspect us; just keep calm and let me handle the situation. You wanted a child so much, so I got one for you."

"And now how are you going to handle this?"

"Just keep him quiet for now. Use your sleeping pills—in small doses, of course—to keep him unaware of what is happening until I figure out what to do."

Her eyes beginning to glisten, Verona asked, "Do you think we will be able to keep him?"

"Of course, we will," Donald replied, lifting his chin as he looked at his wife. "He is ours now. We wanted a kid badly and now we have him; you think I will let him go?"

Verona sat staring at the boy, soaking in his face. "What a beautiful child. Donald, I will be a good mother. I will take care of him." Rushing into their bathroom, she removed a sleeping pill from its container, broke it in two portions, prepared a cup of water, and left them close to the boy.

When the sun illuminated the house on Sunday, Rania was sitting on the sofa in front of the door waiting for somebody to enter, bringing her son to her. It was impossible for her to believe that she had lost her son. The idea was unacceptable, the pain was unbearable, and the fact was impossible to be admitted. Khaled was there at the market looking for them; the employees of the market closed the door and left him inside; he must be crying from hunger and cold; he must be terrified to find himself alone in the dark. She jumped up and rushed into the kitchen to prepare Khaled's breakfast with the hot tea with milk he liked very much. Rania called Omar, who had spent the night outside of the house waiting for his son.

"Omar, let us take breakfast to Khaled, he must be there. I am sure he is there. We shouldn't have left yesterday. We shouldn't abandon our kid and leave him alone. Let us go."

Omar was already in the car. They drove to Pike Street, parked nearby, and went to the market. The market was closed, and they had to wait. Once the door opened, they rushed inside and started looking. They searched everywhere; they went from booth to booth and asked every person they met, but they got nothing. No one could give them any information at all to help. Everyone they met was distraught and saddened for them, but no one recalled anything connected to Khaled's disappearance. Tired and unable to concentrate, Rania and Omar sat close to the door of the market waiting for Khaled to show up, covering the food well to keep it hot, and maintaining the hope alive.

Rania's eyes fixed upon every person as they appeared, hoping she or he would be holding Khalid's hand or at least have some information about his whereabouts. She couldn't understand how she could have lost her son in Seattle, the city she had learned to adore even before coming.

She remembered when Omar's professor, Dr Abdel Akher, encouraged them to move to Seattle. He said, "It is one of the best places to live in America; it is beautiful, charming, and safe city. Your kids will love to grow up there."

And they did, they had been happy since the first day. In the airport, when it was observed that they were troubled by two small kids and a big volume of luggage, they received the help of everyone; even ordinary passengers insisted on helping them until they reached the hotel.

On the second day after his arrival, Omar went to the huge building of Health Sciences of the University of Washington to meet Professor Walton Haig, with whom he planned to work for two years. The meeting with Professor Haig was fantastic; the professor welcomed them and offered his help to find a place for them to live. Rania and Omar found a house in Bellevue to the north of Seattle. Their house was located in the vicinity of a vast park loaded with huge trees that Khaled called the jungle. He used to get up early in the morning, eat his breakfast, collect some of his toys and rush to the park, yelling to his mother, "I am going to the jungle."

Tears dropped from Rania's eyes, and she fell into a desperate crisis. She wept from the bottom of her heart and called Khaled as intensely as she could. Omar hugged her and tried to give her and himself some hope.

"Be patient, he will be back. A father or a mother who loves their kids will find him, and they will think about us and will bring him back."

People gathered around them and tried to give some hope and support, but Rania could neither hear nor see anything. For her, time had stopped the day before at 10:00 a.m. and so had life. Now, nothing would move until Khaled came back. Omar sat beside her, blank-eyed and incredulous. For two marvelous years, he had lived in Seattle, he had every reason to expect a happy end to his stay.

Omar went back to his first days in the university, remembering how, when he took over his project, the professor advised him that he was concerned because the project wasn't going well, and the results were inconsistent.

"I decided to transfer this project to you," the professor told him, "Because you were highly recommended by Professor Abdel Akher, and I badly need the results to be able to renew the research grant. Something is wrong and we are not able to move on, so please do your best."

What the professor didn't expect was to have Omar return to him with a perfect identification of the problem and the right solution in less than one month; after that, it was easy to complete the project and renew the funding.

Omar was truly proud of his work at the university; the result generated an important publication that was greatly appreciated by the scientific community. The work was also valued by Omar's university in Baghdad, and he was awarded more labs to follow up with his work. Now, he was starting his two weeks' vacation and the last thing he could imagine was to be sitting on the kerb of the Pike Place Market waiting for his missing son.

The night returned, but not Khaled. A police car parked near them, and the officers got out of the car and approached the almost comatose couple. The police officers had already been informed about the situation, and the female officer came closer to Omar and said, "Sir, we know how difficult it is for you and your wife, but staying here will not help. We know that your child is not in the market and not even close. We have dusted this place for fingerprints, and there is not a trace of him. Go home and we promise you, we will keep searching. We will do our best to find your child for you."

Crying, Rania answered, "How can I leave my baby alone? He might be hungry or feeling cold. I can't leave him."

It was hard for both officers to hold back tears. The other officer said, "We don't know if he is alone or with somebody. You go home and I promise we will not rest until we solve this case. You need to get some rest."

Omar agreed with the officer and advised his wife, "We need to go home; we need to take care of Dina. We left her with the neighbours, and they must be waiting for us."

Reluctantly, Rania agreed, and they went home.

On Sunday, Donald woke up early thinking about the child. A little time later, Verona came with two cups of coffee and joined him. After a while, she asked, "What is on your mind?"

"Do you remember that adoption guy who confided in us that he smuggled kids from South America across the border? I believe that he is the exact guy to help us."

"You are right," Verona agreed. "He must know how to help in this kind of situation. Why don't you give him a call? What was his name?"

Donald picked an agenda from the phone table and searched for the name. A minute later he answered, "His name is Chick Denney. I'll call him."

Donald picked up the phone and called the man. After a brief chat, he turned to his wife and said, "The guy is in Texas; he will be able to visit us only on Thursday the 12th, so be careful. No one should suspect, no visitors and you never leave home. Keep him sleeping all the time. We can't afford to make any mistakes."

Verona immediately agreed. "Trust me, I will be very careful. We will never lose our baby. What name are we going to call him?"

"We can give him any name we wish; he is ours now. What name do you want?"

"What you think about Donald Jr.?"

"No, no, leave my name out of it. Find another name."

"I like Jonathan, Jonathan McCoolen."

"Okay, that is nice," Donald replied. "Jonathan McCoolen is good."

Verona and Donald spent the days between Sunday and Thursday hidden in their house. Verona never left and stayed close to the boy all the time, keeping him continually asleep or dazed. Donald left only twice to buy food, always at night and taking care not to be noticed. On Thursday, he got up at 6:00 knowing that the man he wanted to speak to would be in his house only at noon. He spent the time pacing back and forth in the living room like a big animal in a small cage. Right on time, Chick Denney knocked on the door, and Donald welcomed him. "Hi, Chick, did you have a good trip?"

"Yeah, it was nice, but I don't have anything for you yet. That is the reason I didn't call you," Denney answered.

Donald was anxious to tell the broker what he really wanted from him, but he lacked the courage. Instead, he asked, "Tell me, when you bring the kids the way you told me, I mean, through the border, how do you resolve the legal issues?"

Chick Denney wondered about the question and responded with one of his own. "What is your problem with that? We haven't found the kid yet. Of course, we help with the documentation."

Chick, having the experience of being a smuggler, smelled the odour of something suspicious; it was clear for him that Donald had much more to say, and he decided to push him hard: "What is wrong with you? I don't think that you called me on Sunday in such a hurry and asked me come here directly from the airport to ask these worthless questions. Why don't you tell me what is your problem, once and for all?"

Donald answered, "I need the documentation."

"What the hell will you do with the papers?" Chick asked. "You need the kid first."

Donald said, almost whispering, "I got the kid."

"Did you hire another person?"

"No, I didn't." That was all that Donald was able to murmur.

Chick looked at him, lost for a moment, and then burst out: "What? The kid from the marketplace— was that you? How did you do it?"

Donald begged him to lower his voice and started to explain. "The kid came to me; he was lost, and I picked him and left the place unnoticed."

Chick warned him, "It is in all the newspapers, radios and TVs, flyers are everywhere, and people are searching all around. You are in big trouble."

"We were very smart, no one suspects us. Now, I need your help; I have nobody else I can trust."

"I don't work for trust, especially when the people are in trouble," Chick snubbed answering in a cold voice. "I work for money."

"I will pay; I need your help. How much that will cost?"

Chick kept thinking for a while, then replied, "Twenty thousand plus expenses."

Donald was shocked by the number, he commented, "That's a lot of money," when he saw the threatening look that Chick pointed to him, he completed, "But I will pay, I will, how we will do that?"

"You must get this kid out of here immediately. Soon, the cops will reach your house and they will find out. You must take the kid as far away as you can."

Thinking for a couple of minutes, Chick came up with an idea. "Find a way to cross the border into Mexico and stay there. I can give you an isolated place where you can stay until I finish the papers for you; it will take about three weeks.

I will meet you there. Give me half of the money tomorrow and the other part you must have when I meet you in Mexico."

Donald asked anxiously, "How will you deal with the situation?"

"What name have you given him?" Chick asked.

Donald answered, "Jonathan McCoolen."

Chick wrote the name on a small piece of paper, then said, "I will find a way to get adoption papers in your name from Brazil, I already have your and your wife's information. How old is the kid?"

Donald tried to guess. "Three or four, I think so."

Chick resumed his orientation. "At the border, when you come back, you will get a temporary permit for him based on the adoption papers. Once you are inside the country, we will finish the adoption process. Will you be able to take him out of the country?"

Donald said, "Sure I will. I have carried a lot of goods to and from Mexico. Give me the address there and I will leave as soon as I can."

"Good. I have got to go. I will be here tomorrow to get the money and to give you the directions."

Chick left and Donald felt relieved. He called Verona and told her, "Chick Denney advised us to leave the country until he brings the adoption papers. We will have to go to Mexico. I am going to check if any of my clients need transport to Mexico or to any city on the way to Tijuana. Be careful with the kid."

Later, about dinner time, Donald came back, tired, and hungry. Verona met him and asked worriedly, "Did you find anything good?"

"Put the food on the table. We can talk while we eat."

She ran to the kitchen and set the table as quickly as she could. After he was already eating, Donald started to tell her what he had achieved. "I couldn't find anything ready to be transported right away, but my clients in the Pacific Electronic Company told me that their branch in Palo Alto needed to transport electronic equipment and machinery to Mexico City."

"What did you do?"

"I took the job of course. We need that. We will be leaving on Saturday. It is a good day because many cars cross the border then, so the control is not very tough." He handed Verona an envelope and said, "Here is six thousand dollars. Add to them, four from the money we have in the safe to make the first instalment for Chick, keep the envelop ready, when he comes tomorrow. Be sure to have all the money that is left in your purse when we leave; I need to pay him ten more grand in Mexico.”

Verona got the envelope and hurried to prepare the money. Shortly after dinner, they heard the child crying. They rushed to the room where he was kept hidden where they found him crying and calling for his father, mother, and sister one after the other. Verona hugged him and told him that they would be here soon, but he had to stop crying and just wait. She gave him food and fruit juice.

“Did you give him a sleeping pill yet?” Donald asked.

“It is already in the juice,” Verona said.

A little after eating, the boy was sleeping again. The couple spent a long time looking at him. He was a beautiful child, and they were starting to feel that he belonged to them in spite of the intense search the authorities were conducting across the state.

Friday at noon, Chick Denney knocked on the door. Donald welcomed him, saying, “Perfect timing; it is exactly 12:00.”

Chick answered icily, “When it is about money, I am never late. Did you get the cash?”

“Sure,” Donald said. He dashed to their bedroom. “Get the money from the safe, please,” he asked Verona.

She already had the envelope with the money in her hand. He grabbed it and hurried back to Chick, saying, “Exactly ten thousand in small bills, as you requested.”

Chick started talking while he was verifying the money. “You need to leave as soon as you can. You will cross the border and in Mexico, don’t stop in Tijuana. On 20, go left to Mexicali, drive until you meet Highway 40. Go all the way down to Guaymas-Sonora. Keep going south until you reach Sanchez Taboada. On the corner of Calle 7, there is a place called Calle Mirador. It is very isolated and safe. A room has been reserved for you there; you just need to call to let them know when you will arrive, and don’t forget to pay for the room.” Chick handed him a sheet of paper with a map and the telephone number of the resort. Then he asked Donald, “When will you be leaving?”

“Tomorrow, I am leaving early in the morning.”

"That is good, because the flyers are already awfully close to you. It is better to speed up."

"Sure, I will. Tomorrow, I am not here anymore."

"Okay, I got to go. Of course, if anything goes wrong, you will never mention anything about us. You don't want your beautiful wife to be a widow early. Am I clear enough?"

Donald answered almost voicelessly, "Yes, you are, I get the message. Everything will be okay, don't worry."

Chick left and Donald advised Verona, "We need to prepare our bags now. We need to leave early. I want to be out of the state before sunrise."

Verona replied, "Everything is almost done. I started to prepare the bags yesterday when you were out."

Heaving a sigh, Donald said, "That was very smart. Then we will be able to leave really early."

At 03:30 on the morning of Saturday, 16 May, Verona and Donald were driving their 18-wheeler truck, on the road to Palo Alto with the boy. Donald decided to avoid I-5, at least inside the state of Washington. Instead, he took 405 heading to Yakima by way of I-90. There, he merged onto 84 back to I-5. He knew that he would have to drive two more hours, but his intention was to escape the rigid police control on I-5 on the border with Oregon. His plan worked well; he was only stopped once by the police close to Yakima. One of the police officers examined his document while the other tried to check the cabin where Verona was resting. She pretended she had just woken up at this moment and was still trying to dress appropriately. The child was sleeping in a box hidden under the seat where she was sleeping. The police officer was embarrassed and quickly told his partner that everything was okay. Soon they were released and two hours later, they reached Portland and released sighs of relief.

"Are we safe now?" Verona asked.

"Not yet. We are far from the Washington police where the search is much more intense, but the risk still exists, and we should be careful."

Donald decided not to take any risks, so he drove another four and a half hours until they reached Medford, where he decided to spend the night. They looked for a motel outside of town, and Donald got the key to the room. He stopped the truck at the door of the room and helped Verona carry the boy and got in without being noticed. Once inside, the child woke up and started crying. Donald cleverly got one of the newspapers he kept in the truck with pictures of

Omar and Rania and started talking to the child, pointing to the pictures and saying, "Look, isn't that man your father? And isn't this your mom? We are going to meet them. Now, if you cry, the police will come and take you, and you will never see your mom and dad again. I am taking you to them, just keep quiet."

Donald left and went to a grocery store to buy food and water. After he returned, they ate, and he advised Verona, "Keep him free of pills tonight. Tomorrow, he will need a strong dose."

It wasn't long until everybody was sleeping. On Sunday at 3:00 a.m., they were up and ready to go and were soon on I-5 heading south to Palo Alto. By 11:00, Donald was parking the truck in the parking lot of a motel in Palo Alto, where he left Verona and the boy and went to Pacific Electronic Branch to pick up the goods. At the end of the day, he was back, exhausted, and with the truck loaded. Verona was relieved to see him. She had been having a lot of trouble with the boy, who never stopped crying and asking for his parents. She was also worried about Donald's delay. He asked her to calm down and tried to calm the boy, telling him that he had called his parents and that they were waiting for him and that soon they would all be together. The child believed this, and they ate dinner and all went to bed.

On Monday, 18 May, they were up around 3:00 a.m., and half an hour later, they were getting onto HWY 101 heading to I-5 south. Donald drove eight hours until the border, stopping only to refill the tank and buy food and water. When they approached the border, Donald advised Verona to sedate the boy with a sleeping pill and to hide him in the box under the seat where she slept. Again, she faked being asleep when they arrived. At the border, Donald presented all his documents and the officers, after checking the loading of the goods, found nothing suspicious, and the truck was released. At the Mexican border, they also checked the documents and released the truck to enter the country. Donald decided to keep driving one hour more until Mexicali. When they arrived, it was about 2:00 p.m. He was exhausted and worried about the kid, who had been hidden in the box under Verona's bed in the cabin for a long time. Donald turned to Verona and said with unmistakable relief, "Now we can relax little, and also, we can give this kid a kind of normal life. We should also start to treat him like he really is our son."

"What will we tell him about his parents?" Verona asked.

"I will think of a story to tell him. We must induce him to forget his parents, his name, and where he came from. Just treat him as a son, teach him to call you mom, and call me dad. Insist on it and he will get used to it."

Donald stopped at a motel in Mexicali and got a room. After showering, they headed to a mall close to the motel to eat and have some fun. Verona was exited; it was the first time she felt like a mother holding the hand of a little kid, that is, her son, or the one that he would be. Back in the motel that night, Donald said to Verona, "Let's have a good night's sleep. We don't need to get up early now."

"If we don't need to get up early tomorrow then we don't need to sleep right away," Verona said.

"I know what you mean. I noticed you were turned on the whole time we were in the mall." Her smile indicated that she totally agreed with his observation and she leaned over him, kissing and hugging. He immediately returned her affection with even more passion and desire. Their love-making indicated they were trying to compensate for the tension and fear they had been living all those days. Donald took her as savagely and intensely as he could, not that Verona objected at all; exactly the opposite: she screamed with pleasure and desire and begged for more.

Chapter 2

For Rania and Omar, Monday night was just like the night before, divided between hope and despair, scattered through prayers and tears. On Monday,11 May, early in the morning, Professor Haig and many of Omar's colleagues and co-workers appeared at his home. They had heard about the tragedy from the newspapers or the TV. All of them were shocked and concerned. Doctor Haig embraced Rania saying, "Rania, I am so sorry for that, I am devastated, I assure to you we will do all and every effort to bring your kid back, I communicated with the president of the university, and he personally is contacting the authority to double the effort to finding the kid as soon as possible."

The other professors tried to help the couple to have some hope and offered all the support they could. Once the professor and his aides left, Rania and Omar couldn't stay home without their child. Again, they headed to the market and placed themselves in the same place and kept waiting and hoping the time would go backwards and Khaled would come yelling 'Mama' as he used to, but time never goes backwards, especially when we beg it to.

Monday passed, sad, empty, and colourless, just like Tuesday, Wednesday, and Thursday, and with them went the hope and meaning of life for Rania and Omar. Thursday afternoon, Omar left Rania at the market and rushed to the university to seek help from Professor Haig. Omar was worried because his stay in the United States ended on Saturday, 23 May, the day he had tickets to leave. His meeting with Professor Haig was very emotional and saddening. The professor told him he had gone to the sheriff's office and asked them to help in this case and had been assured that the sheriff was personally on the case. When Omar asked the professor about the possibility of extending his stay in the country until he could find his son, the professor asked Omar to stop by the international office of the university to seek their help on this question.

"Omar, I also was thinking about that, I already called them to see if they can help, and they are waiting for you," said Professor Haig.

At the international office, Omar was accepted with a lot of sympathy and kindness. The personnel were aware of the situation and tried to give him as much support and solidarity as they could, but what they could do was much less than what they wished. Omar was taken to the director, Mr Robert Whiteside, who told him that they had called the police and informed them about Omar's situation and recommended celerity to solve the case. Omar asked about the situation of his visa and if he could extend his stay until his son was found. Mr Whiteside informed Omar that the university had no authority to deal with that and that Omar must contact the immigration services at Tukwila International Boulevard to change the status of his visa.

On Friday, 15 May, Omar went to the immigration services to inquire about his situation and request an extension of stay. The officer directed him to fill out the specific form for his request and promised that in consideration of the situation, the processing of his request would be expedited and he also waived the fee due for the application. The officer asked Omar to check back on Wednesday, 20 May.

Omar went back home convinced that his son was no longer in the market, and that sitting there would not bring him back. Therefore, he decided to look for his son anywhere and everywhere. He didn't know where to start, but he was certain that something must be done. Arriving home, he had a big surprise; many neighbors and colleagues were there thinking the same thing. Omar was deeply moved and he couldn't hold back his tears. Rania also wept desperately. One of the neighbors suggested calling the police to learn about the development of the case and to ask for help and orientation. The sheriff's department assigned many officers and detectives to help organize the search and to provide guidance and protection.

With hundreds of flyers and many posters, Omar and dozens of police officers and volunteers started a comprehensive search in Seattle and the surrounding area. The police launched a missing child search campaign all over the state and sent the data to the national database program. The TV stations put the matter in evidence asking the public for help, but the days passed with no single sign of the child. To all appearances, Khaled had disappeared and left no trace.

Then it was Wednesday. Omar walked into the immigration building full of hope and fear. He left minutes later, his heart broken and soul shredded. The officer explained to him that the problem wasn't under the immigration authority anymore, and that this matter was governed by an international treaty signed by the governments of both the United States and Iraq precluding the extension of stay for any reason. The officer also told him that any exemption of the treaty in his case must be done by the Iraqi government, and even in this case, he must leave the United States and wait for the decision in another country. Omar left in a state of devastation.

When Omar arrived home, Rania rushed to him.

"They will allow us to find our son, won't they? They will let us search for him, isn't that right? They will help us to…"

In tears, Omar interrupted her.

"They will not, and they cannot. We have no choice; we must go Saturday." Her scream pierced the sky.

"No, I will never leave my son alone, no, for the sake of God, no."

Some neighbors who were there to help her also began weeping. Omar sat in a chair looking at the wall without making any sound. He didn't know what to do. How could he leave the country without his son without even knowing if he is still alive?

One neighbor approached him and said, "Mr El-Dahany, we have a good chance to call for help. The local TV will be here once more this afternoon, and you will have the chance to ask the public for help. That used to be highly effective in America."

Omar thanked the neighbor, murmuring, "I will, thank you, I will ask the public, yes, yes, I will."

That afternoon, three local TV stations gathered outside the home to give Omar and Rania the chance to ask for help. It wasn't easy for either one to speak, but through tears, holding Khaled's picture, they implored the public for help. They explained that they must leave on Saturday and pled for any information that might help them find their son before 21 May. The El-Dahanys answered the reporters' questions with great sadness and emotion, then went inside the house and gave themselves up to despair.

Thursday and Friday, the El-Dahanys, the neighbours, Omar's co-workers, and the police exhausted every possibility they could imagine to find Khaled. They searched every wooded area or abandoned site, they went from home to home asking for any lead, they collected the award amount of $50,000.00 for any information that might help find the kid, but in every case, they came back empty-handed. Finally, it was Saturday, and the El-Dahanys had to leave.

Omar and Rania spent the night waiting for a miracle that they knew would not happen and hoping for something they knew was impossible—somebody knocking on the door and bringing Khaled home. Neither the miracle nor the hope was able to change the painful reality. Khaled had gone, and they must leave. At 8:00 a.m., Professor Haig and many colleagues from the university arrived to take them to the airport. Leaving home without their son was agonising. Rania's screams tore the souls of the neighbors who had gathered to say goodbye. Omar's tears expressed his fear that he would never see his son again. The cars moved to the airport in the shape of a funeral convoy.

At the airport, many other co-workers and neighbors were waiting for them. They swore to Rania and Omar that they would not let the case go cold and that they would work with the authorities side by side until their son was found. No one was sure if Rania or Omar were listening, or they were understanding; they were just looking nowhere, moving without direction, and acting as if they were in a state of deep coma. The check-in was expedited, and one attendant embraced Rania before escorting her gently to the gate; Omar and Dina followed her.

In Baghdad, the situation was as dramatic as it was in Seattle. Rania's parents, Galila and Abdel Fatah, were there hoping that the nightmare would end when their daughter and Omar came out of the gate with the two kids. Omar's mother, Fahima, suffered a heart attack two days before the arrival and was in the hospital, waiting more for her grandchild than hoping for recovery. His father, Kareem El-Dahany, decided to stay with her. A huge number of relatives and friends were there praying for a miracle. But nothing of the sort happened, no miracle, no dream, and no hope. It looked like God wasn't listening. Rania and Omar came out of the gate carrying their daughter and burdened by the devastating reality, Khaled was gone. Everybody wept from the heart. The despair of Rania and Omar was heart-breaking; they tried to explain, they tried to apologize, they insisted they always lavished cared on their children and swore they were never careless or irresponsible. No one could tell if they were explaining to the others or themselves.

At home, the fire that was burning their souls inflamed even more. There was the room where Khaled was supposed to live, those were the toys he used to play with when he was one year old, and there was the bed he used to sleep in.

Everything in the residence had some connection to Khaled and was a piece of fire thrown on their burning hearts.

Rania and Omar left home and hurried to the hospital to see his mother and his father. It was a painful moment. Omar rushed to kiss his mother, asking, "How are you doing, Mother?"

The old lady replied in tears, "Tell me about my grandchild. I don't care about myself. Where is my little boy? How could you come without him?"

His father swung between hope and despair.

"Did you look well for him, son? Couldn't he be in some place waiting for help?"

All the sadness and devastation they had been living with since Khaled's disappearance boiled over, and they all wept. Omar tried to explain.

"Forgive me, Mother, I know it is my fault. I should have been more careful with him and with my family, but I failed. I will never forgive myself."

Rania ran to hug him and said through her tears, "It is the fault of both of us. I was there also, and I should have been more careful, but I wasn't, I wasn't."

Omar's mother tried to say something, but the words stuck in her throat, and she started to feel unwell. They called the doctor, and he asked them to wait outside the room. It took about half an hour for the doctor to come out of the room. He advised Rania and Omar to go home, telling them, "I had to sedate her. Her emotions are overwhelming, and it is very risky for her. Better to see her tomorrow; she might be feeling better."

They accepted the doctor's recommendation and left the hospital.

One hour after their arrival at home, they received the visit of Dr Rashid Basheer Bustani, the dean of the school where Omar was a professor. Dr Rashid informed Omar that the president of the University, Dr Gad El-Damaty, was preparing a petition to the Secretary of State of Iraq asking him to communicate with the American Department of State to guarantee that the case would not be allowed to go cold or be forgotten. Dr Rashid also let Omar know that Professor Abdel-Akher was coming from Egypt on Monday to see Omar and Rania and to meet with the Minister of Science and Technology of Iraq to request his help, since the professor and the minister were colleagues in the doctorate program and had remained close friends since then.

Omar was touched, but still hopeless. In despair, he asked the dean, "Do you think my son is still alive?"

The dean affirmed emphatically, "I am sure he is. If something bad had happened to him, they would have found the body. He must be lost or even kidnapped, but the police will find out, somebody will talk or will send some information and they will discover everything."

"And how will we bring him home?" Omar asked.

The dean replied, "Don't worry about that. We can send you to bring him; we are ready for that."

The talk offered a tiny amount of relief to Rania and Omar. They really hoped that Khaled would be found and they would rush to bring him home. They had a glimmer of hope, and that helped them to get some sleep.

On Monday, 25 May 1981, Professor Abdel-Akher arrived in Baghdad and went directly from the airport to Omar's house. The meeting was deeply sensitive. They hugged each other strongly and wept intensely. They were very close, and the pain was tearing both their souls. Professor Abdel-Akher affirmed to Rania and Omar that on Tuesday, 26 May, he would have lunch with Minister Ibrahim Raslan, and that he would plead for the minister to use all the power of the Iraqi government to put intense pressure on the American authorities to solve the case. He told them that the minister was a very close friend and that they had chatted on the phone already about the problem. After two hours, Professor Abdel-Akher left for his hotel, promising that he would see them immediately after his talk with the minister to tell them what happened.

On Tuesday, Minister Raslan received Professor Abdel-Akher in his home for lunch. After welcoming the professor, the minister asked his guest, "Tell me, what happened to our unfortunate fellow in Seattle?"

Professor Abdel-Akher told the minister how Rania and Omar lost their son in the market in Seattle two weeks before they returned to Baghdad, and that the police and the neighbours and co-workers had made great efforts to find the boy, but it wasn't enough. The professor expressed his fear that the case would turn cold, and that the only way to avoid that was to keep the pressure on the police to keep the case open and active.

The minister was touched by the situation and promised to contact the Secretary of State and request that he use all the means to call the attention of the American Government to the case. The minister told Abdel-Akher that he would authorise the university to raise the reward to US$100,000 for any information that helped in finding the boy. They moved to the table and even during lunch they kept talking and thinking about the terrible situation that Rania and Omar were living at the moment.

About 4:00 in the afternoon, Professor Abdel-Akher was back in Omar's house talking to him and Rania about his meeting with the minister. He affirmed to them that the minister would use all the power of the Iraqi government to press the American authorities in order to keep the case active. He also informed them that the minister promised to get the president involved if he believed that that would help.

Rania and Omar were listening and were grateful, but a huge dark cloud inside them was hindering them from being hopeful. They knew that time was crucial in this kind of case and the police in Seattle had told them that the first twenty-four hours are decisive in children disappearance cases, and Khaled had now been missing for seventeen days. Rania wept in despair, saying, "I know I will never see my child again; I know my son is gone. They didn't let us there to look for him because they knew he was gone."

Professor Abdel-Akher hugged her and said, "Never lose hope. I know how difficult it is for both of you. It is now a long time that we have had no information about him, and that is devastating."

After pausing for minute, the professor resumed, "But at the same time, that tells us that the boy is still alive, and that gives us a big hope. Let us believe; we believe in God and for sure He is watching over you and for him now."

Omar added, "But, Professor, if he is still alive, then how is it possible that no one could see him or recognise him after all the publicity that was in the newspapers, radio, and TV?"

Professor Abdel-Akher answered, "That is our hope. Let us believe that someone will discover him and tip the police. We can't lose hope."

Before leaving, Professor Abdel Akher told them, "If we don't receive news about him in a couple of weeks, I will fly to Seattle. I called Professor Haig and he is ready to help me pressure the police and the media until the case is solved."

On Wednesday, Omar decided to go to work in spite of the permission of the school for him to stay home as long as he considered necessary. He was received with a great deal of love and care by his co-workers and colleagues. Soon, he was told that the president of the university would receive him at noon. On time, the president received Omar warmly and expressed his sorrow and sadness. Dr El-Damaty, the president, read to Omar the petition that had been prepared for the State Department and called his attention to the fact that a huge number of professors had signed the petition. The president told Omar that he had an appointment scheduled for Friday to deliver the petition personally to the Minister of the Exterior in the presence of Dr Ibrahim Raslan, the Minister of Science and Technology. Omar expressed his gratitude and thanked the president for his time and attention.

At home, Rania was surrounded by family members, neighbours, and friends. All tried to give her some relief or at least comfort, but it was very difficult. No one knew if Khaled was alive and they should encourage her to keep hoping for his return, or if the boy was already dead and they should try to comfort her for the loss. The fact was that none of that was touching Rania. Her feelings, thoughts, heart, and soul were there in Seattle in the last moment she saw her son a few seconds before he went running after his father to never be seen again.

"How could I let him go? How could I leave my son alone in that place? It is all my fault, it is all my fault, I let my son go, and I left my son alone."

Rania screamed, crying in despair. Her mother rushed over and hugged her, saying, "No, daughter, don't say that don't feel that way, it was an accident."

Rania's father approached and caressed her hair with his hand, as he said, "My grandson is alive, I feel he is, he will be back, my daughter. The police in America are exceptionally good; they will find him. Have faith in God, Rania."

But Rania was very sceptical. *Hadn't too much time already passed for a little kid to survive alone? How could he protect himself from the cold and the wind? Seattle is a cold and windy city. Is he alone or with somebody? And why does this person not return him to the police? Does he still remember her, his father, and his sister? Does he ask about them*? Thousands of questions were spinning unanswered in the head of Rania, increasing her fear about what might be happening with Khaled and leaving her with a heart on fire. Her neighbours and friends were heartbroken. They tried all that they could do to help, but they could do very little, and even the little they offered was ineffective. Rania knew that when she left the United States, she was leaving Khaled forever.

On Thursday, 28 May, Omar headed to the hospital hoping to check his mother out, but arriving there, he had a huge set back. Dr Gaber Saadi, his mother's doctor, told him that she wasn't feeling well. Her blood pressure was very high, and they were fearing the worst. She had been transferred to the intensive care unit, where she would have to stay until they could stabilise her condition. Omar was allowed to see her for just ten minutes, but he was advised not to expose her to any emotional distress. After Omar entered his mother's room with the doctor, he rushed to hug her and told her that all the officials of the Iraqi government were on the case, and that meant, certainly, that good news would be arriving soon.

Briefly overcoming her illness, the elderly woman asked, "Where is my boy? Will I see him again?" Omar rushed to reassure her.

"Sure, Mother, I guarantee that we will receive good news soon. Please, take care of yourself and everything will be okay."

At that moment, Doctor Saadi interrupted the talk and the visit.

"I think that is enough for today. We can't go any further." Then he turned to Omar and said, "You can come to see her tomorrow. She will be better."

Omar kissed his mother and left. Outside the room, he couldn't restrain his emotions, and he broke into sobs like a child.

The doctor took him to his office and tried to help. "Omar, I know what happened, and I can imagine what you are going through. But we can't increase the damage, as I know you have a daughter to take care of, and your mother is not in good health. You have got to be strong. I know it is strange asking you this, since you are as much a victim as anyone, and you need as much help as they do. But at the same time, you are the one that must help everybody else. You have to struggle to avoid more loss in your family."

Omar replied through tears, "I am afraid that I will never see my son again. The police told me that the first twenty-four hours are crucial to finding a missing child. After that, the situation turns difficult, and now twenty days—it is almost impossible. I don't even know if he is alive or dead. I don't know if I am waiting for my son or for his body."

The physician was touched. He prescribed medicine to help Omar control his anxiety and advised him to try to get some rest.

Omar's mother needed the whole week to recover and to regain a condition sufficiently to be released from the hospital. Omar wanted her to stay at his house to be able to take care of her, but she refused and asked him to take her to her home, saying, "You don't need to take care of me. You need to go and find our boy and bring him back."

Chapter 3

On Tuesday, 19 May, Donald and Verona decided to drive to Guaymas Sonora. In this case, they weren't eager to leave early. They were feeling safe and relaxed, so they decided to stop by the mall they had visited the day before. They got a good breakfast for them and for the kid. Donald stopped by a toy store to buy some toys for the child, and he also asked for a specific video game that the clerk of the store had to help him find. Back at the motel, Donald asked the boy to sit beside him and ran the game on the room TV. The game was a terrifying one with a huge monster that devoured a lot of people. After running the game for a while, Donald looked the boy directly in the eyes and said, "Are you seeing that? The monster, that stole your mom, dad, and sister. See how terrible is he? See what he does with the people? Now he wants you, he wants to hurt you." While he was saying this, Donald repeated the most terrifying scenes of the game.

The boy burst into tears and began yelling, "What did he do with mom and dad? What did he do with Dina?"

Donald tried to feed his fear and terror, saying, "I don't know what he did, but I know that he wants to hurt you. I am trying to help you. Never mention your dad, your mom, or your sister again. If the monster hears you talking about them, he will kill you and them as well. Never mention them again until the monster is gone." He gave the boy a couple minutes to digest what he said, then resumed. "We are trying to hide you from the monster. We have to cheat on him to escape. Your name now is Jonathan, and I am your dad and Verona is your mom. That is the way we protect you from the monster."

Reverting to despair, the boy asked, "And when I will see mom and dad again?"

Rapidly, Donald answered, "If you behave well and help me to protect you from the monster, I will try to find them for you. But you have to be a good boy and make the monster believe that I am your dad and Verona is your mom. If you don't behave well, the monster will kill your mom and dad. You have got to help me protect you and them. Will you do that?"

Believing every word, the boy answered, while crying, "I will, I will."

Fascinated, Verona approached Donald and whispered in his ear, "What a brilliant idea, Donald. Now it will be much easier to deal with him."

Donald replied, "Use that all the time, tell him each minute that his name is Jonathan, his mom is Verona and his dad is Donald, insist until he believes, use the monster story each time you feel any resistance."

"I will, trust me. I will take care of him. Now he is my son."

"Fine, we need to go," Donald said and carried their bags to the truck. Holding the boy's hand, Verona followed him.

Donald headed south to Highway 40 and drove for five hours until they reached the city of Ultimo Esfuerzo, during the trip, Verona's voice echoed in the cabin of the car as she spoke to the boy. "Your name is Jonathan, your dad is Donald, and your mom is Verona. Say that, say with me, my name is Jonathan."

Initially, it wasn't easy; the kid had a hard time to understand, and occasionally he resisted. "My name is Khaled." Immediately, he was interrupted by Verona or Donald, who said, "Look, the monster is coming, never say that again. He will kill your mom and dad. Say my name is Jonathan."

The poor child, overwhelmed by fear and distress, rapidly repeated, "My name is Jonathan," and that was what was heard in the truck all during the trip.

In Ultimo Esfuerzo, they stopped to get fuel, food, and some rest. Donald called Calle Mirador and reported that he would be arriving in six hours. Soon, they were back on the road aiming at 15 South. After another five hours, with Donald driving and Verona teaching, they saw the signs for Guaymas; from there to Sanchez Taboada, they needed only ten minutes. At the corner of Calle 7, they saw the sign for the Calle Mirador. Donald was oriented to park the truck in the trucks parking area behind the hotel, at the reception they asked for an additional bed for the child, then they got the key and rushed to the room.

The room was spacious and comfortable. They all were exhausted, so they had a shower, ate the food they bought in Ultimo Esfuerzo, and went directly to sleep.

The following day, Verona and Donald spent the day enjoying the place, which was really fascinating. Guaymas was surrounded by mountains and water. The Mirador was a few steps from the water, with a gorgeous view. It was the perfect place for relaxing and a vacation, and for hiding, as well. Verona and

Donald and their 'son' spent the day on the beach enjoying the sun and the water. At the end of the day, Donald told Verona, "I will be leaving early tomorrow. It is a long trip that probably will take the whole week. Be careful; insist to the kid all the time, his father is Donald, his mother is Verona, and his name is Jonathan. Repeat this as often as you can. It's the same old story: lie, lie, and lie again; the lie becomes true. Is that clear?"

Verona replied with an apprehensive voice, "Yes, it is, I'll do my best."

Donald, sensing her concern, tried to encourage her. "Don't worry. By the time we go back, the situation will be calmer. I read in the newspaper that his family will have to leave the country, and soon everything will be forgotten. Calm down. We have already done the most difficult part."

Verona, feeling a little better, replied, "You are right. Trust me and take care of yourself during the trip."

Donald reminded her, "Be careful with the money we brought for Denny. Is it well hidden?"

"Definitely, I hid it in a safe place. Don't worry about that." Verona snuggled closer in the bed to Donald and said, "I will miss you during the week."

"Me too," Donald answered, "but we still have tonight to enjoy."

Verona jumped all over him, kissing and hugging. Donald wasn't any less eager to make love than her, so he reacted with heat and passion and soon the sound of love-making filled the room.

The next morning, Thursday, Verona was torn between the happiness of being a mother, a feeling that she had yearned for since she got married, and the fear of being alone with the boy and having to turn him into the son she wanted. During breakfast, she did her best to please the child, offering him food, fruits, and sweets. After breakfast they had a very nice walk on the beach, and of course during the tour, she remembered to warn him about the monster and advised him to recall as much as he could that his father is Donald and his mother is Verona. She stopped by a toy store and bought a nice car for him.

Khaled, now Jonathan, spent the afternoon playing with the car. Verona was happy and relieved; she realised that her mission wouldn't be very difficult. In fact, it appeared to be easier than she had imagined. All that she needed to do was to keep watching him playing and reminding him occasionally that his name was Jonathan, and his parents were Verona and Donald, and for sure he would learn.

Verona was enjoying her success and decided to repeat what she had done on Tuesday every day that is, having a nice breakfast with Jonathan, then taking him to the beach and encouraging him to play, run, and swim until he became exhausted. After that, she bought a toy for him and spent the evening watching him playing with his toys until dinner was served. Everything went smoothly and easily; the kid was feeling her warm care, she was enjoying his company, and it was clear they were navigating in the right direction.

On Saturday, 23 May, Verona got up about 8:00 a.m. She called Jonathan and, after taking showers, they went to the restaurant of the hotel for breakfast. The place was full of people enjoying the variety of food offered. Verona seated Jonathan at one of the tables and went to bring the food. Soon she was back with two plates with omelettes, toast, and fruits for her and the boy. She asked Jonathan which kind of juice he preferred, and he chose apple juice, his favourite. Verona brought the juice for him and coffee for her, and they started eating their breakfast.

Suddenly, Verona was torn from her breakfast by a terrifying scream coming from very close to her; it was the boy screaming desperately. "Mama Rania, baba Omar, Mama, Baba, Dina!"

When she turned around to see what was happening, her eyes landed on the big television placed on a table in front of them. The TV was broadcasting the international news from Seattle-Tacoma airport, where a reporter was interviewing Rania and Omar and stating that they were being forced to leave the United States without knowing about their son, who had disappeared two weeks ago.

Verona grabbed the boy to stifle his cries and began whispering in his ear. "The monster, he'll kill your mother if you do not stop crying, stop now. It will come here and kill you; the monster will come. Stop crying now."

And without waiting, she pushed him and began running with him to the room, leaving the food behind.

At the room, Verona continued terrifying the child.

"See what you did? Now the monster is angry, and he will come after you. Now he will gobble up everybody. Your dad Donald went to fight the monster. If you don't stop, the monster will find us."

Fear started to dominate the boy, and he stopped crying and began mumbling, "Dad Donald, fight the monster. The monster is bad. The monster will come."

Verona trembled when she heard someone knocking on the door. She ran to the kid and said, "See? Now hide yourself and call for your dad Donald to save us."

Hiding himself under the blanket, the boy repeated, "Dad Donald, come here, help us. The monster is coming."

When Verona opened the door, two security officers were standing there. They introduced themselves and asked Verona if she and the boy were okay. She explained that the boy had a bad dream about a monster attacking him, and that that was normal every time his father travelled for work. The officers, hearing the kid mumbling about a monster and Dad Donald, believed the story and offered any help she might need. When they left, she couldn't restrain herself and started crying frantically. She went under the blanket and hugged the boy firmly, and both kept crying for a long time.

Verona needed a huge amount of time to recover. She wasn't able to leave the room for the whole day. She was afraid, terrified, and frustrated. She realised that all her teaching and indoctrination during the week had evaporated in seconds when he saw the image of his parents. That meant for her that everything was back to the very beginning and that all the brainwashing she had applied to the boy was in vain. Verona was distraught. She remembered that Donald would be back in two days and he would be disappointed if she failed, and she knew that failing could mean much more than losing the kid. Verona decided to intensify her efforts to condition the boy. She ran the game of the monster on the room's TV and made the kid watch with her, as she insisted:

"Look, Jonathan, the monster is very bad. He will kill your dad and your mom if you mention their names. Don't forget, your name is Jonathan, your dad is Donald, and your mom is Verona. If you don't remember that, the monster will kill everybody."

For hours and hours, the boy had to watch the monster killing people, destroying buildings, and burning everything around. Hours and hours the kid had to listen to Verona reminding him that his name is Jonathan, his dad is Donald, and his mom is Verona.

On Sunday, Verona ordered breakfast to be served in the room. After eating, they went directly to the beach, but in this case, she chose a distant and isolated spot far from the crowd. When the child asked why he wouldn't be able to play with other kids, the answer was obvious, "We are hiding from the monster; he might be close looking for us."

Finally, it was Monday, the day Donald said he would be returning. Verona again ordered breakfast in the room, then spent the day working with Jonathan thinking about Donald. She knew that her husband would be anxious to see what she had achieved in training the kid to be their son, and she wasn't willing to fail. Therefore, she ran the game and made the boy watch while she repeated in his ears uninterruptedly, "Your mom is Verona, your dad is Donald and your name in Jonathan, say that to me, what is your name, your name is Jonathan."

At 7:00 that evening, Verona heard the knock on the door she was waiting for. She jumped from where she was to open the door to Donald. Once he entered the room, she threw herself in his arms and began to cry like a child.

As he hugged her, Donald asked, "How are you? Is everything okay? Why are you crying?"

Verona couldn't hold herself back anymore. She told him how the boy had exploded when he saw his parents on the screen, and how she rushed to hide with him in the room. Verona told him about the security officers' visit and how she was able to dupe them by saying that the kid had a bad dream.

Donald hugged her firmly. Then, taking care that the boy couldn't hear him, he said, "Calm down. Now I am here, and I will help you take care of him. His parents are gone already, and it is just a matter of a few days before the story will be entirely forgotten. This kid is ours, and no one will take him away. Just relax and start really feeling that you are his mother."

The tenor of her voice conveying her fear, Verona asked, "Do you think we will be able to do it?"

"Sure, we will. We have to change his mind. But, by teaching him English, we can make him forget his language and he will forget everything about his family."

Verona started to be calmer and asked Donald about his trip. He answered, "It was good. As a matter of fact, it was very good. We made a lot of money, which will help us in our project."

He said the last sentence looking at the boy. Verona understood and said, "Thanks to God. Then you think we are safe now?"

"I do believe that, but we still have to be careful. I thought about that a lot during the trip, and if you agree, I think we should find another place to live."

Verona was taken by surprise. She asked, "What do you mean?"

"I mean move to another city, smaller and quieter."

"Do you think we need to do that?"

"It will be better for us," Donald said, confirming Verona's question. "Moving to another city will avoid questioning and suspicions. The neighbours will believe that he has always been our son."

"How will we do that?"

"I am thinking about calling our real estate agent, Linda White, and discuss with her selling our house in Everett and see what she has available in the cities nearby."

Verona thought for a while, then she said, "If you think it is better, it is okay with me. I will miss that house, but to have a baby, I am willing to do anything."

"You will have the baby," Donald assured her. "I mean, you already have the baby. Just relax and act naturally. He is now Jonathan and he is ours. Now, I will take a shower and we will go to dinner."

Verona, Donald, and Jonathan went to a stylish restaurant located at Benito Juárez Garcia. They acted like a real family. They treated the boy as their son and forced him to call them mom and dad, and the boy, having the image of the monster in his mind, behaved exactly as they demanded. Donald, who was monitoring him all the time, praised him.

"Good, Jonathan, good, this way we can beat the monster, now you can have dessert. Do you like chocolate ice cream?"

"Yes," he answered in a subdued voice.

They finished their dinner and returned home. Later, Donald tried to sleep, but he observed that it would be impossible. Verona had scooted over on his side of the bed, eager to have sex, without being coy or evasive. Turning to her, Donald said, "I see that there is no excuse tonight, not even after driving for eleven hours."

"I put in a lot more hours than that waiting," she replied.

While she was talking, her hands were undermining his resistance. When her mouth took over, Donald succumbed completely. In a few seconds, they were nude and in a complete state of madness. Donald devastated her with power and wildness, and she moaned like a wounded cat, in a few seconds.

Verona's moans turned to screams expressing the mixture she was feeling of pain and pleasure.

After the storm, the two lay on the bed powerless for a while, then Donald turned to her and asked, "Are you happy now?"

Smiling, Verona answered, "For today, it is enough, but just for today." A few minutes later, both were sleeping.

Tuesday, the three of them went to the hotel restaurant to have breakfast. Calm and relaxed, they got a table and had their meal. Donald wanted everybody to see them as a nice and happy family.

Back in the room, Donald called Linda White. "Hi, Linda, it is Donald McCoolen from Everett."

"Hi, Donald, how are you and your wife?" Linda replied.

"We are okay; I am now in Mexico City working, and I am calling to request your help to sell our house."

"That is surprising. Is something wrong with the house?"

"Not at all, the problem is that I am travelling a lot, and Verona is starting to have a problem with that. We are worried she might develop some kind of depression. The doctor's recommendation is to move to a quieter place."

Linda asked, "And do you already have in mind where to live?"

"Not really. We would ask you to help us buy a new home in a smaller city in the area."

"And what about the loan? You will need to finance the new house, is that right?"

"Yes, I will, but I think it will not be a problem. I have good credit, and I am in very good standing with my financial institution. Anyway, I will call them tomorrow to find out."

Linda thought for a moment, then she said, "Buying is not a problem; there are plenty of homes on the market. Selling is the issue, but we might be very lucky. I have a client who has just been hired by Boeing, and he wants a home in Everett, the problem is, how can he see the house?"

"There is a key under the mat close to the back door. You can keep it until the house is sold."

"Do you or your wife have an idea which city you would like to live in, and about the kind of home you would prefer?"

"Not really," he replied, "but we would like to live in a small and quiet city, not very far. The house should have three bedrooms, two or more bathrooms and a good yard."

"What about Kirkland? I have two homes for sale and both fit your description."

"Kirkland is a nice place to live. One of those houses might do."

"Okay, Donald," Linda concluded, "let me work on that and I will get back to you when I have any information. Thank you for calling."

"Okay, Linda, thank you."

The following day, Donald bought many beautiful children's books and a lot of paper and collared pencils and said to Verona, "Keep him busy all the time. Get his language out of his mind. Teach him English. There are a lot of books here for drawing, colouring, and learning. Keep him busy all the time."

"Do you think it will work?" She asked.

"Sure, it will, just do like I say."

Two days later, on Friday, Donald received a phone call from Linda. "Hi, Donald, how is your wife now?"

"Hi, Linda, Verona is better now. She is excited by the idea of moving to a new house."

"I believe I have good news for you. The man fell in love with your house, and when he discovered that your house is walking distance from the factory, about twenty-five minutes, he authorised me to place an offer. He asked me about the price and I informed him about the average in your area, but of course you are free to set the price for your house."

Donald answered with great enthusiasm, "That is very good. I also got good news about the loan; the same company will finance the new house. They recommended making it a pending transaction, so they can liquidate the old loan and approve the new one very quickly."

"Well, then, we are very close. Okay, Donald, talk to Verona and call me later to give me the price of your Everett house."

"Will do, thank you, Linda."

"Take care."

The next day, Donald called the agent, "Linda, Verona, and I see that the right price for the house is ninety-five thousand dollars."

Linda commented, "This is a reasonable price. The prices of similar homes in the area range from 90 to 100,000. I will inform the buyer and come back to you in two days. On Wednesday, 3 June, Linda White called Donald to let him know that the buyer had made a full price offer and now it was up to the seller to decide.

"Great, we accept. What should we do now?"

"I will open the escrow, but I need your decision about the house you will buy, so we can process both operations in the same escrow."

"I will fly to Everett in two days to deal with that."

"Wonderful. I will arrange the appointment to see the homes in Kirkland."

"If you can arrange everything for Friday that would be good for me."

Linda replied, "I think it is possible. What time will you be in, Everett?"

"Around 11:00."

"Good. We can do everything in the afternoon. Is that okay for you?"

"Perfect, see you on Friday."

"Bye, Donald."

Thursday, 4 June, at night, Donald requested the hotel transportation to Guaymas International Airport, to take his overnight flight to Seattle. Friday, 5 June at 11:15 a.m., he entered Linda's office.

"Hi, Linda, I am here. Is everything ready for today?"

"Hello, Donald," Linda said, "nice to see you again. How is Verona?"

"She is not feeling so good," he replied. "I invited her to come with me, but she refused. I hope the move will help her to get better."

"I hope so. Well, I have here some papers for you to sign, and we have appointments to see two homes, one at noon and one at one o'clock."

"Very good, I intend to fly back tonight, I don't want to leave Verona alone."

Donald signed the papers and they left to visit the homes. Donald liked the first house very much; it was very close to what they desired.

After the visits, they returned to Linda's office, and here Linda asked him, "What do you think at home? Did you like anything about what I saw?"

Donald replied, "In fact, I liked the first house very much, but I would like to contact Verona before I give you the final response."

She said, "Sure, you can use the office phone."

Donald called Verona.

"Verona, I do believe I found the perfect house for us. It is three bedrooms, two baths, and a huge lot of seven thousand square feet. It is in Kirkland close to schools, malls, and all that we need."

Ending the call, he turned to Linda and said, "Verona is very excited. You can place the offer. I will put you in contact with my financial agent. He is awaiting your call."

Linda commented, "We are lucky. The price of this house is six thousand less than your house in Everett. This way, you don't have to worry about the down payment.

"Okay, Linda. Please place the offer as soon as you can. I would like to bring Verona to the new house very soon. Can I put you in contact with my financial agent, Robert Warden?"

"Yes, please. I need to talk to him to initiate the processing."

Donald dialled his financial officer. "Hi, Robert, we just found the home we want. My real estate agent, Linda White, will give you the details." He passed the phone to Linda.

After talking to Mr Warden, Linda turned to Donald and said, "Don't worry, I don't see any problems. It will be a smooth and fast transaction."

"Thank you very much, Linda," Donald said and left for the airport.

Chapter 4

Verona was thrilled by the news Donald brought from Everett. She asked, "Then you think that we will be able to return directly to the new home?"

"I am working on that," Donald said. "I am sure we will be able to do it. Our house is almost sold, and we placed a full offer for the one in Kirkland."

"Tell me about the place in Kirkland. Is it nice?"

"It is a beautiful place, called Queensgate. Everything is close; there are supermarkets and drugstores close by, and we are less than two miles from Totem Lake mall."

"Thank you, Donald. You did a great job. I am really excited."

Smiling, Donald said. "Every time you get excited, I get worried."

Verona returned his smile with a significant one and said, "You'd better be."

And she was serious. Donald had to use all his energy and power to make Verona happy.

On Friday, 12 June, Linda informed Donald that his offer had been accepted by the seller and that the escrow was working on both transactions. She also told him that she expected everything to be completed by 27 June, by which time he and Verona should be back to conclude the transactions. On the same day, Donald received another call he also was waiting for, this one from Chick Denney.

"Hi, Donald, it is Denney, Chick Denney. How are you?"

Donald answered anxiously, "We are fine. How are things going with you?"

"Not bad. We may have some delay, but no reason to be worried. I believe that in one week we will get the papers issued. So, stay where you are and wait for me."

"We need to move back around 20 June. Do you think we will be able to?"

"Yes, you will, don't worry. Everything will be fine. Bye."

"Thank you, bye."

On Friday, 19 June, Chick Denney knocked on Donald's door around 10:00 a.m. Verona and Donald were delighted with the surprise. "Hi, Chick," Donald said. "What a great surprise. Tell me, are we all good?"

Chick replied, "Everything is okay. Now, we will go take some pictures of this kid. Did you bring your passports like I asked?"

Verona immediately affirmed, "Sure, we have everything."

Chick requested her to give him the passports, and all of them left to take the boy's picture. After, Chick left them, recommending, "Tomorrow at noon, I will see you in your room. Be ready with the money."

"We will be waiting, the money as well," Donald confirmed.

Saturday at noon, Chick was back with the completed documents. He instructed Verona and Donald, "Pay attention. You have been in Brazil, where you adopted the kid. All the papers are in his name. Everything is here, including his Brazilian birth certificate. He was born on 15 June 1978. They will give you a temporary entry for him at the border, and you will complete the documentation from the immigration in Seattle. You don't need to do that right away; it is better to wait a couple months until everything calms down. You understand, right?"

Donald agreed. "We will wait three or four months. We will be very careful."

Verona came with the money and handed it to Chick. He took the money, counted it, and left.

Early in the morning hours of Monday, 22 June, Verona and Donald and Jonathan were on the road heading to Washington State. They knew it would be a tough four-day trip, but their minds were focused on Nogales, six hours from Guaymas, where they would cross the border. Donald decided to enter the United States through Arizona. He drove onto Boulevard Benito Juàrez and merged with Highway 15 heading north. They spent the six hours thinking and praying. When Donald spotted the border ahead, he told Verona, "Be calm and quiet, act like a happy mom. Prepare the kid. I want both of you smiling."

Verona hugged Jonathan with affection and replied to Donald, "Okay, everything will be fine. He is good."

At the border, they had an easy time. The immigration officers checked the papers, issued a temporary entrance to the boy, and directed Verona and Donald on how to proceed to obtain permanent residency for the kid. A few feet from the border, they exulted, yelling, crying, laughing, and sighing.

"We did it, we did it," Donald shouted.

"Now we are really family," Verona replied. "We didn't make any mistakes. He will have a much better life here with us than he would have in his country."

Donald agreed. "For sure, don't worry about that. We needed a kid, and we got one. It doesn't matter how."

After a while, Donald asked Verona, "Are you ready for a long drive?"

"Do you intend to make it all the way to Washington?"

They laughed and Donald answered, "I am excited, but not that much. I am thinking of sleeping in Nevada. That is about seven hours from here."

"Go ahead. I have food and water here and everything we might need."

The trip went smoothly and was even enjoyable. Seven hours later, they entered Las Vegas. It was a little after 6:00 p.m., and the city was gorgeous with lights and colours. Verona was thrilled; she had always loved Las Vegas, but they had had few chances to visit it. She jumped on Donald, hugging and kissing him. "Donald, you are marvellous, thank you. You couldn't have found a better place to celebrate. I love you."

Donald looked at her and said, "I see it will be a long night. I thought that the kid would make you calmer."

She smiled and replied, "During the day maybe, but at night, it is you who makes me calmer."

She turned to Jonathan and said, "Look, Jonathan, how beautiful this place is. See the colours and the buildings."

The boy appeared fascinated with everything around him. He noticed the spectacle of water, music, and light on the Strip, and he couldn't hold back. He screamed, "Look, the water, it is pretty!"

Verona was delighted. She promised him, "Later on, I will take you there."

Donald parked the truck in a parking lot of a fancy hotel in the Strip. They got a room and minutes later, Donald was in the bed sleeping and Verona and Jonathan were on the Strip enjoying the city. They walked everywhere on the Strip. They visited all the hotels and stopped to see the famous Bellagio Fountain show. At 10:00 p.m., they returned to the hotel, exhausted. Donald was waiting for them. Verona handed him a lunch she had bought for him. While he was eating, she put the boy to sleep and jumped on the bed close to Donald. "Should I wait until you finish eating to start our celebration?" Verona asked.

Donald answered, "If I am right, you already started."

Verona replied, "If I am already started, I must go on."

Tuesday morning, Donald told Verona, "I am thinking of staying the day here. We have time. Let's relax and enjoy the city with the kid."

Verona loved the idea. "I was hoping for that. Thank you, Donald."

Finally, they had a nice and relaxed day in Vegas. Before leaving the hotel after lunch, Donald called his real estate agent. "Hi, Linda, It is Donald."

"Hello, Donald, good to hear from you. I was waiting for your call. Everything is perfect. I arranged the first appointment for the escrow on Friday 26 at 11:00. You and Verona must be there to sign. The money will be deposited and distributed on the same day, so the loan of the new house will be released on Monday, and you and Verona will close the transaction on Monday the 29th. Is that good for you?"

Thrilled, Donald said, "That is more than perfect. You are fantastic. We will be there."

Linda added, "I have better news. The buyer will allow you to stay at the home until Friday, 3 July, so you can move directly to your new home."

"Oh, Linda, that is marvellous. Thank you very much."

"I am glad you are happy; that is my job. Have a safe trip."

After that, everything seemed to be working well for Donald and Verona. The trip was very nice and comfortable. On 24 June, they stayed in Boise, Idaho, and on the evening of Thursday, 25 June, they arrived in Bellevue. Donald decided to stay in a small motel close to 405. He told Verona, "We will stay here until we receive our house."

Verona agreed. "Yes, it is wiser to stay far from Everett now."

"Of course, we will never go with him there. I will hire two people to help me move our belongings from Everett on Tuesday. When I am done, I'll take you and him to the new house."

On Friday, Donald requested the management of the hotel to find a babysitter for Jonathan, so he and Verona could sign the sale of their house in Everett, and since everything worked well with the babysitter on Friday, they hired her again on Monday of the following week. Donald and Verona signed for and received the keys of the house they bought in Kirkland. On Thursday, 02 July 1981, they moved to their new home.

Verona was very happy with her new life. The house was nice with a huge yard. She had a loving husband and the son she had always wanted. She also now could live a normal life with her son; she could go out with him without raising unsettling looks or embarrassing questions. Verona also received a tough mission from Donald. "Verona, I will go back to work on Monday. That means I will be travelling most of the time. You have an important mission. The kid still has all the past in his mind, and we need to get that out of him. It will not be easy and will not be fast. This is your job, and you can't fail." She promised him, "I will not fail; I will make him forget his family and his old name."

"You have got to do that. Keep working with him. His name is Jonathan McCoolen, his mother is Verona, and his father is Donald. One other thing: Be careful if you need to open the safe for any reason. All the newspapers and magazines about the case are there. Don't let him or anybody else sees that."

"Do you think we need to keep all that?" Verona asked.

"I really don't know, but I like to have all the information about him. We might need that. Just be careful."

"Don't worry, everything will be fine."

On Wednesday, July 8, Donald was back on the road with the truck loaded and heading to Jacksonville, Florida. He told Verona, "It will be a long trip. I will be out for about three weeks. Be careful. I accepted this long trip because we needed the money. I will do my best to be back as soon as I can."

Trying to be strong, Verona said, "Don't worry, we will be fine. Focus on your trip and take care of yourself." Laughing, she finished by saying, "You are a father now and need to be careful."

Verona really was feeling much better than she had in Guaymas. She believed that the riskiest part of their scheme was already over, and that the kid was more accustomed to them than he had been yet. He was more easy-going, and he was calling her mom more often. The time went by gently and effortlessly. Donald travelled a lot to make as much money as he could, but now Verona wasn't complaining about being alone anymore. She had the company of the son she had wanted so much, and she was always busy teaching him and educating him, as she had been asked to do. She was so busy with Jonathan that Donald started to claim, mock-provocatively, "You got the baby and forgot the husband."

Verona laughed and said, "But when you are here, I take very good care of you. You can't deny that."

Donald protested, "You take care of yourself; you kill me every night, that is what you do."

She couldn't deny it. "Sure, but you like it, don't you?"

"Of course, I do."

Chapter 5

On the other side of the world, in Baghdad, the situation was very different. There was no joy, no happiness, and no son. Omar and Rania were living a bleak and endless nightmare. Their nights were filled with tears, regret, and strong feelings of guilt, and they spent their days running after a miracle they knew would never happen. They knew that Khaled was gone forever, but they couldn't stop trying, running from office to office, knocking on every door that might lead to something or shed any kind of light. At the end of the day, they used to come back home with their hands empty and their souls shattered and bleeding. On Saturday, 8 August 1981, Professor Abdel-Akher came from Cairo to Baghdad to collect all the information about the case. Twenty-four hours later, he resumed his trip to Seattle to meet with Professor Haig. On Wednesday, 12 August, the two professors held a long meeting in the sheriff's department and pleaded for help. The sheriff was deeply touched and assured his visitors that the case was considered a high priority by his department and that he had designated his best officers to solve it. However, he made it clear to them that the situation was very difficult considering the age of the child and the time elapsed since his disappearance.

In spite of the attention of the sheriff and his aides, the two professors left with great disappointment in their hearts. Professor Haig commented, "Professor Abdel-Akher, I am sorry to say it, but I don't see any ray of light. It now has almost ninety days. That is too long for a three-year-old to survive by himself."

"I agree," his Egyptian colleague said. "I do feel that there is something wrong. How can it be that no one saw anything? Why did none of the people who were there remember the face of the guy who walked away with him?"

"This is another part of the puzzle. The police tried hard to produce a composite of his face, but it was impossible. The people had been worried about the child and nobody focused on the image of the man," added Professor Haig.

Upon returning to Baghdad, Professor Abdel-Akher had to deliver the sad news to Omar. "Look, Omar, we did all that we were able to do. We begged the sheriff to double his efforts. I told him about your situation, the despair of Rania, and the illness of your mother. The man was really touched; I could see the tears in his eyes. But I can't hide the truth from you; the police are very pessimistic, the boy has been gone for a long time now, and they believe that any hope is much diminished."

On Tuesday, 18 August, three days after Professor Abdel-Akher had left Baghdad, Omar was struck by another severe blow. He was called urgently to his parents' home because his mother wasn't feeling well. He rushed there, but when he arrived, the neighbours informed him that she was no longer there; his father had hurried her to the hospital because she was feeling very unwell. Omar ran to the hospital; his father was sitting in the hall crying while she was with the doctors in the emergency room. After two agonising hours, the doctors came with the information, "She is in a coma. We had to put her on life support. Now, we need to wait and hope."

The words fell on their hearts like pieces of fire. Omar and Kareem remained, looking at each other wanting to say something, but they could not find the words, the voice, or the courage. They were fearful and hopeful, they were devastated and helpless, they needed to do something, but nothing could be done. In a few seconds, Omar burst into tears and said, "I lost my son and now I am losing my mother. Why, God? What wrong have I done to go through this?"

Kareem hugged him and whispered in his ear, "I do believe you should call your brother Rafik and your sister Ghada."

Wednesday and Thursday were a continuous and silent torture for Kareem and Omar, sitting and waiting, hoping and fearing. For them, time passed slowly, and the hours seemed endless. On Saturday, they were joined by Rafik and Ghada, who came from Basra. Finally, the agony ended in a way they didn't want. On Friday, 21 August 1981, early in the morning, Fahima was pronounced dead. Fahima's husband, daughter, and sons had to listen to the doctors saying what they didn't want to hear. "Sorry, we did all that we could do, but she passed away." The earth started to turn faster and Omar couldn't digest the news. To make matters worse, he saw his father collapse in front of him, forcing the doctors to rush Kareem back to the emergency room.

Within the hour, dozens of relatives, friends, and neighbours appeared to provide solidarity and help in the preparations for the funeral. Kareem regained consciousness and decided to attend the burial.

"I can't leave Fahima alone," he said. "We were never apart. I must be with her. She might need something, and I have to be there," Kareem insisted.

At 4:00 in the afternoon of the same day, they were at the cemetery giving the last goodbye to Fahima. It was a deeply affecting ceremony. Everybody was crying from the bottom of their heart, but no one knew if they were weeping for Fahima's loss, Khaled's disappearance, or Omar and Rania's despair. After the burial, Omar tried mightily to bring his father to spend the night at his house, but it was impossible. Kareem, without saying a single word, walked to his house accompanied by Rafik and Ghada.

When Kareem entered his house, he had a strange feeling. Everything was the same, but nothing was familiar: the rooms, the furniture, the walls, the rays of light coming through the window. Everything was equal, but all was strange. Fahima wasn't there, and without Fahima, nothing was familiar. Fahima was the colour, the brightness, and the meaning of everything. Fahima was the light, the guide, and the sense of life, and without her, nothing was real, genuine, or meaningful. He walked from room to room; he moved from place to place; he knew that he was looking for something he would never find. Early in the morning, Kareem woke up, prepared breakfast, and sat at the table waiting for Fahima to join him. Later on, Ghada woke up and saw her father sitting at the table with his coffee untouched. She hugged him and wept.

Two days later, Rafiq and Ghada were forced to return to Basra. Before leaving they had a long and sad conversations with Omar, the three were very worried about Kareem. Their father seemed sluggish, oblivious, and distant. They were hoping that time would help him accept the reality of Khaled's disappearance, but the time was not as useful as they had hoped, Kareem was still searching for Khaled and asking why his return was delayed, and now with Fahima's departure, what remained of his consciousness was gone. He was looking for Fahima to tell her what he had done in the morning, what he was going to do in the afternoon, and they often heard him asking her if she wanted him to do something else. The emptiness that Fahima left in his life was immense and nothing could change that, not even all the efforts his children made to help him. Kareem's life became vacant and meaningless, and he remained fraught with mixed feelings of fear, loss, and vulnerability.

Sadness was the colour that painted every day in the Al-Dahanys life. It was difficult to keep hoping, but it was impossible to live without hope. Every day started with the hope for something, a piece of information, a ray of light to help crack the darkness, but nothing happened. Every day started with the hope that someone would bring new evidence, somebody would mention Khaled's name, anything to move the stagnant water, but nothing happened. Every day started with the hope that somebody would knock on the door with something to tell them, someone would call on the phone looking for them, or a letter would arrive by the mail with information about their son, but nothing happened. Every day started with hope, proceeded with apprehension, and ended with despair, tears, and desolation. But they had no option; that was the thin thread that connected them to life. It was the tenuous and fragile hope that would give them reason to live. But the days turned into weeks, the weeks into months, and the months became years, and nothing happened until the end of 1983.

On 23 November 1983, Omar received a call from his brother Rafik. "Omar, I have some important news for you. Next month, a very important American envoy will visit Baghdad to meet with the president."

"What kind of envoy?" Omar asked. "What will he be doing here? And how can that help us?"

"You know we are here at the front and we receive the information to process the security issues. His name is Mr Rumsfeld, Donald Rumsfeld. He will be representing the president of the United States to discuss with President Saddam the war with Iran and the military help we need."

Omar asked his brother, "What do you think I should do?"

"Don't you think it is a good opportunity to request his aid in the search for Khaled?" Rafik replied. "Why don't you prepare a complete file about the boy's disappearance and deliver it to him and appeal for his help?"

"Do you think it will work?"

"Brother, we can't give up. We need to find our son, alive, God willing, but we have to know."

"You are right. I will check the information and prepare the document. Thank you, Rafik."

"God bless you, Omar. Goodbye."

Omar and Rania started to collect all the information available about the expected visit of the American envoy. Soon, the news started to appear in newspapers and TV news programs. Omar learned that the United States intended to send a high-level presidential envoy named Donald Rumsfeld to meet with President Saddam. The goal of the visit was to renew ties and provide intelligence and aid to ensure that Iraq would not be defeated in the war against Iran. Omar also discovered that the meeting of Mr Rumsfeld with President Saddam was scheduled for 20 December. Omar worked as hard as he could to prepare a complete file containing all the information about Khaled's disappearance in the marketplace in Seattle and the search and the great effort of the police and the population to find him. The file also exposed the devastation of the family, the death of Fahima, and the desolation of Rania and Kareem. Omar added many pictures of Khaled to help in identifying him.

With the help of the university, Omar was able to make an appointment with the U.S. General Consul in Baghdad for Monday, 12 December at 10:00 a.m. Rania and Omar were very happy; they felt like they were closer to Khaled than they had been in months. They started to feel him, to smell him, and to hear him calling again, mama and baba. They counted every second, they lived every day running to the following day, their hope was again relit and the desire to see their son was overwhelming. They were anxious and hopeful as if they were expecting to see their son waiting for them at the meeting.

Rania and Omar appeared at the American embassy at 9:00 and had to wait until the time of their appointment. At the time, they were invited to speak to the consul. Omar explained their case in all its details, and at the end he presented the file to the consul, saying, "Sir, you can find everything in this file. All the information related to the case is here. All we are asking for is to have the opportunity to talk to Mr Rumsfeld to seek his help."

The consul expressed his sorrow for their loss, but he made it clear that he could not help. "I am really sorry. Mr Rumsfeld's agenda is fixed by the Department of State with the Iraqi Government, and no one is authorised to introduce any alteration."

Rania and Omar fell into despair. Rania wept and pleaded in an agonised voice, "We need help to find our son. We want him back. Please help us."

Omar added, "Please, sir, we won't take too much time, just a few minutes. We beg you."

The consul affirmed that he understood their pain and despair. "I am really sorry for your suffering, but unfortunately, I can't do anything."

Omar tried to preserve his hope. "But could you deliver this file to Mr Rumsfeld with our request?"

The consul was firm. "Sorry, that could be considered as a commitment from the embassy. I can't accept that."

Rania screamed with a voice thickened by tears, "Where can we find some kind of help?"

The consul answered, "The only thing I can do is to talk to the ambassador to check with Mr Rumsfeld if he has time to talk to you out of the agenda. I am not promising, but that is all that I can do."

They thanked him and left, stripped of hope. They had been expecting more and hoping for something more effective. In frustration, Rania asked, "Couldn't he be more helpful? It is our son who is missing."

Omar shared her disappointment. "I also was expecting a warmer reception, but I am sure that Mr Rumsfeld will be more interested in helping."

"What makes you think that?"

"He is a higher-ranking government officer and should be more willing to deal with our problem."

The pain and the anxiety enlarged the tiny particle of hope they nurtured in their hearts, and they started to believe that Mr Rumsfeld would bring Khaled back.

Omar rushed to his father's house to tell him what had happened in his meeting with the consul. Omar tried to give his father the impression that everything was under control and that they might get the help they needed. He told his father that the consul promised that the ambassador would seek the envoy's help, and that Mr Rumsfeld, as a high-ranking officer, would be able to speed the search for Khaled.

During all the time he was talking, Omar wasn't sure if his father was listening, and if he was listening, how much he was understanding. Really, Omar wasn't sure if his father was there. The old man kept looking at nothing and saying, "God help you, son, God help you."

Life for Rania and Omar became a routine of waiting, counting, and hoping, waiting for the time to pass, counting the seconds as they dashed past and hoping for a miracle to happen. Every morning was one further step toward paradise and hell; each night was a move in the direction of happiness and devastation. Each day, Rania and Omar lived the joy of the expectation of succeeding and the fear of being declined. They scoured the newspapers, TV programs, and every news source for information about Mr Rumsfeld's visit to Baghdad. Every moment they lived, they were affected by all the information, and they collected all the pictures.

Rania and Omar waited desperately for a call from the embassy that never came. Finally, it was December 20 and they saw President Saddam Hussein on the TV shaking hands with Mr Rumsfeld. Both men were smiling and looked happy and pleased. Omar couldn't restrain his agony and screamed like a wounded animal. "And our son, they owe us an answer. Where is our son?" Rania kept crying without answer. On the second day, early in the morning, they were at the gate of the embassy begging to speak to anyone. Around 9:00, an employee of the embassy came outside and informed them that nothing could be done. That was all, nothing could be done. Now, Rania and Omar felt that their son was gone, forever.

Rania yelled from her tearful soul, "What can we do now?"

Through tears, Omar answered, "Maybe we should bury our son."

Chapter 6

The years 1982 and 1983 were especially plentiful for Verona and Donald. Jonathan was five years old now, almost six, a beautiful and handsome child. He also seemed to have been well integrated into the family, bringing much joy and happiness to his parents. Donald also was able to acquire two more big trucks, allowing him to incorporate the McCoolen Transportation Company (MTC Transportation) and hire four aides to operate his expanded business.

September 1983 arrived, and it was time for Jonathan to start school. However, Verona and Donald weren't sure they could take that step. The boy still had many memories in his mind, and, even if it wasn't very often, he used to mention his parents and call for mama and baba. Verona and Donald did not want to take the risk and decided to keep him home for one more year.

In March 1984, Verona told Donald, "I am not feeling very well. I am tired and sleepy. Something is bothering me; I am too late. You understand, don't you?"

Donald laughed and said, "Should I start looking for another woman?"

Verona shouted, "Don't you dare! You are mine and that is that. I am serious. I do not feel well." Donald tried to calm her. "No problem. Let's call the doctor and make an appointment."

Verona made an appointment with her doctor for Wednesday, 14 March, choosing a day that she knew Donald would be home and so would be able to be with her at the doctor's office. On the day, after a long and detailed examination, the doctor called them to his private office and began talking. "There is no reason to be worried. On the contrary, you have reasons to celebrate; congratulations to both of you." Then the doctor turned to Verona and said, "You are pregnant."

Both Verona and Donald were stunned. Verona murmured, "What a surprise. We have been trying for many years."

Donald couldn't contain himself and asked, "But how could this have happened?"

The doctor answered by joking, "I do believe that you are the one who can tell us how that happened."

They laughed, and the doctor resumed. "You ought to be happy. Finally, you did it."

"Doctor, are you sure?" Verona asked. "We had given up all hope of having a natural baby. That is why we adopted our son."

The doctor explained. "That is not rare. You tried unsuccessfully, you adopted a child, you relaxed and got pregnant, I am very sure. Enjoy your second baby."

The surprising news took the couple to the brink of delirium. They hugged and kissed each other; they laughed and cried as madly as they could. Finally, the doctor interrupted, joking, "If the celebration is going to go further, you had better go home."

Verona's face turned red and Donald replied, "We are going as soon as we can."

On the way home, Verona and Donald were in a state of ecstasy. They were driving, dancing, and singing at the same time. Donald expressed his joy. "Verona, we will have a baby of our own, a real one."

Equally joyous, Verona said, "Yes, Donald, I will give you the baby you always wanted. I am so happy."

At home, Donald reminded Verona of the doctor's recommendation to be careful and to get as much rest as she could, especially during the first three months of pregnancy. They prepared the master bedroom to offer all the comfort to Verona. Donald moved to the adjoining room, which used to be Jonathan's room, moving him to the third room of the house.

Verona initially protested. "Are you leaving me?"

"Never, I will be here all the time. I will have to consolidate our project as much as I can."

With a smile, Verona said, "But the doctor said that everything is okay."

"No, no, no, I must keep working until the baby is born. It is my duty." They laughed, enjoying the happiest moment of their lives.

Donald also changed his work schedule, avoiding long trips that kept him far from home for an extended time. He tried to be at home most of the time to take care of Verona. He would not allow her to do any hard work or carry anything heavy. It was delightful for her, but she used to joke, saying, "Donald, you are spoiling me too much."

"You are making my dream come true," replied a thrilled Donald. "How many years have we waited for this?"

Despite all their efforts and excessive care, the pregnancy wasn't an easy one. Verona often felt very tired, and most of the time she was sick with an upset stomach and felt a deep malaise. But Verona's major worry was to lose the baby. Donald and the doctor had a tough job to convince her that the risk was exceedingly small and her fear was only worsening her situation. One week after Verona ended the third month of the pregnancy, the doctor called the couple in and assured Verona that she could relax now and all that she needed was to follow his instructions. He assured her that everything would be all right. The doctor then looked at them and said, "Are you both ready for a surprise?"

"What surprise, Doctor?" Verona asked suspiciously.

Donald, also anxious, asked, "Yes, Doctor, what is it?"

Smiling, the doctor replied, "Are you interested in discovering the gender of your baby?"

Both Verona and Donald answered immediately, "Yes, Doctor, please."

The doctor pointed to the ultrasound on his desk and said, "You are having a boy."

Their happiness was overwhelming. Donald hugged and kissed Verona with passion. Then they thanked the doctor and left his office delighted.

Over the subsequent months, Verona had a better time. She was more confident and happier, which helped her to deal with the physical problems she eventually faced. She was also very busy buying clothes and furniture for the new baby. At the seventh month, they started to think about a name. Once more, Verona suggested Donald Junior, a suggestion that Donald rejected immediately. "No, Verona, let him have a modern name of his time. Donald is not adequate for his time."

Verona admitted, "I have been thinking about this for a while."

"Then you must have a name by now. Please tell me; I am anxious."

"I can't make up my mind. I have a list of three names. Help me choose from Alexander, Andrew, and Tayler."

Showing a big smile, Donald said, "You did a good job. All of them are nice, but I like Andrew the most."

"I also prefer Andrew."

"Then he will be Andrew Gaston McCoolen, the real McCoolen. Is that good for you?"

"Yes, that is wonderful," Verona answered, and kissed him.

⎯⎯⎯

10 September 1984 was Jonathan's first day at school. Verona had deep and mixed feelings of joy and fear. She had been waiting for this day since a long time ago, dreaming about preparing his lunch, taking him early to school, and waiting for him at the door of the school at the end of the day. These thoughts brought her so much happiness. But she was afraid, too. It would be the first time he would be alone by himself and far from her eyes. All the way to the school, Verona kept advising the boy, "Be careful, and don't talk too much. The school doesn't like kids who talk too much. When the teacher asks you, what is your name, what do you say?"

The boy answered, "Jonathan McCoolen."

"Good, smart boy. If you do well, I will take you to the ice-cream place after school."

At the door, she left the boy and her peace together in the school. She was fearful, tense, and stressed. She kept looking at her watch and wondering why the time was passing so slowly. For Verona, the time wasn't running; it was walking. As a matter of fact, the time was plodding, inflaming her fear and anxiety. Finally, it was time to pick him up, and she was the first mom to be at the door of the school. Minutes later, he came running toward her, followed by a teacher. Verona hugged him and asked the teacher, "How was his first day?"

"Very good, he is a lovely and beautiful kid," the teacher answered.

Verona released a sigh of relief and exclaimed, "Thanks, God."

The teacher understood her reaction as the exaggerated concern of a loving mother and said, "Don't worry, Mom. Your son is doing very well." Then she turned to him and said, "Bye, Jonathan, see you tomorrow."

"Bye, teacher."

Verona was exhilarated. At that moment, she was confident that she had passed the most difficult test of her life. Now, he was Jonathan and now he was her son.

Four days later, when Donald returned from his trip to Denver, she was in ecstasy, telling him how Jonathan behaved in the school and that he answered to his name, Jonathan McCoolen, when asked. "Donald, we can relax. The kid learned everything we taught him, and we have nothing to worry about anymore," she said.

Donald hugged her and said, "That is good. We can enjoy our life now, but keep working with him. Make him happy. I brought many toys for him. We will be happy with him, and we will make him happy as well."

Verona decided not to lose the moment, and asked, "And when will you make me happy? I haven't been happy since you left."

Donald warned her, "Better to be prepared, because I also haven't been happy since then. I will make you happier than you can handle."

Verona laughed loudly and asked, "Is that a threat?"

"No, it is a promise."

On Monday, 29 October, the doctor told Verona, "This is your last visit before delivery. Be prepared; your baby will be here any day next week. Please report to the hospital when you feel it is time and they will call me."

Verona answered happily, "Thank you, Doctor, your care has been fundamental for me to have a healthy pregnancy."

"I am happy to hear that. Now, we just have to wait for the baby."

The night of Saturday, November 3, 1984, Verona began to experience delivery symptoms. The contractions were frequent and started to occur closer together. She felt the baby was lower and her vaginal discharge was copious, pink, and bloody. Donald rushed her to the hospital where she was admitted immediately. Soon the doctor arrived and visited her in her room. Donald decided to watch the delivery, and early on Sunday, 4 November, he rejoiced to see the birth of his son. Verona cried deeply when the doctor laid the baby on her chest, flooded by a wave of emotion that she could not withstand. Donald also sobbed and laughed and hugged everybody in the room. It was the moment they had desired for almost ten years. Donald asked the doctor, "When can she come home, Doctor?"

The doctor laughed and said, "Now that you got what you wanted, you are in a hurry to leave, right?"

They laughed and the doctor added, "She will stay with us for two days. Now, we will move her to the room; better to wait for us there."

At the room, the doctor congratulated them again. "I am glad both are happy; the baby is healthy and beautiful, just like his mom."

They laughed and Donald protested, "The father is not that bad."

The doctor replied, "No, you are okay, Donald. Did you decide about the name?"

Verona answered, "Andrew, we chose Andrew. Isn't that a beautiful name?"

The doctor agreed, "A very nice name, congratulations."

Then he turned to Donald and said, "Now, I recommend you leave her to sleep and get some rest. You can stay with her tomorrow as long as you want."

Donald agreed. "I will be leaving in a few minutes."

The doctor left the room and Donald turned to Verona. "I am thinking of placing Andrew's crib in the room beside yours. He will need to be close to you."

"And you? Where you will put your bed?"

"I will take over Jonathan's room. I will find a place for his bed in the basement. I am sure he will be okay there."

Verona's silence indicated her consent, and Donald soon left.

Two days later, Verona was back home with Andrew and experiencing all the happiness of the world. The house was different, her feelings were different, the walls appeared to be smiling at her, the flowers in the yard were more colourful, and everything had a new shape, colour, and taste. Donald also was feeling like a new man; his eyes were shining, and his joy was overwhelming. He guided Verona to see how he had prepared the room for Andrew. She was impressed. "You did a good job, Donald; the room is wonderful."

He answered, proud of his achievement, "Our son deserves this, doesn't he?"

"He certainly does. And you, what about your room?"

"It is okay. Come on, have a look."

Verona liked what she saw and asked, "Did you find a place for Jonathan?"

He said, "There wasn't room for his bed in the basement. I put a small mattress instead; he will be fine."

Verona placed Andrew in his crib and walked around her house like a queen on the day of her coronation. She hugged Donald and cried on his shoulder, saying, "I am the happiest woman in the world. I couldn't be happier. Thank you, Donald."

Deeply moved, Donald said, "I also am very happy. We dreamed about this all our life, and now it is real. He is here in the room between us."

"We will take care of him; we will prepare him to have a great future."

"No doubt about that, he will be a great man," Donald confirmed.

Verona looked at the clock on the wall and told Donald, "It is about 3:00, time to pick Jonathan up from school."

Donald replied, "It will be tough to take him to and pick him up from school. It might be better to put him on the school bus starting tomorrow."

Verona agreed. "Yes, I think we need to do that. Just inform the school administration."

"Okay, I'll do that. Be back soon," Donald said as he left.

Half an hour later, he was back with Jonathan. Verona hugged him and said, "Jonathan, come see your brother, your baby brother is already home."

They went to the room where Andrew was sleeping. Jonathan looked on with a smiling face and said, "He is very cute. Look how small his hand is. Will I be able to play with him?"

Donald answered quickly, saying, "No, be very careful with him."

Verona tried to soften the response. "He is still a baby. When I am with you, we can play with him together."

"I am happy I have a brother," Jonathan said. "All my friends in school have brothers."

Verona smiled and said, "Now, you have one."

Donald pushed him out of the room, saying, "Go to your place now. Andrew needs to sleep. Go downstairs and do your homework."

For Donald and Verona, life began to revolve around Andrew: the time he slept, the time he cried, the time to breastfeed him, and the time to bathe him, all arranged around were the most convenient times for Verona and Donald. Verona was living twenty-four hours to care for him, and Donald rearranged his trips to be home as much as he could, focused on playing with the baby and helping Verona to take care of him. Every change that he manifested was registered, every new movement or expression was celebrated, and the smallest evolution was a huge achievement. The time went by so fast that suddenly they were talking about Andrew's first birthday.

"Donald, it is almost Andrew's birthday. What do you think about that?"

"We will prepare a big party, and we will invite all the neighbours. What do you think about hiring a caterer to take care of everything?" Donald asked.

"I was thinking about that, but I am worried it might be very expensive."

"Don't worry about that. We are good. He is our son, and he deserves the best."

Verona smiled, showing her happiness, and added, "Though we still have three months, I think we should start working on that."

"Sure, go ahead. I want him to be proud of his first birthday. I will hire somebody to record the party."

Verona decided not to lose any time and started immediately working on preparations for Andrew's first birthday party, and she did a good job. On 4 November 1985, the McCoolens' house was full of joy and happiness. Children, neighbours, and guests gathered there to celebrate Andrew's birthday. The McCoolens hired a band to play music and arranged to have a children's theatre group to entertain the kids. The party was superb; everyone was pleased, and all the child guests were rewarded with small toys and gifts.

Life went by happily and smoothly for the McCoolens. Each month, there was something new about Andrew. Each year brought so many things happening about or related to Andrew, always ending with an outstanding party to celebrate. Everything was going the way the McCoolens had dreamed; the business was doing very well and Andrew was growing fast. But at the same time, they had some problems. Donald could never find the time to watch Jonathan playing on the school football team anymore, and Verona never had time to attend the school meetings or to help him in his homework, but that wasn't big enough to disturb their happy life. Suddenly, when Verona and Donald least expected, it was 1989, and Andrew was getting ready to start elementary school.

"Donald, I can't believe it; our son is ready to go to school. I am delighted."

"So, am I. It is the happiness we have been living for. I was thinking about that. What do you think about Bellevue Lakeview Elementary School?"

"Wow, Bellevue Lakeview. It is the most expensive school in the area; our son will have the best education," Verona answered, excited.

"Of course, he will. We can visit the school tomorrow and talk with the administration," Donald said.

During dinner, Donald told Andrew with a great deal of pride, "Tomorrow, we will visit your school. The name of your school is Bellevue Lakeview. It is a very good school."

Verona added, "Oh, Andrew, it is a marvellous school. Many courts, many places to play, it will be a lot of fun."

Jonathan's eyes shone, and he said, "It is a very nice school; they have the best football team. Will I be able to finish my school year there also?"

Donald said, "Andrew will go there; you, no."

Jonathan, who was almost twelve years old, insisted, "The coach says that if I join their team, I can be a professional player. You know I play well."

Donald was fast and swift to reply. "The coach can say what he wants, I don't care. You will stay where you are. And now don't disturb our dinner."

Jonathan left the table weeping and ran to the basement.

Jonathan spent hours crying and wondering why his father was so unloving and even cruel to him. For years now, his life had been one of suffering and isolation. Years ago, Jonathan started to be alone and isolated, having almost no contact with his parents. His greatest relief came during the few moments he was able to spend with Andrew when he was asked to take care of his brother. Once more, Jonathan found himself alone in the company of his tears.

Later, when everybody seemed to be sleeping, Jonathan heard somebody coming downstairs to the basement. When he looked, he had a great surprise: it was Andrew carrying a piece of cake. Andrew offered the piece to Jonathan and said, "I saw you left your food on the table; you must be hungry."

Jonathan hugged his brother and said, "I am hungry, thank you. I love you very much."

Andrew answered, also crying, "I love you too. You give me all your toys and you play with me." Jonathan enjoyed the cake, hugged his brother, and both went to sleep.

Chapter 7

From this point on, Jonathan's life went in opposite directions. On one side, his relationship with his parents was deteriorating every day. Donald treated him rudely and carelessly, and Verona appeared to be okay with that. During the following three years until Jonathan graduated from school, Donald never watched a single football game. Ignoring Jonathan's appeals and begging, he was always busy or tired or not interested. The distance grew greater between the two, increasing Jonathan's disappointment and frustration. Each year they had a battle because Jonathan wanted to transfer to Bellevue Lakeview School and his wish was promptly rejected by Donald, sometimes because it was expensive, sometimes because it was too far, and many times without any explanation at all. At the end of the eighth grade, the tension between the two, which was already high, exploded, as could have been expected. Soon before graduation ceremony day, Jonathan discovered that his father would be travelling to Texas during this period, and he couldn't contain his anger.

"How could you do that to me? You never go to my games; you don't even look at my grades and now you won't be in my ceremony, even knowing that I will make the speech representing the students."

Donald answered coldly, "Good luck to you."

The situation got worse when Andrew tried to give support to his brother.

"Dad, I think all of us should be there. It is his graduation day. Please."

Donald replied, "Andrew, it is not your business."

"But he is my brother, and I love him."

That was enough for Donald to lose patience. "Andrew, no more interference, go to your room."

He turned to Jonathan and said, "You see, you are always creating confusion and trouble for the family. I won't change my schedule. I won't go to your graduation ceremony, and that is that."

Jonathan looked at his mother, begging for help, but Verona again did what she had gotten used to doing for the last three years, almost nothing. She looked around vaguely without saying a single word. Jonathan realised that he was defeated, and nothing would change. He left for his place in the basement accompanied by his frustrations.

The graduation ceremony was held on Friday, 2 July 1993, in the school gym. The interior was ornamented with designs, poems, and pictures drawn by the graduates. The families were filling the auditorium with pride and joy as they anticipated honouring the heroes of the moment. The students were introduced in the place to the music of the third symphony of Beethoven, the Eroica. After the speech of the director, Jonathan was called to speak for the students. His speech was entitled "A great man starts in the school." He began by thanking his school and his teachers. He mentioned that a great man started as a good kid, good student, and good athlete. He said that a great person should start learning at an early age to be honest, responsible, and caring for his family, teachers, and classmates.

The speech was well received by the audience, and he felt a mixture of sadness and pride responding to the applause of everybody there. To his joy, he saw a small hand raised in the middle of the crowd trying hard to be noticed; it was Andrew. Jonathan's joy was overwhelming. When the ceremony ended and the students were free to join their families, he rushed to find his brother. They hugged each other tightly and Jonathan asked, "How did you come here?"

Andrew answered, "I would never leave you alone. You are my brother and my best friend. I feel how much you care about me, and I also care about you."

"But dad will be angry with you, I mean, with both of us."

"I know that, but I don't care."

"Thank you, Andrew. You have saved my day."

Soon after the graduation battle between Donald and Jonathan, they had another big confrontation, this time about high school. Jonathan wanted to study in a private school with a great reputation. Therefore, he approached his father and said, "Dad, I am thinking of joining Eastside High School in Seattle. Will you help me?"

Donald replied, dropping a bombshell. "It is better to start looking for a job. You're big enough to take care of yourself."

Jonathan was stunned. He never expected that kind of reaction. He knew that his family's business was going very well, and he had planned his next three years thinking about studying and playing football with the aim of winning a fellowship at the University of Washington. In despair, he said to his father, "But dad, you know that I will be studying and playing football. I won't have time to work."

Donald was unreceptive. "You must. I need to take care of Andrew."

Already crying, Jonathan implored his father, "Please, Dad, I can't give up football. I am the quarterback of the team, and I have a good chance of being drafted if I keep practicing."

Unmoved, Donald shouted, "Find a job and take care of your life."

Jonathan realised that he had no option. He joined the school closest to home because no one was willing to take him to school, and he found a job in a drug store in Totem Lake. In the beginning, Jonathan tried to make it studying, working, and practicing, but soon he understood that it would be impossible. He got tired, exhausted, and unable to fulfil his duty as well as he should have. Soon, he had no choice but to quit the football team. It was very painful for him. Football was his joy in the present and his dream for the future. Now, he was living without joy and without dreams, and without understanding why these events were happening to him.

While the struggle between Jonathan and his father intensified over the following three years, his relationship with his brother was his haven, as they became closer every day. Jonathan acted as Andrew's guide, idol, and second football coach. Hidden from their parents, Andrew used to visit Jonathan in the basement almost every night and bring many good things to him that the McCoolens would buy only for the younger child. The brothers used to meet out of their home, at the Totem Lake mall, and spent a lot of time talking and strengthening the ties between them.

Life for Jonathan became a continuous marathon. He had to get up early at 6:00 and rush to be in school at 7:00. At 3:00, he had to run to catch the bus to be in the mall to start his shift from 4:00 to 10:00. After that, he had to hurry home to keep up with his homework. He had no time for anything else, not even for living. One day in May 1995, he was at the bus stop when he saw a car coming in his direction. The car stopped and the driver opened the passenger's window.

When Jonathan looked, he saw it was Meagan, his classmate and one of the few people he used to talk with.

"Hi Jonathan, are you going to work?"

"Yes."

"Get in. I will give you a ride."

Jonathan got into the car and said, "Thank you, Meagan. I was running late."

Meagan replied, smiling, "Hold on, it is not for free. I need your help."

"No problem. I will be happy to help you."

Meagan started talking. "I know you work in the mall. I need your help. Things are not going very well between my mother and my stepfather, and sometimes I find myself in the middle of their arguments. As a matter of fact, my home life has never been good. My stepfather has a drinking problem, and he is overly aggressive when he loses his temper."

She stopped a little to control her emotions and resumed. "I think I need to move out. I need to find a job and place where I can live. Can you help me find a spot in the mall?"

Jonathan was touched. "Sure, Meagan, there are lots of stores in the mall. One of them might need help. I will contact them during my break, and I will leave your name at as many as I can."

"Thank you, Jonathan. You see, I told you the ride wasn't for free," Meagan said, parking in front of his store.

They laughed and Jonathan added as he got out of the car, "Thank you, Meagan. I enjoyed talking to you."

"Me too."

A few days later, the 'Photo & Camera store' contacted Jonathan asking him to call Meagan for an interview. On the following day, he informed Meagan and she asked, jokingly, "Is that an excuse to get a ride today?"

"No, it is serious. They have an opening and they want to talk to you."

"That is very nice, but I would have given you the lift anyway. Thank you."

At the mall, Meagan left Jonathan close to his store and walked to 'Photo & Camera store.' She introduced herself, and the manager welcomed her. "Hi, Meagan, we really need a salesperson. Are you ready to start immediately?"

"I am," she said, "but to be honest with you, this will be my first job. I don't have experience selling anything."

The manager smiled and said, "Thank you for being honest. That is exactly what we need; everything else you can learn. If you are ready, you can start tomorrow."

Meagan was delighted. Now, she could find a place of her own. The next day, she ran up to Jonathan when he arrived at school. "Jonathan, thank you. I got the job. I'll start today, and the best thing is, they gave me the afternoon shift. It is almost the same time as yours. You know what that means? You got a ride every day."

Jonathan's happiness was also great. He liked Meagan and he had always felt comfortable talking to her, although that happened infrequently. In the afternoon, he got the ride and congratulated Meagan again for the job. She said, "I am happy that we will have more time together." Then she looked at him and said, smiling, "I hope you will talk a little more now."

Jonathan laughed and said, "I have been talking with you more than anybody else in the class."

Meagan replied, "You don't talk with anybody else in the class." They laughed deeply.

The ride with Meagan opened a small window in the hard life Jonathan was living at home. He was surprised to find himself talking a little more, and, soon, really it was more than a little more. He told her about his problems at home and how his parents were unfair to him. "I feel I am no son at home; my dad doesn't care about me; he is always angry and ready to explode for no reason. Mom is always busy, and she never has time for me," Jonathan said.

Touched by his revelations, Meagan asked, "Did you ever ask him about that?"

"I tried, I tried, but I never got an answer."

"Did you ever think about leaving home?"

"I did, but I can't. I love my little brother Andrew too much, and he loves me too. He is the best thing that ever happened in my life. He begged me not to leave home, and I promised him I wouldn't."

The friendship between Meagan and Jonathan was a big relief for both, and they began to spend most of their time together when they weren't working. Soon the year ended, and the summer vacation gave Meagan and Jonathan more time to meet, to talk, and to share hopes and frustrations. The free time also enabled Meagan to find a place to live. She got a room with Jessica, a newcomer to the school who had moved recently from Spokane. Jonathan and Andrew helped

Meagan move and to place her belongings in the new place. Meagan was delighted to meet Andrew, and soon they became good friends.

The third year went fast, and before they knew it, Meagan and Jonathan were preparing for graduation. "Jonathan, this is June; our graduation will be next month. Can you believe that?" Meagan said as she drove to the mall where they worked.

"Yes. In one month, we will be done with high school. Are you serious about going to LA?" Jonathan asked.

"Yes, please understand that. I need a fresh start. Moving out of my house helped, but not enough. I need to be far from my family. I need to be myself and here I never will be."

Jonathan said, with great sadness, "I will miss you very much. I wish I could move with you, but my dad refuses to give me any help. I have no choice; I must stay here."

Meagan tried to console him. "I will miss you too, but I know you will be happy going to UW. It is a great university, and you might get a fellowship there."

On Thursday, 18 July 1996, the school gym was ready for the graduation ceremony. The stage was full of flowers and colours, and the administrative staff and teachers were all there dressed in academic wear with bonnets, hoods, and gowns. All the graduates were standing on the left of the stage, and the gym was packed with families and friends. The graduates were called one by one. They had to step on the stage, get their diploma, face the audience, and step down at the left side of the stage. The director congratulated the graduates for their achievement, and after the speech of the president of the student union, the ceremony ended, and the students were freed to receive the compliments of their families and colleagues.

Jonathan was happier in this ceremony than the one he had experienced three years ago, and he had a good reason for that: his parents were present. However, they had come only after a huge effort by Andrew, who was now about twelve, and he had had to make a clear and frightening threat to his parents:

"If you don't go to Jonathan's graduation, you won't be welcome at mine, either."

They had no choice, but to go. When Jonathan was ready to leave the graduates to join Andrew and his parents, he observed somebody cutting through the middle of the crowd in his direction. It was Meagan. When she arrived, she jumped on his neck embracing him, and when he least expected it, she kissed him passionately. Jonathan noticed that he not only enjoyed the kiss but also responded with a more passionate and avid kiss. When they came back to earth, all the people in the gym were applauding and congratulating them.

With a red face and tremulous voice, Meagan said, "Forgive me, Jonathan, I couldn't hold it in anymore. I love you too much."

"You couldn't have done anything better," Jonathan said. "For a long time, I have been trying to find a way to tell you how much I love you."

They kissed again and each ran to meet their family.

For Meagan and Jonathan, the gap between high school and college was full of activity and emotion. They had acknowledged the love they had held in their hearts for a long time and now they wanted to enjoy it every second, and they tried. They were together almost all the time and everywhere. They were loving and caring all the time. But they also had a problem, and they had to deal with it. Meagan had decided to study in California, and that meant she needed to move soon.

"I really don't know what life will be like without you. I am used to seeing you every day. I never go to sleep before saying good night to you," Jonathan said with a tremulous voice.

Meagan hugged him and said, "We will keep doing the same things. Our love is real and deep in our hearts, so it will be always the same, real and truthful."

"But I am afraid of the distance; distance and loneliness can soften feelings."

"Not mine, I hope not yours either. When I crossed the crowd to kiss you on graduation day, I wanted God and everyone on earth to know how much I love you."

"I want you to know how much I love you, too. You are the best thing that ever happened in my life. You helped me to support the hard life I have with my parents. I will be forever appreciative for you and Andrew," Jonathan said.

"We helped each other. Life would have been much harder for me and for you without our mutual support and encouragement. And we will keep doing that," Meagan said with love and determination.

On Thursday, 3 October, Meagan invited Jonathan to go with her to the camera store to say goodbye to her friends there. Jonathan agreed. "Certainly, I need to go there. Andrew is starting to show great interest in photography, and I promised to give him a camera for his upcoming birthday."

"Cool. You will find a great variety of cameras there. One must fit in your budget," Meagan said.

At the store, her co-workers congratulated Meagan for having been accepted at UC Irvine and wished her success. Jonathan chose a nice camera for his brother, and he got a good discount from the manager who also awarded Andrew a free training program to learn how to use the camera.

On Friday, 11 October, Jonathan was driving a small truck with Meagan and her belongings heading to Los Angeles. He had offered to drive Meagan to LA, and she immediately accepted. "It will be wonderful to enjoy the trip with you," Meagan said.

"And you can take all your belongings and books all together," he replied.

"Sure. It will be great starting my California adventures with you. Can I dream that one day you will join me there and we will finally have happiness together?"

"That is exactly what I intend to do once I get my college degree."

"Is that a promise?" Meagan asked.

"Sure, it is. When I am done with college, Andrew will be sixteen, and I am thinking to invite him to study in California. He is very interested in photo, video, and all kinds of pictorial arts. California would be the best place for those studies."

"Oh, Jonathan, you couldn't think of a better idea, having your brother with us in California. You love each other so much. I love him too."

"I am working on that, Meagan. We will finish our college degrees and start our family and have children, and I swear to God, I will love all of them the same way."

Meagan saw the tears in his eyes and couldn't help but respond; she wept and said through the tears, "I am sorry, Jonathan, for what you are going through, and I can't understand why your parents are doing that, but I promise you, I will give you all the love they didn't."

He looked at her and asked, smiling with tears in his eyes, "Is that a promise?"

She smiled and said, "Of course it is, just like I have your promise. I will live with it and for it, and now you have mine."

At that moment, they were close to Portland. Jonathan asked, "Meagan, should we stop to eat something and get some rest?"

"Good idea. We need that."

On Monday, they arrived where Meagan had arranged to live in Tustin. It was a small apartment with two bedrooms, but it was a perfect fit for her, plus there was one other big advantage. "Rent is lower in Tustin than Irvine. I will be by myself, but when you come to visit me, it will be just the two of us," Meagan said, smiling.

"That is why I am thinking about bringing Andrew each time I come to visit." "No problem; I will pay for him to go see a movie," Meagan retorted.

They laughed and embraced passionately.

Chapter 8

Monday, 14 October 1996, was the beginning of the fall quarter. Jonathan was happy; entering UW had long been his big dream. Now, he could let his passion for math and physics flourish and design his future. He had developed a great passion for math, especially the spectral theorem. During the summer break, he read some articles published by Professor Gregory Martin Moore, one of the most respected professors in the UW math department. Jonathan's joy and happiness were greatly increased when he discovered that Professor Moore would teach a subject entitled 'Basic Theorems and Applications' scheduled for the winter quarter.

On the very first day of the winter quarter, Jonathan enjoyed his class with Professor Moore. At the end of the class, he hurried in the direction of the professor and introduced himself. "Professor Moore, my name is Jonathan McCoolen. I have read many papers about your work on the spectral theorem, and I wonder if there is any chance for me to learn more with you as a trainee."

The professor was very kind and receptive. "Thank you for reading my work. I hope you enjoyed it. Why you don't stop by my office tomorrow in the afternoon and we will see what we can do."

"Yes, Professor, I will be there. Thank you very much," Jonathan answered, delighted.

The next afternoon, Jonathan arrived at the professor's office. The professor welcomed him and asked him to talk a little about his background and his interests. Jonathan spoke about his passion for math and his interest in pursuing a career in this field. When he finished, he asked the professor about the possibility of joining the math department for a training program. The professor encouraged him to keep reading and studying, and informed him that, "Having you here in the department can be discussed only after you finish the class 'Basic Theorems and Applications,' and, of course, your grades will be a fundamental factor."

That would be a huge achievement for Jonathan. Having the opportunity to learn with Professor Moore was beyond his dreams. It wasn't easy for him to understand how the spectral theorem provides conditions under which an operator or a matrix can be diagonalised. Jonathan was fascinated by Professor Moore's work, where he proved that every real, symmetric matrix is diagonalisable. Jonathan also believed that the spectral theorem, as generalised by Professor Moore, is today perhaps the most important result of operator theory, and he badly wanted to learn more about that.

With the beginning of the spring quarter, Jonathan was living his dream. He had been accepted by Professor Moore as a fellow trainee. The professor was impressed by his grades and his persistence. "Jonathan, you have good grades and a real desire to learn. That is enough for me to have you here. You will work on the spectral theorem for the Hermitian matrix. I recommend you start reading about that."

Jonathan replied, "Yes, Professor, I will start immediately. Thank you for giving me this opportunity."

"No problem. I am glad to have you here. You will have a desk and place to work. Let me know if you need anything."

On the first available weekend, Jonathan flew to California to meet Meagan carrying the news he kept to surprise her personally. "Meagan, I have been accepted by Professor Moore to work with him. Now I am part of the UW math department."

Meagan was delighted. "Congratulations, Jonathan. You deserve it. You work hard, and I am so happy for you." Then she added, "I am also now working. It is not in the math department, but it is still good."

They laughed and Jonathan asked, "Where will you be working?"

"It is a huge department store. I will be working in the video and audio department. They liked my experience in Seattle."

"That is good. That will help you pay your bills and have an unstressed life."

"For sure, it hasn't been easy managing my budget these last six months."

Jonathan hugged her and said, "Everything will be ok. Sorry, I couldn't help you, but I am sure everything will be all right."

Meagan hugged him passionately and said, "You don't have to be sorry. Both of us are having a hard time, but we will make it. We are doing it; we are getting our college education, and soon I will be the wife of a great scientist, maybe the new Isaac Newton." They laughed loudly.

Meagan was taking a dual degree program, studying administration and economics. It hadn't been easy before getting a job, and now it was going to be even tougher, but she was determined. Jonathan was her biggest supporter. They used to talk with a great deal of pride about their achievements.

When Meagan asked Jonathan about Andrew, he said, "Andrew is now thirteen. He is my lovely and dear brother. We become closer every day, but something about him has me worried."

"What is that?" Meagan asked.

"He is now thirteen; he is not a kid anymore, and I have noticed that he is being aggressive with our parents because he doesn't like the way they treat me."

"Have you talked with him about that?"

"Of course, I did. I told him I was not happy about the way he was acting, but I know he loves me, and I can see him suffering when they hurt me."

After a moment of silence, Jonathan continued talking. "I don't want him living with hate, and I don't want him to hate our parents, even if they are wrong."

Placing a comforting hand on Jonathan's arm, Meagan said, "It is hard when you suffer twice from the same problem. You don't know if you feel sorry for him or for yourself."

Andrew was growing fast and becoming a handsome young man. He was already as tall as Jonathan, with black hair and beautiful green eyes, and an athletic and robust body. Andrew also had developed a strong and determined personality. The relation between Jonathan and Andrew had continued to be strong and was a relief for both youths. Andrew had long looked up to Jonathan as his older brother, friend, and idol. He used to consult his brother about everything and it was clear that he took any advice he received from Jonathan very seriously. Verona and Donald, however, were very uncomfortable with the close relationship between Andrew and Jonathan. They tried by every possible means to separate the brothers or divert Andrew's interest in his brother, but without success.

The relationship between the two brothers was strong, real, and joyful. Andrew was no longer a kid and he was starting to be irritated by the fact that their parents had always treated Jonathan in a very bad manner. The situation came to the surface when Andrew interrupted the dinner one day to announce, "Mom, Dad, I am going to swap my room with Jonathan."

The food stuck in Donald's throat, almost suffocating him, and Verona looked stunned. After a moment, Donald Rattled rasped out an almost voiceless, "What?"

Andrew ignored his parents' dismay and repeated firmly, "I will change my room with Jonathan. I don't think it is fair for him to sleep in the basement while all of us have rooms."

Verona tried to justify their living arrangements. "But we don't have room for everybody."

Andrew replied firmly, "That is not true," and he turned to his father and said, "I don't understand: Why you don't sleep with mom like every normal couple? Why do you keep a separate room for you while Jonathan sleeps in the basement?"

Donald was on the verge of losing his temper. He turned to Jonathan and shouted, "What the hell have you done to the mind of our kid? Are you trying to turn my son against me? Is that what you want?"

Jonathan replied, "I am as surprised as you. I would never try to turn him against you or mom. Why would I do that?"

Andrew intervened. "It is me, not him. I am not a baby anymore and I see that both of you are very bad to my brother and I can't see why. He is very good to everybody here; he helps me and protects me everywhere."

At that moment, both Jonathan and Andrew were crying. Verona hugged Andrew and tried to cool him down. "Calm down, Andrew. This is not the way you believe. We are good with both of you."

Andrew interrupted her and said, "No, you and dad are not good to Jonathan. If there is no room for him, I will give him mine or I will sleep with him downstairs."

Verona looked at Donald, and he caught her unspoken message. Making a huge effort to disguise his real feeling of hate and anger towards Jonathan, he said, "Okay, Andrew, I will do it; I will move to your mom's room and he can take mine."

The relationship between Jonathan and Professor Moore was a blessing in the young student's life. He was able to find the recognition he needed and the care he had been lacking at home. On his side, Jonathan worked as hard as he could and impressed the professor with his achievements. Professor Moore also admired his analytical competence and his ability to extract unexpected results connecting the great variety of factors and considering all the possibilities. On Monday, 13 October 1997, at the beginning of the second year, the professor called Jonathan for a talk.

"Jonathan, I believe it is very tough for you to distribute your time between your job and your work here, and I think we can help you on that. We have arranged to pay you $800.00 a month. It is not much, but also, I talked to the people in student affairs and they will hire you to work in the library earning almost the same amount. I think that can enable you to quit your job at the mall and concentrate on your efforts here."

Jonathan was delighted. "Thank you, Professor. Now I can spend more time in the lab. I am really grateful."

Professor Moore said, "You are most welcome. I am glad we have you with us."

During the second and third years of his college education, Jonathan developed a memorable body of work under the guidance of Professor Moore. He was delighted to see his name on his first published paper. Jonathan's work in the library was nice and easy. He was there, close to all the books he liked, and, when possible, he could study during work hours. At the library, Jonathan could invite Andrew to enjoy the numerous photography albums and books. Andrew was greatly impressed by the work of the renowned Brazilian photographer Sebastião Salgado, and he spent hours in the library studying Salgado's pictures.

His third year sped by, and soon Jonathan was finishing the last quarter. However, Professor Moore informed him that there would be no long vacation this year: the entire team would be working through the summer on the final report, applying for a bigger budget for research for the next couple of years. Jonathan asked Meagan to plan to spend the summer in Seattle so they could be together.

On 1 July 1998, Meagan arrived in Seattle to see her mom and to spend the summer with Jonathan, but she never expected the surprise he prepared for her. On 4 July, Jonathan invited Meagan for dinner at the Salmon House on Lake Union. After dinner, Jonathan surprised Meagan with a ring and a proposal. Meagan was thrilled by the surprise. She stood up from their table and hugged him, whispering between tears and smiles, "Yes, yes, you are my man, my love, and my future."

In tears himself, Jonathan replied, "You are everything for me." All the guests in the restaurant started yelling and congratulating them.

On 11 October 1999, Jonathan started his fourth year with the status of a student fellow with considerable participation in Professor's Moore work. He already had the trust of the professor, and that was his goal. Jonathan had lost any hope of things getting better at home with his parents, so his life turned to Meagan, Andrew, and math. His plan was to do his best in the school to get his degree with the best grades, find a good job, and marry Megan, and he worked hard to meet that goal.

On 12 June 2000, at the end of his fourth year, Jonathan was called by Professor Moore for a talk. "Jonathan, I called you to talk about your future. You are almost done with your college studies, and I am sure you must be thinking about your future."

Surprisingly, Jonathan's eyes filled with tears, and Professor Moore quickly understood why. He had had some talks with Jonathan and he knew what was going on between him and his parents. Accordingly, the professor resumed. "I know you wished it was your father instead of me asking about your future."

Jonathan admitted, "I wish I knew why they don't care about me. You know, Professor, I am not a bad son. I try to do everything to please them, but they are never happy with me."

"I have no doubt you are a good son. You are a good man, and that is the basis for all your behaviour. You are one of the best trainees we have ever had, and that is why I wanted to talk to you today."

Jonathan thanked the professor with deep emotion. "Thank you, Professor. You have given me most of what I am missing at home. I am ready to listen."

"Look, Jonathan, as I said, you have been one of the best trainees here, and we are now selecting our graduate students for the master's and later for the doctorate degrees. Our interest is to have highly qualified students, and our trainees are our first choice. I am thinking seriously of recommending you remain with us and to work with me; this is the right place for you. The list will be put forward in one week; if you agree, your name will be on it."

Jonathan was taken by an overwhelming rush of joy and pride. "Thank you, Professor. It is an honour for me. Thank you for your trust. Most of what I am now I owe to you. Thank you very much."

The professor smiled and said, "You earned everything you have achieved, and you deserve the success you are reaching. I am confident both you and the university will be happy." They shook hands and Jonathan left, delighted.

Jonathan rushed home to tell his parents about the huge recognition he had just been given. When he arrived, Donald was on the couch watching TV. In his excitement, Jonathan said, "Dad, the professor will recommend my name to go on the list for a master's degree next year."

Without deviating his eyes from the TV, Donald mumbled, "Good for you." Coming out of the kitchen, Verona said, "Time to pick up Andrew. Don't make him wait for you." Jonathan turned around and left with his vision blurred by tears.

In the car on the way home, Andrew noticed that Jonathan seemed out of sorts. "What is wrong with you? Why do you look so upset?"

"Today I was informed by my professor that I will be recommended to join the graduate studies program after getting my degree."

"Wow! Isn't that great, are you upset about being good at what you do, and recognised as important?"

"No, I am very proud, but I wish our parents were also."

"Now, I get it, you told them, and they didn't pay attention, right?"

"Yes."

"That is their normal. They didn't know what a master's degree is, and why should they? They don't mention advanced degrees in the soap operas our parents watch all day."

They laughed, then Andrew added, "Don't lose your moment, brother. I am happy for you. Did you tell Meagan?"

"Not yet. I will wait for her to come. I want to see her reaction."

"She will be very proud of you, me too. You are our hero."

Finally, Jonathan felt some joy. He smiled and said, "Thank you, brother, I love you a lot."

Andrew answered in a quavering voice, "I love you too, Jonathan."

On 15 July, Meagan arrived in Seattle to attend Jonathan's graduation ceremony. Jonathan met her at the airport that same day, and he couldn't wait to tell her. "Meagan, the professor told me he is going to recommend I join the graduate school to get my master's degree. Isn't that great?"

Meagan jumped on his neck, kissing him and talking at the same time. "That is much more than great, that is fabulous. That means your future is guaranteed."

"You mean our future. You know, Meagan, this means that I am a good student and researcher, but it also means that I will stay here in Seattle."

"And, overall, you are a good man," she continued. "They don't recommend just anyone for those important positions, and I am with you anywhere that is good for you."

"Thank you, Meagan. That means a lot to me."

Meagan added, smiling, "It also means something else."

"What?"

"That we can get married soon."

"That is my sweet dream," Jonathan replied, his face beaming. "I can't wait to see you as my wife, my partner, and my lover, I mean my everything. Meagan, you are all my life."

Meagan was already in tears. She hugged him fiercely and said, "I swear I will give you all the happiness you missed; I will make it up for you. I will give you some beautiful children, I mean many of them if you want, and the warmest home in America. I do promise."

"We will be happy. I have no doubt about that."

The graduation ceremony was very good, particularly for Jonathan, who graduated with honours. Andrew and Meagan were very proud of him.

Meagan and Jonathan had a wonderful time during the days she spent in Seattle. They visited British Colombia by ferry and drove to Vancouver, and in Seattle, enjoyed visiting the UW library and the hub and eating in the many ethnic cafes on University Way.

Meagan spent only fifteen days in Seattle and had to return to California and her job at the end of July. "Don't be sad," Jonathan said to console her. "Next month I will be with you for fifteen days. I saved my vacation time to watch your graduation ceremony. We will have a wonderful time in California."

"I will be waiting for you," she replied. "I will always be waiting for you."

Jonathan did his best to finish all his tasks in the lab before leaving. In the middle of August, he delivered his report to Professor Moore. "Professor, I hope you like it. The results look good."

"I am confident I will; you are always precise and accurate. Just keep going the way you are now, and I am sure that you will be one of the best scientists of this country."

"Thank you, Professor. I will be gone for fifteen days, then I'll be back soon to start my master's."

"Go ahead. You deserve some time off; enjoy yourself."

Thursday, 17 August, when Jonathan arrived at John Wayne Airport in Irvine, Meagan was there waiting for him. "I told you I'd be here," he told her.

"And I told you I'd be waiting for you."

"That's what I came for."

They tried to make the best of their time together. They enjoyed walking on Hollywood Boulevard and loved spending time on Santa Monica's Third Street promenade. They visited the famous LA beaches, rode all the rides at Disneyland, and took pleasure in watching the panda at the San Diego Zoo. Everything was going their way, everything was perfect: the weather, the places, the people. Even the panda seemed to smile at them as it munched on bamboo.

During his visit, Meagan told Jonathan that she had the opportunity to start her MBA degree in October. Jonathan was delighted and asked, "Meagan, why not? That is wonderful. Have you accepted already?"

"I am thinking. The grant will cover only half of the tuition, and I am not sure I can afford it."

"Sure, you can. My contract with the university will grant a good salary, and all my research costs are covered, so I can help."

"But it is my life and I should be able to take care of myself."

"No, Meagan, it is our life. Starting now, it will always be our life. Please make me happy by accepting my offer."

With tears in her eyes, Meagan said, "I will do anything to see you happy."

"Then we agree: you start next October, and we will finish our degrees at almost the same time."

Both started working in October 2000, Jonathan in Seattle and Meagan in Irvine. Their tasks were intense and demanded a lot of effort, but they were in love and doing their best to fulfil their goals. In July 2001, Meagan returned to Seattle for the celebration of Andrew's graduation from high school. In a very beautiful and elaborate ceremony, the young man received his high school diploma. The McCoolens were in ecstasy, but only briefly.

Once they were back home, Andrew told his parents, "Mom, Dad, I will be studying in California."

Donald and Verona hated the idea. They wanted him close to them all their life, but they knew it was useless to argue. They were aware that he wanted to study arts, especially photography, and they couldn't stand against his wishes. Andrew told them that he had applied for several schools in Southern California. One of them, California Coast College, was ten minutes from Meagan's place, and this one was his first choice.

In August, when Andrew received a letter from California Coast College announcing his acceptance, he ran to the lab to tell Jonathan the news.

"I am very proud of you, brother; you will be a great artist," Jonathan said.

"Thank you, brother. I have a good example to follow."

They hugged each other and Jonathan asked, "Where are you thinking about living?"

"I was thinking of sharing the place with Meagan. Do you think she would be comfortable with that?"

"She will be very happy to hear your idea; you know she loves you. And having you as a housemate will help her meet expenses."

"Will you talk to her about that?"

"I intend to visit her on September 8; I will let her know. When will you be moving?"

"The quarter start on October 15, I intend to be there couple days before."

"I don't see any problem; I will take care of it."

"Thank you, brother. You are the best," Andrew said, Jonathan smiled.

On 8 September 2001, Jonathan arrived in Irvine. Meagan was thrilled to see him, and they headed directly to Meagan's place and started talking about their achievements in their work. They were almost halfway to finishing their master's and they had plenty to talk about. When Jonathan had a chance, he asked Meagan, "Would you like to have a roommate?"

Meagan immediately caught his meaning and asked, "Are you talking about Andrew?"

"Yes. He was accepted at California Coast College."

"Wonderful," Meagan yelled. "It is in Costa Mesa, ten minutes from here. He is most welcome. I will love having him with me."

Jonathan agreed. "I told him he will be good company for you, as well as help in the rent and expenses."

On Tuesday, 11 September 2001, Meagan and Jonathan were woken violently by sounds and screams coming from the street. Jumping out of bed, they rushed to the window, where they were shocked by what they saw. It seemed as though the world had turned upside down: People were running in all directions, yelling, screaming, and shouting loudly. Police cars rushed past, their sirens wailing insistently. Jonathan turned the TV on and in a few minutes, he was stunned. In a shaking voice, he called Meagan. "Meagan, come see what is happening. There is a huge fire, but where is it?"

Meagan was terrified as she saw the image on the TV: Two huge buildings towered above other skyscrapers, and one of them was enveloped in fire and a huge cloud of dark smoke. Listening to the newscasters, they learned the scene was of the World Trade Towers in New York. They gaped, speechless, as the TV newscasters explained that an airplane had just crashed into the building. All the TV channels were there, and emergency vehicles, ambulances, and fire-fighters were already on the scene, while a huge crowd of people had gathered in the surrounding streets.

While Jonathan struggled to understand what had happened, Meagan screamed. "Jonathan, look!" At nearly the same moment, a scream was echoed from the TV. Jonathan realised that another explosion had just erupted from the other tower; another jet liner had just crashed into the second World Trade Tower. Meagan and Jonathan were dumbfounded. What is really happening? Is this the third world war?

As it quickly became clear that no one in the street was safe, people's despair turned to madness. On the TV, agitated commentators were talking and yelling, transmitting the sudden panic of the crowd as they began running away from the buildings. Soon, the talk on the TV shifted from speculation about a possible accident to the possibility that this was a deliberate action. At that point, they heard news of a third crash at the Pentagon.

"What?" Jonathan screamed. "The most protected building in the world? How is that possible?" Meagan was speechless. She kept turning her eyes from him to the TV to the streets of New York. Then, suddenly, they saw something they couldn't imagine: one of the buildings started to collapse, and in just a few seconds, the tower of 110 floors was gone.

Megan screamed, "The building is exploding!"

Jonathan was shocked and horrified, but he had some difficulty understanding what he was looking at. "Something is strange; it is not an explosion. It looks like the building is crumpling. That is different."

"What do you think is happening?" Meagan asked.

"I don't know. I really don't know."

At that moment, they were struck by the news that another airplane had been aiming at the White House, but it had been shot down. They felt a brief flash of relief; finally, there had been some reaction, but it was only for a very short time. Soon, they watched the second tower collapsing the same way as the first. Another 110 floors looked like each one was melting into the one below it. The chaos was total and absolute. America was under fire, and it seemed that no one had any idea what to do. On TV, the newscasters and commentators started to talk about a terrorist attack, and certain names and words like Al-Qaeda, radicals, and extremists started to be mentioned. Jonathan called home to talk to his family. Andrew told him that their father was furious about the attack and that their mother had been crying without stop. Meagan also called her mother, and she told her how shocked they were.

The rest of the week was tense and stressful. It was established that an extremist organisation known as Al-Qaeda was the mastermind of the attack, and a passport found in the rubble of one of the melted towers was offered as a smoking gun. A dark wave of hatred and anger covered the country, and some innocent people paid with their lives for that. The country started to move to war, and the call for vengeance quickly became a national demand, expressed overwhelmingly by the media and government agencies. Military cars and personnel were seen everywhere. It was clear that a confrontation of some kind was inevitable.

On Sunday, 16 September, Meagan left Jonathan at John Wayne Airport to catch his flight back to Seattle. Arriving home, Jonathan was anxious to see everybody and to be sure that they were doing well. What he never expected was to be greeted by his father in a state of fury. "Where have you been all this week? Did you forget the family you claim you love so much?" Donald shouted.

Jonathan was shocked. Everyone had known he was with Meagan and that he would be back home on Sunday, so why was his father so angry? Jonathan tried to explain. "You knew I was with Meagan, and you know also that I love my family."

Donald replied with even greater anger. "No, you don't, you don't care about this family, and you don't care about the country. The country is burning, and you are in bed with a girl. You only care about yourself; you have no feeling for anything else."

Almost in tears, Jonathan insisted, "I love my country and I do love my family; the question is, does my family love me, especially you? Do you see or feel about me like a son?"

Donald exploded, shouting, "What you just said, you want the truth? No, I don't, and I don't want to see you anymore. Take your belongings and leave this house immediately. This family is not…"

The words stuck in Donald's mouth with Verona's desperate yelp, "Donald, stop…"

Donald immediately realised what she wanted to warn him about and changed his words. "This family doesn't want you here anymore."

Advancing toward his father, Andrew yelled angrily, "This family is not only you; I am part of this family and I want him here."

Verona started weeping intensely and Donald looked at Jonathan and said, "Can't you see how much harm you are doing to this family? My son is opposing me, and my wife is almost dying from sadness and frustration. What else are you going to do with us? What are you waiting for? Just leave us."

Jonathan ran to his room and started to collect his belongings. Andrew ran behind him begging, "No, Jonathan, don't leave, I need you. I love you."

"I love you too," Jonathan replied, "but I have no place here anymore. I have been expecting this for a long time. I just don't understand why now."

"I don't know either. I asked those many times why they act the way they do to you, but they never say why. Sometimes I feel that even they don't know."

"God knows I did everything to win their love. I wish I could, but now I must go."

"I'll go with you," Andrew shouted.

"No," Jonathan screamed, then he said, "You don't have any reason to do that. They love you, and you are still seventeen years old. You can't leave home now."

"Then stay with me, please. You know how much I need you. I love you, brother."

"I know, and you know that your love is the most valuable thing I have, but I need to leave. Things have reached the breaking point and started to be dangerous. I must leave before it gets worse."

After Jonathan finished packing his clothes, he hugged his brother and left, feeling his tears mixed on his face with those of his brother.

Chapter 9

Jonathan had nowhere to go, no home, no family, and a lot of sadness in his heart. After wandering around for a couple of hours, he stopped at a low-cost motel to spend the night. Early on the second day, he went to the student housing division of the university to ask for help. The supervisor was nice enough to find shelter for him for two weeks at a reduced fee. Jonathan left his bag in the room and rushed to the lab. He had a very hard time paying attention to his work. It was difficult to understand why his father was so furious with him, why he had been ripped out of his family and thrown away without any affection or kind feeling. At the end of the day, he found himself alone in his room asking the same old question: What did I do wrong? Why do they not like me if I love them so much?

Later that day, he met with Dr Moore, who welcomed him affectionately. "Welcome back, Jonathan. One more year and you will be done with your master's work. We have a lot to accomplish."

Jonathan could not hold back his tears. The doctor approached him and said, "I see you have more problems at home. What is it this time?"

"I was thrown out of my home; my family doesn't want me anymore."

"You know, Jonathan, I have great difficulty understanding your problem with your parents. You are a good person. I can't see why they act the way you tell me they do. Anyway, you have your life to live. If you need any help, let me know."

"Thank you, Professor, I am fine," Jonathan said, but in fact he was far from fine; he was sad, frustrated, and depressed.

The country was living through days of fear, anger, and uncertainty. The smell of blood was everywhere, and America's feeling of invincibility was definitely shattered. Newspapers expressed this sense of upheaval in their headlines: Terrorists attack New York and Pentagon; War on America; Hijacked jets destroy Twin Towers and the Pentagon in day of terror; A Thousand feared dead. Everybody was looking for an explanation, to understand how what had happened could be real. The madness was generalised, and the call for retaliation came from every corner. The military opened many centres to recruit volunteers.

The madness also found a home in Jonathan's head. He fell into a state of despair about the country, his family, and himself. He wasn't doing well in his research; he wasn't doing well in the lab; and he wasn't doing well when he was alone in his room. Jonathan was living with hell burning in his head and he was going through a deep and continuous depression. After an intense inner struggle, Jonathan decided to enlist in the army. On 25 September 2001, instead of going to the university, he went directly to the nearest recruiting centre and presented himself. Back at the school, he went to Professor Moore's office and told him, "Dr Moore, I am sorry, but I will not be able to help here anymore. It is impossible for me to finish my master's degree. I joined the army and I will be leaving tomorrow."

Dr Moore needed some time to absorb what he had just heard and took a couple minutes to answer. "We have a lot to accomplish here. I still believe that your battlefield is not that one. You are a scientist, but it is your life and only you know what to do with it."

Jonathan left and went to his room to write a letter to Meagan:

Love, I am sorry I didn't talk to you first, and I am sad I won't be able to see you before, but soon I will be leaving to Indiana military training centre and from there I will be deployed to the battlefield abroad. Now you know that I joined the army and my life doesn't belong to me anymore. I hope you know that you have been the greatest happiness I ever had. You gave my life the brightness, the hope and the love, your love gave me back the tomorrow that I didn't have before meeting you, your love gave me the desire to live that I didn't have before loving you, your love regenerated in my heart the feelings of caring, sharing, and joy that I never knew before I knew you. You are the light in my eyes, the sun of my days, and the star of my nights. You are the meaning of my life, the reason for my fight, and all that I live for. But I have no option; it is my destiny and I need to go. Please forgive me.

Jonathan called home, and Andrew picked up the phone. "Jonathan, I am glad you called."

"Andrew, I need to meet you. We need to talk."

"What has happened? Is something wrong?"

Jonathan repeated, "Andrew, please, I need to talk to you."

"Where are you?"

"I will be in the library of the university in twenty minutes; I'll be waiting for you there."

"I am on my way."

Twenty minutes later, Andrew arrived, and Jonathan immediately started talking. "Andrew, you are a man now, and I am sure you will understand. I am leaving tomorrow."

"Where are you going?" Andrew asked.

"I joined the army. Soon, I will be going to Indiana for basic training camp. After that, I don't know where I'll be; probably out of the country."

Andrew was stunned. He had never imagined his brother being far from him. Since the day Jonathan was forced to leave home, Andrew had met him almost every day, and he was hoping to fix the situation and bring his brother back home. He said, almost crying, "What are you telling me, Jonathan? And your research? What about your future?"

Jonathan answered, "All that can wait. My place now is at the front, and there is where I must go."

"What will I do without you?" Andrew said, in tears. "Can you imagine how much I'm going to miss you?"

"I will miss you too, Andrew, you know how much I love you. But I need to go; everything will be okay. I'll come back to you."

After a couple minutes of silence, Jonathan told his brother, "I hope that my decision will not change your plans, I mean the move to California. Meagan is waiting for you to arrive on 12 October. Promise me that everything will go as we have planned."

"Sure, I promise."

The brothers hugged each other and wept long and hard.

On Wednesday, 26 September 2001, at exactly 6:00 a.m., Jonathan presented himself at the Seattle Naval Base as he was ordered to do. After registration, he received his clothing and gear and was directed to his place in room seventeen. In the room, he met three other young men who had registered before him.

"My name is Carterwhite, Geoffrey. Nice to meet you," the one on the bottom of his bunk bed introduced himself.

"Nice to meet you too, my name is McCoolen, Jonathan." The other two guys jumped out of their beds and welcomed him.

"I am Glaver, Marcus."

"Welcome aboard. I am Garcia, Victor, but if I am promoted to sergeant, I will change my name." They all laughed, and Marcus commented, "We would love to call you Sergeant Garcia." They laughed again and Jonathan started to relax.

Geoffrey offered to give him some information. "Look, Jonathan, we have been here since Monday, so we will let you know about the routine here. In a few minutes, we will be called for 7:00 a.m. line-up for flag hoisting. There you will receive the instructions of the day. You must be wearing your uniform and boots, so it is better to start dressing now. You can't be late. After the line-up, you will have fifteen minutes for breakfast, then you start executing the instructions you received."

Jonathan quickly put on his uniform and once the siren of the call was heard, the four of them left the room in a hurry to join the others in the courtyard for orientation. There were about a hundred volunteers, and the base was expecting more until Friday. The ceremony took exactly one hour. After breakfast, they ran to start the training schedule. At noon, they had thirty minutes for lunch. Afterwards, they rushed back to the training site and worked hard, stopping only at 7:00 p.m. Tired and exhausted, they only had time to have dinner and fall into bed. On Thursday and Friday, they repeated the same screening of Wednesday. More people joined them, elevating the total number to approximately two hundred young men and women, all of whom were subjected to the same programming. Saturday, all the volunteers participated in a unified training session ending at 7:00 in the evening. Sunday, they had a free day to prepare for the trip to Indiana.

On Monday, 1 October, the recruits boarded an airplane, which soon left Seattle and headed to Indiana. At noon, they arrived at Indianapolis International Airport, from where they were transported by bus to the military base of Columbus. At 6:00 a.m. on Tuesday, 2 October, more than one thousand young men and women were lined up on the training field to hear the speech of the base commander lieutenant Colonel Jaxon Fulton Hunter. The commander welcomed them briefly and then gave them a promise:

"You are here to defend America. You think you are here to fight. Wrong. You are here to win. You think you are here to die for your country. Wrong. You are here to kill the enemy of your country. We are at war, and the one who will win the war is the one who survives the war. There is no other choice: Either we or the enemy will win, or we have got to prevail, for America and for the victory. Here, you will learn how to be a soldier, a fighter, and a winner. There is no other choice, no alternative but victory. I have sixty days to turn you into soldiers, and that is a very short time, almost impossible, but I have no intention to fail."

After the speech, they had fifteen minutes for breakfast. After, they were divided into groups, each under the command of a sergeant and several aides. Immediately, the volunteers started the hard task of being transformed into real soldiers. They had nine weeks. Eight would be dedicated to physical performance, training with small weapons, training with combat vehicles, and tactical training. Each modality would be concluded in two weeks, with the last week scheduled for lectures and studying political and security issues. There was no time to lose, so they worked as hard as they could to get the job done. At the end of each section, the performance of each volunteer was evaluated to be qualified to proceed. Jonathan did his best, and at the end of the nine weeks, he was at the top among his mates.

During the training period, Geoffrey, Jonathan, Marcus, and Victor, or the four of seventeen, as they called themselves, developed a wonderful and joyful relationship. Geoffrey was twenty years old. He was the older brother of two sisters and came from Bellingham, a beautiful city of eighty-five thousand residents close to the Canadian border. Geoffrey was very proud when Jonathan praised the Bellingham Festival of Music. "I always wanted to visit Bellingham during those lovely summer days to enjoy the festival, but I never had the chance."

"Yes, you would love it. There is marvellous music everywhere. Bellingham is a magic city during the festival. I have an additional pleasure in July: my father is a cellist, so for me it is a double joy."

Marcus came from Spokane. His parents had a big farm where he and his two brothers and sister used to work. Marcus had the simplicity and innocence of people who works on the land; he was very friendly and cooperative and always willing to help the others. Marcus made every effort to convince his roommates that his family descended from James N. Glover, the so-called father of Spokane, and that the difference in the name, from Glover to Glaver, was just a pronunciation accident, but no one was sure, especially Victor.

Victor, or Sergeant Garcia as he was nicknamed, came from an immigrant Mexican family. They had arrived in Seattle in the late eighties, when he was six years old, and his sister Gloria was three. The family was awarded one more brother, Anthony, two years later. The family opened a Mexican restaurant on University Way, and they had to work as hard as was needed. They couldn't afford to hire anyone to help and had to do all the work themselves. His father took over the kitchen and his mother had to wait tables and act as the cashier at the same time. Time passed and Victor started to help, and his sister also went to the kitchen to help their father. Eventually, the family's hard work paid off, and the restaurant became one of the favourites in the area. Victor's dream was to go to dental school, and while his father offered him all his support to achieve his goal, he had to postpone his dream to serve his country. The friendship among the four of seventeen helped them to beat all the challenges they faced in this period. The support and encouragement they offered to each other was fundamental for them to maintain their performance at the highest level possible.

On Sunday, 7 October, all the trainees were gathered on the patio of the centre for an important announcement. Soon, the commander in chief informed them that the United States was at war. "Fellow Americans, your country is at war. Your country has been attacked, and our president demanded that the Taliban hand over Osama bin Laden and his aides. The Taliban declined, arguing that they needed evidence of his involvement in the 9/11 attacks. The United States considered the request for evidence a delaying tactic and was dismissed. Today, our country and the United Kingdom launched Enduring Freedom Operation." He paused for few seconds and resumed the talk, asking, "Are you ready to defend your country?"

The answer coming from one thousand volunteers was thunderous. "Yes, we are."

The commander ended his speech by recommending, "Then practice, practice with all your strength and power, because your country might need you very soon."

On Saturday, 17 November, they received the information that the next week would be their final week in Indiana and would be the most important and dangerous part of their training. They were informed that they would go through realistic war conditions, during which the fire would be live. They were also informed that immediately after, they would be transferred to a combat zone. It was a very difficult week; they had to finalise their program as best as they could, and they had to fight against the stress and strain. The four of seventeen tried to offer each other support, but it was impossible to avoid the tension and curiosity.

What you think we will do there?" Garcia wondered.

"Kill our enemies," Glaver said.

"How we will know who our enemy is and who is not?" Garcia insisted.

Marcus replied, "All of them are. We are training to kill, not to question."

Carterwhite tried to help. "Look, fill yourself with the sense of duty to defend your country and think about the opportunities the army gives you to do things with your life."

On Wednesday, 28 November, a huge airplane landed in the airport of Kabul with four hundred privates, among them the four of seventeen. There was no reception ceremony, no welcome speech; it was the war. That what was waiting for them and what they began living from their first day in the Afghani capital. The war was everywhere. The airport was heavily secured with soldiers, tanks, and armoured vehicles. Security checks were rigid and unyielding, and the recommendation was to be very careful; any carelessness could be deadly. The group was transferred to a nearby air base in several strictly escorted convoys, where Jonathan and Marcus joined the infantry forces, Victor was designated for the communications division, and Geoffrey was nominated to aid the 5th Special Forces Group. They were also told that they would soon be engaged in a huge and vital battle.

On 3 December 2001, 5th Special Forces Group supported by the CIA National Clandestine Service was inserted by helicopter into the city of Jalalabad to start the battle of Tora Bora. Two days later, the fighters of the Afghan Northern Alliance joined the battle. Heavy uninterrupted air strikes targeted the enemy fighters using laser-guided bombs and missiles for seventy-two hours. One week later, ground forces composed of Delta Force's A Squadron and Air Force units, lately embedded by two British divisions, arrived to support the bombing campaign. Fires, which the Afghan fighters had lit to heat themselves, were used by the laser-guided, air-launched weapons to reveal their specific locations. On 12 December, the fighting spread, and within a few weeks, the U.S.

ground and air forces with the CIA and Northern Alliance had captured several key cities from the Taliban. The battle of Tora Bora was the first major battle to face U.S. troops in Afghanistan, and it was also the first big test for Jonathan and Marcus. They were part of the front lines of the ground forces with the mission of expelling the enemy from the Tora Bora terrain. The American troops had all the maps and information they needed about the Tora Bora caves and their defensive positions. In the eighties, the CIA helped Al-Qaeda and the Afghani fighters in extending and shoring up the caves in the fight against the Soviet occupation. Of course, all of these maps and relevant information were forwarded by the CIA to the troops. Jonathan's performance was noticed and praised by his commander, who noted that he showed himself to be smart, brave, and full of determination.

After the battle of Tora Bora, the Taliban and Al-Qaeda forces went into hiding and started to prepare for the next battle. According to intelligence reports, one of their leaders fled to Pakistan and called fugitive fighters to join him. By the beginning of Operation Anaconda, the estimation was that the forces he had gathered totalled over 1,000 combatants. On 2 March 2002, the United States, leading a coalition of eleven countries, started the first operation in the Afghanistan theatre involving many conventional forces. A total of 30,000 coalition soldiers participated in direct combat activities. The main purpose of the operation was to destroy Al-Qaeda and Taliban forces, which were estimated at 600–1,000 fighters, and obtain control of the Shahi-Kot Valley and the Arma Mountains. At midnight, the units of TF Hammer left their base heading to the Shahi-Kot Valley. After reaching its pre-established point about 6:15 a.m., the company paused and waited for the planned intense aerial bombardment of enemy positions. Unexpectedly, the aerial attack failed, frustrating the assault. Due to heavy small arms and mortar fire, combined with the lack of the planned massive air support against the enemy, the coalition's attack stopped short of entering the valley.

The troops designated to block the eastern and northern edges of the valley were transported via helicopter to their positions to await fleeing Taliban and l-Qaeda fighters. These troops also had a hard time fulfilling their mission. Once they landed, they encountered concentrated fire and became locked in a fierce fire fight. Due to the heavy fighting, only two of the planned eight helicopters landed. Fire support for the troops was provided by two Apache attack helicopters. Though the Apaches faced fierce resistance and suffered serious damage, they were able to destroy many enemy positions that were confronting the U.S. troops. The disarray among the troops continued during the battle over the following days. Also, when the two SEAL fire teams, Mako 30 and Mako 31, tried to establish an observation point on either end of the valley on 3 and 4 March, they failed to fulfil their mission.

The first group was picked up by an MH-47 Chinook helicopter and attempted to land atop the mountain at 3:00 a.m. As they approached, they noticed signs of human activity. The helicopter was hit by rocket-propelled (RPG) fire, receiving damage that prevented proper control, and the helicopter was forced to crash-land in the valley below. Exiting the aircraft, the team immediately lost three of their men. The survivors were joined by Special Forces and engaged in fierce battle. With the aid of very intense air support, the troops were able to defeat the enemy and consolidate their position. The second team, Mako 31, also faced serious difficulties due to their proximity to the enemy, which prevented the use of sufficiently concentrated firepower. In their first attempt to reach the landing zone at the peak of the mountain, two of the forces were killed and two injured. Finally, Mako 31 discovered an adequate spot for landing. Subsequently, the team established suitable defences and started to take care of the wounded.

Over the following days, the mission was to clear the valley of any remaining enemy forces. The plan was for the troops to sweep through the valley under heavy bombing by U.S. strike fighter aircraft. But, to the attackers' surprise, the mission wasn't that easy. The enemy put up ferocious resistance and was unwilling to be easily killed. After Sergeant Williams Valdez, Jonathan was second in command of the twelve members of their group; Marcus was also one of the twelve. On 17 March, the group received an order to clear a passage on the eastern side of the valley from the enemy in order for the other troops to advance. The passage was covered by snow, and the strong wind made clear vision difficult. Valdez organised his men in line, trying to hide from the enemy. He positioned Jonathan at the end of the line to protect the rear of the column.

The group advanced in the passage under strong fire. After two hours of intense combat, the enemy considerably reduced the intensity of the fire, giving the impression that they were retreating. Valdez decided to take the opportunity to advance and eliminate the enemy. However, some short time later, Jonathan noticed suspicious activity behind the group. He realised that the withdrawal of the enemy was a plan to push the group forward and cut the way between them and the main troops. Jonathan immediately called Valdez on the radio. "Sergeant, the enemy is trying to infiltrate behind us."

Valdez answered immediately, "They are trying to surround us; we can't let them succeed."

Jonathan asked, "May I have your permission to deal with that?"

Valdez agreed. "We don't have time. Go ahead. Take one man with you. Be careful."

"Yes sir," Jonathan replied, "moving to comply immediately."

Jonathan tried to pass his position to Marcus, but Marcus asked him to transfer the position to another soldier and insisted on being his companion in the mission he had just received. Jonathan agreed and the two started to move in the direction of the enemy.

Jonathan asked Marcus to move on the other side of the road, a few steps behind him. Soon, they were received by a blast of bullets, and an intense fire exchange started that lasted for a few minutes. Through binoculars, Jonathan saw the enemy's fighters trying to install a machine gun in a strategic position to isolate the group from its main contingent. Jonathan approached Marcus and whispered, "We can't allow that. If they get the machine gun, they will control the passage. Continue firing and keep them busy. I will turn around and approach them. We need to blow everything up."

Worried, Marcus said, "But you will be very close. It is very risky."

"I must do it. I need to blow them up using grenades, so I need to be close. Give me protection, fire and move fast, change place to keep them confused and make it look like many people are firing." Having said this, Jonathan began moving in the direction of the machine-gun position, Marcus did his best to keep the attention of the Afghans in his direction. Meanwhile, Jonathan moved stealthily, trying to flank the Taliban fighters, approaching their position until he reached a point, he judged within throwing range. Pausing, he activated a grenade and threw it into the middle of the position where the machine gun had been set up. The grenade exploded, reaching the heavy weapon and killing several fighters. To be sure that the weapon was completely destroyed, Jonathan activated a second grenade and stood up to throw it. Just as the grenade left his hand, he was shot several times in the chest. The grenade exploded, killing the rest of the enemy fighters.

Marcus watched the explosion of the enemy's position in ecstasy. He looked in the direction Jonathan had gone, expecting him back, joyful for his great achievement, but Jonathan never came. A few minutes later, Marcus started to worry. After looking around carefully, he started to move forward slowly, calling his friend, but there was no answer. Marcus hurried his passes searching for Jonathan. There, close to the explosion site, he found his friend in a pool of blood. He ran hoping to do something to change the situation, but nothing could be done: Jonathan was dead. Marcus dropped in grief. He knew he was fighting a war; he knew there would be killing, he was surrounded by dead bodies, but not his friend, not Jonathan, Jonathan, no. His despair was interrupted by the arrival of the other soldiers. Marcus was directed to the commander's vehicle to report what had happened, and the soldiers started to take care of Jonathan's body. On March 18, 2002, Operation Anaconda was declared over.

Chapter 10

On 8 April 2002, at around 10:00 a.m., two officers knocked on the McCoolens' door. When Donald responded, one of the officers asked, "Mr McCoolen?"

"Yes, that is me."

The officer said, "May we come in? We need to talk to you."

Donald asked, "What is this about?"

The officer insisted, "Can we come in, please?"

Donald moved aside, allowing the officers to enter. They sat in the living room and one of them started talking. "Should we wait for your wife to join us?"

Donald said, "No need for that. She is sleeping, and I don't want to bother her."

The officer continued. "I am Lieutenant Harris, this my partner, Lieutenant Clark. Sir, we are sorry to inform you that Private First-Class Jonathan McCoolen, posthumously promoted to corporal, is dead. He was a hero who offered his life to save America."

Donald did not show any reaction; he just asked the officers unemotionally, "What am I supposed to do now?"

The officer replied promptly. "Nothing, sir, we are here to inform you that the army will take care of everything. The body will be transferred to the mainland on Friday, 26 April, and the funeral can be arranged any time after that. We understand that you need time to think about that."

The officer handed Donald a portfolio and said, "Here is all the information you need to contact us. Just let us know how you want to proceed."

Donald, standing up, answered coldly, "Okay, thank you."

The officers left, and once they were out of the house, one of them said, "Did he understand what we said? It was like we were talking about someone he didn't even know."

The second officer replied, "His reaction shocked me too; I mean, the lack of any reaction. Anyway, we did the first part of our mission, we communicated to our soldier's parents. Now, we need to finish our mission by contacting his fiancé as he requested in his will."

Verona entered the living room and asked, "Donald, is that true? I overheard the officer saying he had been killed."

Donald placed the portfolio on the table and answered, "Yes, it is true. Now we are definitely rid of him."

"What will we say to Andrew?" Verona asked.

"Say nothing, just ignore it," Donald grunted.

The officers flew to California on the same day, 8 April. Early on the following day, they knocked on Meagan's door in Tustin. When she opened the door and saw the officers, she collapsed, and the officers had to catch her before she hit the floor. They seated her while she was sobbing. "What happened, tell me. No, don't say anything. Why are you here?" Then she yelled for Jonathan's brother, "Andrew, help me, please."

Andrew came running from the room. Seeing the officers at the door, he felt that something bad had happened. Blinking, he asked, "What happened? Is something wrong with my brother?"

The officers remained standing, it was clear that they were having a hard time to keep their military posture in spite of the huge uneasiness they were experiencing, their concern reflected strongly in their eyes. They realised that their mission would be very difficult, but they had no choice. Lieutenant Clark stepped closer to the pair and said, "We can see how difficult this will be for both of you. It is difficult for us too, but we need to tell you that Jonathan is dead. He gave his life for his country. He was a hero."

"No!" Meagan's cry tore the souls of the officers. "No, tell me that you are mistaken. No, I don't want him a hero, I want him to be the lover I need, the father he dreamed of being. I want my Jonathan. He is the only thing I have."

Andrew's reaction was no less emotional. His expression was that of a man who had lost any sense of reality. He kept yelling, "My brother, Jonathan, my brother, no! My brother could not die. Jonathan is my brother, no, dead, no, please no."

At that moment, several neighbours entered the apartment, asking what had happened. These were Lesley, Alicia, and Larry, the right-side neighbours, and Joanne and Adam, from the third apartment on the same floor. The officers informed them about the death of Jonathan. Lesley hugged Meagan and said, "I am so sorry. I know how much you love him. I am devastated."

The two girls wept deeply on each other's shoulders. The other neighbours tried to help Andrew, but he was inconsolable; he kept crying and calling for his brother.

The officers were deeply affected. Lieutenant Harris approached Andrew and hugged him, saying, "We are really sorry. He was a brave man. He recommended in his papers that we contact both of you personally if something happened to him. Certainly, he loved you very much."

Weeping, Meagan said, "We had so many plans. We should be preparing for our wedding. We intended to have children and a beautiful family. Now everything is gone, everything is lost."

Clark attempted to offer her some relief. "You can still have a beautiful family."

She cried from the bottom of her heart, "Not without Jonathan, never, not without him."

Lieutenant Harris called Adam to the corner of the room and informed him that they had left the instructions for the funeral with the parents. He also left his card with Adam, asking him to give it to Andrew. "Please, tell him that he can call us any time." The officers then left, deeply moved by the sorrow they had brought.

Suddenly, Andrew felt the ground softening under his feet. Everything in the room started to turn around and abruptly everything disappeared. Hours later, Andrew recovered and opened his eyes. He was in his bed. Meagan and the neighbours were there, sad and worried. His voice came weakly and wounded. "What happened? Where are the officers?"

"You fainted and fell on the floor," Alicia told him. "You are okay; our friend Mathieu from the fifth floor is a doctor. He has already been here and said you are okay."

Adam added, "The officers left a message for you; they left their phone number in case you need to call them."

Two days later, Andrew told Meagan that he would fly to Seattle. "I am travelling today. I need to talk to my parents."

Meagan looked at him through her tears and said, "Please, take care of yourself. Did you call them?"

"No, I didn't. I will take a cab home. I hate to leave you alone, but I need to go."

"Don't worry about me. I need to learn what it is like to be alone now."

Andrew hugged her and mumbled, "I don't know how we will live with this for the rest of our lives."

Meagan replied, "We will have to. We have no choice."

Arriving home, Andrew met his parents in the living room as they watched TV. Everything was normal, as if nothing serious had happened. Shocked, he shouted, "Have the officers been here? Did they tell you about Jonathan?"

The tension rose in the room. Donald looked at Verona fearfully, and she returned his look. The silence prevailed for a few minutes until Andrew shouted hoarsely, "I am asking: What did the officers tell you about my brother?"

Donald and Verona's fear turned to despair. They realised that Andrew was appalled by their apparent indifference. Verona struggled to answer. "It is sad, but they told us he was killed in the war."

Andrew felt like the bottom of his heart was in flames. Through tears, he tried to say, "My brother…my only brother was killed and you sit here watching television like nothing has happened …Jonathan is dead. What will be life without Jonathan?"

Suddenly overwhelmed by rage and disgust, he snarled, "You killed him. It wasn't the war; it was both of you. You sent him to the war to be killed."

Verona again tried to deflect the turmoil of Andrew's furious storm of emotion. "No, son, he volunteered for the army. It was his own choice."

Andrew interrupted vehemently. "No, it wasn't, it was your choice, not his. He was never a man of war; he was the most peaceful person I have ever met in my life…"

He was interrupted by an overwhelming fit of weeping. After a while, he spoke again. "My brother was a good man. He would have been a great scientist; he would have been a brilliant one. You killed him."

He turned abruptly to Donald, yelling, "Especially you, you killed Jonathan. Your hate and your cruelty to him, you killed him. Do you think I believe you when you say you love me? No, I don't. He was also your son, and you hated him. How can you love one and hate the other? You love nobody; you love no one."

Donald tried to defend himself. "You can't say that, you are wrong. I always loved you. Everything I did, I did to please you."

Andrew interrupted. "And everything you could to displease him. You are a killer, you killed your own son, your flesh, and you are a murderer."

Donald screamed, "Don't call me a murderer. I demand more respect."

But Andrew wasn't intimidated. He replied, "I hate you and I will hate you for the rest of my life. For, me you are nothing but a killer, a murderer. You killed my brother, the person I loved most in the world. I will never forgive you for the death of my brother."

Donald lost his temper and shouted, "You don't know anything. He is not your brother, and he never was. You are crying for nothing. He is no one, and it is good that he is gone now."

Verona grabbed Donald around the neck and tried to shut him up. "Donald, watch yourself! What are you saying? Please leave now. It is better to leave right now," she said and pushed him out of the room. When she came back, Andrew was still stunned; Donald's words were reverberating in his head like a rock crashing to the ground:

"He is not your brother and never was. You are crying for nothing. He is no one, and it is good that he is gone now."

"What does that mean? Is Jonathan not my brother? Can you tell me the truth now?"

Andrew asked Verona for the truth, but she was willing to do anything and to say anything to keep her and Donald's secret from being revealed, so she tried to persuade Andrew that Donald was out of his mind and didn't know what he was saying. "Don't say that, Andrew, of course, he is your brother. Your father lost his mind and spoke foolishly. He didn't mean what he said. Please forget about that."

But Andrew was far from believing her. The power and strength of Donald's speech showed that he meant what he said. It was clear to Andrew that the statement wasn't a manifestation of anger or lack of control. Andrew turned to Verona and said, "If you don't tell me the truth, I will go to the deepest spot in hell to find it."

In desperation, Verona implored him, "I beg you, son, get that out of your mind. Your dad lost his mind; he didn't mean what he said."

Andrew insisted, choked on his own tears, "I will find the truth about my brother. I will never quit. I owe him that; I owe him that."

The following days were exhausting for Andrew. He was struggling against the fact that he had lost his brother and best friend. His need to refuse to believe that Jonathan had gone elevated the fight inside him to the highest level, making healing almost impossible. At the same time, another fight was going on with great intensity between Andrew and Verona. Donald had arranged a long business trip to Guatemala and left Verona to face the storm alone, as much as he could. Andrew insisted that Verona "Tell me the truth about my brother. I need to know. I will stay here until you tell me. I am quitting school and everything else until you tell me the truth."

Verona kept answering that there was nothing to be said and that Donald had lost the ability to be rational when he said what he did. Andrew never accepted that; he was sure that something remained, and he was determined to find out what it was. Therefore, he asked Verona, "If dad said that Jonathan is not his son, what about me? How could he be the father of one and not of the other? Who is my father?"

Verona went crazy when she heard that. She cried, "No, Andrew, never say that again. Donald is your father."

Andrew retorted, "You told me all my life that Jonathan is my brother, and now I have been told otherwise. You lied to me before, and you are lying to me now. Tell me who my father is."

Verona felt that the problem was growing bigger, and doubt was taking root in Andrew's mind. Trying to remove the mistrust from her son's mind, she ran in despair to her room and returned in a few minutes carrying a sheet of paper and presented to Andrew. "Look, Andrew, look son, this is your birth certificate. Look, here is the name of your father. You could never doubt that."

Taking the paper, Andrew looked it over thoroughly and saw the name of his parents and all the other information. But just when Verona was starting to feel some relief, Andrew dropped a bombshell. He looked firmly in her eyes and demanded, "Then let me see my brother's certificate of birth."

At this moment, Verona realised the huge mistake she had just made. She remembered that the only birth certificate she had for Jonathan showed him as having been born in Brazil, and it was a forgery. She tried desperately to find an excuse, but the only thing she could do was increase the doubt in his mind. Finally, her only way to get out of the trap she had built for herself was to promise him that she would find the certificate and let him see.

Andrew returned to California, where Meagan met him at John Wayne Airport in Irvine, and they drove to their place in Tustin. Once there, they dissolved yet again in tears and needed time to get control of themselves. Meagan hugged Andrew affectionately and said, "Tell me how your trip was. Did you talk to your parents about the funeral?"

"No, I didn't," Andrew answered. "We had something much more serious to discuss."

With a puzzled look on her face, Meagan asked, "What is happening?"

Andrew told her what Donald had said and commented, "I believe that they are hiding something. What my dad said explains why he treated Jonathan so badly. No father would be so cruel to his son the way he always was to Jonathan. I need to know the truth; I owe that to my brother."

Meagan was shocked. "What could be wrong with your brother? I met Jonathan in high school when we were sixteen years old. He has always been a good and kind person. Of course, he was sad for the rejection he suffered from your parents, but nothing else caught my attention."

On Tuesday, 30 April, Andrew got a call from Lieutenant Harris. "Hello, Andrew. I hope you and Meagan are coping. I am calling to inform you that the body of your brother is already home. We called your parents and their choice was to leave to the army the task of taking care of the funeral services and burial."

Andrew interrupted him. " That will never happen. If they don't want to take care of him, I can do it."

Harris replied, "I am sorry, Andrew, but you can't. Only the parents can make this decision. I understand your sadness, but the only thing I can do to help is to send you the tickets to join us at the ceremony in honour of your brother. If Megan wishes to be here, we can send her tickets too."

Andrew's sadness was overwhelming, and tears hindered him from answering, so Harris added, "The services and burial will be on Saturday 18 May 2002, at 11:00 a.m., in Point Lookout Confederate Cemetery, Point Lookout, and Ridge, Maryland, 20680. You will receive the tickets and the hotel voucher in three days."

Barely able to speak, Andrew answered, "Thank you, we will be there."

On Friday, 17 May, Meagan and Andrew arrived at Washington Dulles International Airport. Lieutenant Clark and Lieutenant Harris were waiting for them. In the hotel, Lieutenant Harris told them, "Everything has been taken care of. A car will be here tomorrow at 08:30 a.m. to pick you up." Clark handed Megan his card and said, "If you need anything, please contact us." On Saturday, Meagan and Andrew arrived at the cemetery around 10:40. They were immediately directed to the gravesite. The ceremony started when the flag-draped casket arrived at the cemetery, where a six-man honour guard transported the casket to the gravesite. After the committal service, the American flag stretched over the casket was lifted and held by the honour guard. The firing party fired three volleys, and one member of the honour guard folded the American flag, which he ceremonially presented to Andrew and Meagan.

After the ceremony, Lieutenants Clark and Harris with two other officers approached Meagan and Andrew. Lieutenant Clark said, "I wish to introduce those two brave soldiers to you, Carterwhite, Geoffrey and Glaver, Marcus. They were the closest people to Jonathan on the front. Victor Garcia, their third companion, is in the hospital, which is why he is not here."

Carterwhite and Glaver hugged Meagan and Andrew and expressed their deepest sorrow for the loss of Jonathan. Marcus told them that he was the last one to be with Jonathan. Geoffrey said, "Jonathan will live forever in our hearts. He was a man who won't be forgotten."

Chapter 11

Back in California, Meagan and Andrew had to prepare for fall quarter finals, scheduled to start on Monday, 16 September 2002. Andrew hugged Meagan and said, "We have to get over the loss, the sadness and the emptiness Jonathan left. We need to be prepared for our finals; we need that."

And they tried, though it wasn't easy. Many times, one was caught crying alone in their room, and the other had to struggle to take them out of the sad moment. They did what they could to get ready for their exams, and it was a great relief when the tests ended on 25 September.

On Saturday, 28 September, they headed to Seattle. Since his disastrous encounter with his parents and Jonathan's funeral, Andrew had accepted very little contact with them. When she opened her door and found Andrew standing there, Verona broke into tears and hugged him. "Son, are you still blaming us for his death? You won't talk to us; you don't take our calls. What can we do to fix our relationship?"

Andrew's answer was sharp and unforgiving, "Bring Jonathan back to me."

The days went by in a nervous fugue, reflecting the sad and unfriendly atmosphere of the family's home. Andrew spent almost all the time isolated in his room. Any contact between him and Verona was painful and troubling. Donald did again what he had done before, arranged a long business trip, and left.

Nights were especially tough for Andrew. That was when he used to sit with his brother and talk about everything. They would exchange ideas and dream of the future. Now he was alone in his room missing his brother and best friend. One day he couldn't resist the impulse; he walked to his brother's room, opened the door, and entered. The room had been abandoned since Jonathan left the house; everything was the way he had left it. He sat on the bed and called to mind the battle he had fought so that his brother could use the room. He looked around; everything was there; books, notes, and papers, all his brother's life was there.

Andrew started to examine the books and notes, trying to bring his brother to life through memories. The books and notes that Jonathan used in his first school were particularly interesting; they were full of designs and strange words. He started flipping through the books. Hidden inside the pages in the middle of one of the books was a piece of a page of an old newspaper, folded many times to fit in the middle of the book. The book was one of the first Jonathan had ever used, one that kids learning to read used. Andrew unfolded the paper and tried to understand what it was saying and why Jonathan kept it so carefully. The page was a part of a local newspaper with a photo of a couple. Around the photo, the words 'baba Omar, mama Rania, baba, mama' were scrawled in primitive and tremulous letters, along with some other words he couldn't decipher.

Andrew tried to read around the photo to extract the maximum he could understand. He couldn't understand very much; the paper was old and almost yellow, but the little he grasped was enough to leave him gasping.

The subject of the newspaper article was the disappearance of a little boy. The caption below the photo indicated that the man and the woman were the parents of the lost child, and Andrew understood that the words around the photo had been written by Jonathan. A storm of terrible questions blew across his mind: *Who are these people? How did they lose their kid? When and where did that happen? How that could be related to his brother? What was the meaning of the words that Jonathan wrote and why did they point to these people?*

Driven almost to madness, Andrew searched the room thoroughly to see if he could find more information to help him understand, but all that he found was a date, on the top of the page where the strange words were written, indicating the day the newspaper was published: Friday, 15 May 1981.

Andrew was unable to close his eyes even for a moment. He spent the night in a state of terror, thinking, trying to understand the meaning of what he had found. Early in the morning, he ran to Meagan's house asking for help. Meagan was shocked to see him exhausted and terrified. She asked, "What happened? Why do you look so terrible?"

"Something terrible, unbelievable," Andrew told her, his voice harsh and quavering. "Look what I found in Jonathan's room."

He gave her the piece of the newspaper with the strange words written on it. Meagan looked thoroughly, then after reading the caption below the photo many times, she turned to Andrew and asked, "What are you trying to tell me? Does this have something to do with Jonathan?"

Andrew answered promptly, "Why did he have this hidden in his stuff?"

Her own voice almost a strangled scream, Meagan begged, "Please tell me what you are thinking. I am confused."

"I don't know, Meagan, but there is something very wrong about this. We need to know the meaning of these words."

"The people at the Department of Anthropology in my school should know; they speak many languages and are familiar with different cultures."

"In two weeks, we will be there. I hope we can learn what my brother wanted to tell us."

Her forehead wrinkled with confusion, Meagan asked, "Are you sure this is Jonathan's handwriting?"

"There is no doubt in my mind. We have to discover what these words mean so we can understand better."

Monday, 14 October 2002, was the first day of winter quarter, and on the same day, Meagan headed to the Department of Anthropology with the scrap of newspaper. At the department, she was directed to Professor Badrkhan Ahmed Razy, a respected specialist in Middle Eastern languages and cultures. The professor welcomed Meagan very warmly and encouraged her to tell him the problem. Meagan told the professor about the problem Jonathan had with his parents, and she also let him know about the doubts she and Andrew had, especially after what Donald had said. Finally, Meagan let the professor know about Jonathan's death on the field of battle and handed the paper to him, saying, "We found this hidden in his stuff and we are anxious to know if it can help us discover the truth."

The professor was intrigued by the story. He spread the newspaper out on his table and started to examine it thoroughly with a magnifying glass. He grabbed a huge dictionary, opening it to the letters b and m. After a while, Professor Razy said, "Initially, I can tell you what the words mean. Baba Omar means Father Omar; mama Rania means Mother Rania. But I can tell you more if you give me a couple of days. I feel I need to request the help of Professor Swanson, Charlotte C Swanson. She is a Ph.D. in psychology, and I am sure she will have much more to say about this picture."

Meagan agreed immediately. "Of course, Professor, can I come back on Friday?"

"That will be fine," Professor Razy said. "I will see you on Friday, at noon."

Andrew was terrified when Meagan let him know. "I am scared. It looks like the truth is exactly what we have been thinking it is," he said.

Meagan replied, "Let us wait. It is a very terrible thing if it is real. I really hope we are wrong."

"Good to see you again, Meagan. We have a lot to talk about," Professor Razy said as he welcomed Meagan upon her arrival at his office on Friday.

"Thank you, Professor," Meagan replied. I hope I am not taking too much of your time."

"Not at all, things are as serious as I suspected when I saw the picture, and the notes of Professor Swanson allowed us to draw a complete and sad picture. She was able to identify a strong and intimate relationship between the child and the couple in the picture. They must be very close and intimate to him; it would not be going too far to believe they are his parents. She also felt that the child was torn from his parents with much violence. His writing represents a cry for help, an appeal for aid from a frightened and solitary child wanting to get back what he has lost. The way of writing and hiding reveals something very serious. It looks like he fears someone who is close to him."

Professor Razy stopped for a moment, then asked, "Does that tell you anything?"

Meagan was shocked and frightened. Barely murmuring, she answered, "That tells too much, Professor, too much that is scary and terrifying."

"What do you intend to do now?"

"I need to talk to Andrew; it is his problem, and I will respect his decision."

"Of course, tell him that everything I and Doctor Swanson know is confidential. Good luck."

Meagan left Professor Razy's office dumbfounded. How could that have happened, she wondered? She started to put the pieces of the puzzle together, what Donald had said, the hell that Jonathan had gone through living with Donald and Verona, and what the psychologist had told her. Putting all that together, it was hard to avoid her and Andrew's worst conclusions. Finally, she arrived home and was relieved to see Andrew.

"Andrew, I am afraid to tell you what I just heard from the Professor. He and the psychologist believe that Jonathan might not be the McCoolens' son."

She released her despair as she recounted to him the details of her talk with the professor. Without saying a word, Andrew listened speechlessly. After a long time, he said, "That was my fear, I wish it was anything but that; he is my brother and they are my parents. It is hell for me any way I look at it."

In tears, Meagan asked, "What should we do now?"

Andrew answered promptly, "Search for the truth, the complete and full truth. We need to know the whole story. We can't leap to any conclusions before that."

"You are right," Meagan said. "We need to know, but where can we find the truth?"

"Jonathan gave us the lead, although he didn't know he was indicating where to look. The photo in the newspaper tells us that is where we can find the story. We need to find newspapers from around May 1981. That is where we will find the answers to our questions."

Meagan asked, "Where can we find those?"

"Public libraries, schools of history, art and literature, the repositories of newspapers."

"But all that should be in Seattle."

"Yes, here there will be very little."

"Only during the winter will we have time to do that."

"Yes," Andrew agreed, "we will have to wait, but we will do it. I owe that to my brother. I hadn't been born yet, but I have the feeling that he left the message for me. I wish he were here now."

Andrew could no longer hold his tears and broke down in sobs. Meagan tried to help him, although she was as overwhelmed as he was.

Andrew and Meagan experienced the quarter as much longer than it really was, probably because they were anxious to see it gone. Finally, January 18, 2003 arrived, and they were back in Seattle, where they began the search on the second day of their arrival. Andrew focused on the resources of the public library, and Meagan went through the newspapers' archives. The idea was to check newspapers, magazines, and any information source about an accident involving a child or a foreign couple. They decided to start on 1 May 1981, with the intention to examine every page, go through every subject, and look at every picture. At lunchtime, they would meet at a nearby restaurant and talk over what they had found.

One week later, on Monday, 27 January, their efforts paid off when Meagan dropped a bombshell over lunch. "Andrew, you should come with me this afternoon; I think I discovered everything."

After momentarily freezing, Andrew was able to wheeze out the question, "What did you find?"

"I'd rather you see for yourself, but it seems that Professor Razy was right."

They left the café with lunch unfinished and rushed to the newspaper building. In the archives room, Meagan showed Andrew the edition of May10, 1981. Displayed in the middle of the first page was a picture with the prominent title, "Iraqi boy disappears in Pike Place Market." On page 8, the full story reported that the three-year-old child of Professor Omar Assad Al-Dahany and his wife Rania disappeared in thin air during their visit to the marketplace. The internal page featured a picture of the missing child and his name: Khaled Omar Al-Dahany. The article stated that several witnesses reported that a man had walked away with the child after stating that he was returning him to his family.

It was too much for Andrew to take in, and he began crying uncontrollably. Meagan escorted him from the building to a nearby park, where they sat on a bench.

"We can't jump to any conclusion," Meagan said. "We aren't sure about what happened."

"The picture matches the one Jonathan left, and the names," Andrew said.

"Yes, things are adding up, but we still need to learn much more."

"I agree; we need to keep digging. We need to know everything."

Meagan suggested, "Let's stop here today. We need some rest."

Andrew agreed. "Okay, but please, don't mention this to anyone else. We need to know the truth, the whole truth, first before deciding what we will do."

"That is perfect. I think the same way. Tomorrow, we restart our search to see what happened next."

For two more weeks, Meagan and Andrew went through all the information published in the newspaper. They discovered the story of the Al-Dahany and read about Khaled's disappearance in the marketplace. They were deeply touched by Rania and Omar's appeal for help, and their souls were torn by learning that the family was forced to leave the country without their son. Andrew and Meagan had no doubt that Jonathan is Khaled, the small boy who was abducted at the marketplace. Though it was difficult to admit the facts, they were impossible to ignore.

"Do you think the man mentioned by the witnesses is your dad?" Meagan asked.

"All the evidence points in that direction. It is horrible to admit that your dad was capable of committing such a horrendous crime."

"It is your dad, not you."

"Still, knowing it is painful, and shameful as well."

"And now, what are we going to do?"

Andrew thought without speaking for a while, then said, "They will have to tell me the truth. They will have to tell me everything."

For the next three days, the secret burned in Andrew's heart. Donald was travelling, and he wanted both his parents to be present. Once Donald arrived, Andrew called upon him and Verona for a talk. He looked at Donald challengingly and said, "One day you told me that Jonathan is not my brother and never was. Now, I want you to explain what you meant."

For a few minutes, Verona and Donald gave the appearance of being struck by a very high voltage electric shock. They remained silent, looking at each other and at Andrew, their faces cycling a mixture of fear, astonishment, and anguish. Finally, Verona said, "I told you; your dad lost his mind. What he said doesn't mean anything. Why don't you forget that once and forever?"

On a coffee table, Andrew placed the photo of Rania and Omar, with the annotations made by Jonathan, flanked by another of his brother at the age of five.

"Can either of you tell me if Jonathan had anything to do with this?"

The couple's fear turned to terror, and their anguish was converted to agony. Simultaneously, they began whimpering and sniffling.

"What is this? Where did you find these? I don't know what you are talking about."

They were stopped by Andrew's shout, "Of course, you know! This kid is Jonathan, I mean, Khaled, pleading for his parents. Isn't that true? Will you tell me the real story now?" As he spoke, Andrew laid out on the table copies of the newspapers, magazines, photos, and articles he had brought.

At this moment, when they knew that *the cat was out of the bag* and that their secret had been discovered, Donald tried to defend himself.

"He was lost in the marketplace, and I tried to help him."

"No, that is not true. Many people saw you taking the kid away saying you would deliver him to his parents. You kidnapped him," Andrew shouted.

Donald insisted, "I gave him a family and shelter." He was interrupted by his son.

"You stole him from his family and his shelter. He didn't need yours."

"I gave him a better life, our way of life. What would he have had where he was born?"

"That is arrogant and presumptuous; it is insolent. Who told you that your life was better than his? Who told you that he wanted your way of life? You know what he would have had where he was born? A loving family, friends, happiness, and people that don't kidnap other people's children."

"You called me a murderer, and now you call me a kidnapper. I can't accept that."

"I am ashamed. You are my father, but you are both murderer and kidnapper, and, I don't know, maybe much more."

Verona was in tears, fearing how the argument might end, so she intervened. "Now he is gone, and it was his decision."

Andrew replied, "He was gone the moment both of you ripped him from his life, he was killed when both of you slashed him from his family, and now for you he is gone, without any feelings, any remorse, any regret. It is too ugly, too cruel. It is disgusting. I don't want to see you again; I don't want to see you ever again."

Andrew turned around and left the house.

When Andrew came out of his family's house, he had to face a country as agitated as the home he had left. Talk about war was everywhere. President Bush was pressing for war against Iraq on the basis of information guaranteed by Mrs Rice, his security advisor, confirming that Iraq possessed huge arsenals of nuclear, chemical, and biological weapons of mass destruction, and that Saddam

Hussein was harbouring and supporting Al-Qaeda. The commotion and uproar were uncontrollable because a great section of the population and the country's traditional allies were thinking exactly the opposite. They questioned the veracity of the war supporters' allegations. For twelve years, Iraq had been under a tight siege of international sanctions; everything that went in or came out of the country was thoroughly inspected by the United States under the United Nations flag, making it impossible for the Iraqis to acquire such an arsenal.

The heat of the discussion was burning everywhere, but the drums of war were pounding loud enough to deafen people's ears, blind their eyes, melt enough consciences, and drive the nation to war. The fierce opposition of France and Germany to the war and their complete denial of the allegations of weapons of mass destruction enflamed the discussion. But the president and his principal aides, Dick Cheney, Donald Rumsfeld, and Condoleezza Rice, alleged that the Iraqi government was capable of posing an immediate threat to the United States and its friends and allies. They were also determined to bring freedom and democracy to Iraq. The march toward war was escalating and the call to join the army was intensifying, and that was what Andrew decided to do.

"How could you do this to me, Andrew? Don't you see how much suffering I am going through for the loss of Jonathan, and now you are going to leave me," Meagan said angrily when Andrew told her that he had enlisted.

Andrew had no answer and no expression on his face, giving the impression that he felt nothing inside. Meagan was stupefied and incredulous. "What they did to your brother, you are now letting them do to you. They ripped him from his family, his future, and finally his life. And now, in one way or another, they are doing the same thing to you. Please think again. I couldn't stand to lose both of you."

But Andrew couldn't hear any voice, couldn't see any image, and couldn't feel any emotion. On Wednesday, 12 February 2003, at 6:00 a.m., he presented himself to the registration section of the Seattle Naval Base, as he had been ordered to do when he enlisted two days before.

Inside the Naval Base, the war was everywhere. Soldiers ran in all directions, training was intense, and the time was always short. It was clear that the war was coming, no doubt, and they had to get ready as fast as they could. On Wednesday, 5 March, Andrew and hundreds of other soldiers were transported from the Naval Base to the nearby airbase, where many others were already boarding the huge C-130 Hercules planes to take them to Kuwait.

The first impression of the soldiers in Kuwait was that they had left the world behind. The desert was enormous, and so was the emptiness. The only companion was the wind hitting the desert and moving a huge wave of sand. The high temperature just increased their discomfort.

The troops were soon advised that they could not afford to feel uncomfortable or to worry about sand and weather, because they were there to save America from the devil who lived beyond the border. They were alerted not to have pity or mercy because on the other side there were only inhuman and delinquent terrorists. They were also educated about the shock and awe doctrine that would be imposed during the war. They learned that the idea was to use overwhelming power and spectacular displays of fire and human force to paralyse the enemy's control of the battlefield and crush its will to fight. They were instructed to act strictly under this guidance. Many of the soldiers did not fully understand this doctrine, including Andrew, who questioned the need for so much hatred and violence against the Iraqi people. He had only known one Iraqi in his life, his brother, and he was a good man; he even died for America. But they were trained to be good soldiers, and a good soldier never questions, just executes.

On 20 March 2003, the coalition launched simultaneous air and ground assaults preceded by an airstrike on the Presidential Palace in Baghdad. The following day, from their massing point close to the Iraqi-Kuwaiti border, coalition forces invaded Basra Province. Andrew found himself marching on Iraqi soil. The troops moved into southern Iraq, occupying the region. The big surprise was that the war was far from what they had been told: The Iraqi army was literally in shambles; they encountered no effective resistance, and the only battle that occurred was in Nasiriyah, which happened because a convoy of thirty-one soldiers led by a supply officer with no training as a combat officer mistakenly entered the city.

From Basra to Baghdad, the troops had no trouble in their advancement. What really attracted attention was the huge amount of destruction that had been inflicted on the cities on the way to Baghdad. It was clear that the goal was to annihilate the basic conditions of life to force the citizens of the country to struggle to survive. It was learned later that the advancement of the troops had been preceded by massive air and missile strikes across the country. By the beginning of April, Baghdad was completely under control of the American troops, the dreaded fierce battle of Baghdad never happened, and the rare and feeble pockets of the Iraqi army were easily defeated. With the help of Kurdish fighters, who had been armed and trained by the CIA, the troops needed only a few days to complete their domination over all Iraqi territory. At that moment, the war itself was gone, Iraq had no government, had no army, and had no Central Command, but still had people and they decided to confront the occupation. The American soldiers were warned repeatedly about that.

Chapter 12

The first challenge for the command in Baghdad was to deal with the people who were trapped in the hotels located in the so-called Green Zone. This consisted of about two hundred people of various nationalities. The hostages were divided into two groups, one restricted and one unrestricted. The first group consisted of people from Middle Eastern, Arabic, and Muslim countries. Many Africans were ordered to join this group, and the command handed this group to the CIA to conduct a rigorous background check of each person and suggest their fate. The other group, the unrestricted, was formed by people from Europe, Japan, and three men from China. A commission was formed to facilitate their return to their countries. General Millos Brenmann, the commander-in-chief, gave Colonel Harold Walsh, one of his aides, his first order:

"Get the files of the hotels, here and in the Meridian, and find the address of the employees of both hotels. I need all of them here tomorrow morning. Especially those who speak another language; we will need them, no matter how we get them. They must be here tomorrow."

By the second day, Colonel Walsh had under his custody eighty-three people. They were Iraqis, Egyptians, and Pakistanis, who used to work in either one of the hotels. General Brenmann was concise and clear:

"We need help, and you have only one choice, which is to work with us. We will pay for your work. That is not an offer; it is an order."

Colonel Walsh began assigning the newly appointed translators, some of whom spoke good English, which was very useful for the troops. It was made clear to them that it was not an optional matter; America needed them, and they had to cooperate.

Andrew was assigned to the technical support office located on the twentieth floor of the Ishtar Sheraton Hotel in downtown Baghdad. The building was huge and very fancy, and was mirrored from the other side of the square by another sophisticated building, the Palestine Meridian Hotel. The first thing that caught

Andrew's attention was that this zone had been preserved from bombing; the buildings and the roads were in perfect condition. Immediately, the Americans closed off the area and called it the Green Zone.

Andrew was introduced to Mr Philippe William Adams, a well-respected journalist from New York who was appointed to run the media office in the Central Command. Adams welcomed Andrew.

"Good to have you here. I'll need a photographer, and I was told you are a good one."

"Thank you, Sir," Andrew said. "I'll do my best to help."

Andrew shared a unit of two rooms and reception with Sergeant Ronald Campbell, a forty-year-old army veteran with huge pride to be from Texas, the same state of President Bush. Three Iraqis were assigned to aid the two soldiers, Yusra Rashid Kaidany and Amin Abdalla Amin, for Sergeant Campbell and Adnan Mahmoud Salem for Andrew. Yusra was a very beautiful woman with dark hair and big, black eyes. She had graduated in history and was working on her master's degree and spoke very good English. Amin was the front desk manager at the hotel before the war. He had a degree in administration, was married, and had two teen girls.

At almost fifty, Adnan was the oldest of the three. Standing five foot three, he was a man of very few words, especially when he needed to speak English. However, he was very efficient. The relationship between the two soldiers and their Iraqi helpers began on a tense note. Andrew was luckier than his boss; his relationship with Adnan was much easier, and they soon established a functioning modus operandi: Andrew gave an order and Adnan obeyed, without a single word of question. The communication between Sergeant Ronald and his aides wasn't easy, especially with Yusra; the sergeant was arrogant and aggressive, and so was Yusra.

Once the troops established control over the country, the commanding general had to deal with some urgent problems. First and most important was the rejection of the invasion by the population and the willingness to fight against it. The intelligence reports confirmed that the invasion had been hated from the beginning, in and out of Iraq, principally because all the allegations about developing weapons of mass destruction and supporting Al-Qaeda terrorists by the Iraqi government turned out to be false. Surprisingly, in spite of the terrible tales about Saddam's cruelty and unkindness as a dictator, for many people he was a hero, and, amazingly, a great many of the Iraqi people were aligned with him, while the thinking of other groups seemed to be, if it is against the Americans, I am ready to join the evil, that is, Saddam Hussein.

The command was convinced that firepower was useless. Saddam adopted a campaign of resistance, and he was working to form a league that would combine the different groups of guerrillas under his name. The biggest triumph of the Iraq War wasn't the result of pulling triggers, launching drone strikes and air attacks, or wreaking more destruction; the biggest triumph turned out to be finding Saddam Hussein, demolishing his aura and thereby eliminating him. It was the old story: cut off the head and you kill the body. It was determined that all possible efforts must be focused on this goal at any cost.

Remote from this discussion and despite the difficult times, the population of Baghdad was trying to move on with their lives. In Al Mansour, the most populous district of Baghdad, life remained intense and noisy. Al Mansour was a peculiar district in Baghdad; it wasn't the fanciest district in the city or the most modern, but, undoubtedly, it was the most fascinating and the most visited in Baghdad. The district was formed on the sides by the charming Al Mansour Street, a huge avenue that begins in Arabian Knight Square and ends at 14 Ramadan Street. There, the essence of Baghdad could be found, especially the typical food starting with the popular falafel, fried fava flour, cookies served with tahini and sesame oil. You could also find baked lamb and even masgouf, fish roasted over low heat, taking hours to cook. In Al Mansour Street, you saw Iraqi fashion mixing on different levels, Western and Eastern influences; for example, women wearing veils along with a dark robe that covers the entire body walking with friends wearing long pants and short-sleeve shirts, women wearing the hijab and others exhibiting the wonderful work done by their hairdressers. Men's clothing styles also displayed the same intercultural interaction; for example, while some men wear a head cloth and ankle-length robes with long sleeves, others sport the most sophisticated European brands.

Al Mansour offered stores for everything, including clothing stores with half of their stock displayed on the sidewalk, music stores with all their tapes playing at the same time at the highest volume, toy stores displaying the toys in the middle of the street. All in all, a great variety of stores contributed to making Al Mansour Street an unforgettable experience.

One of those special places in Al Mansour was the Al Saah restaurant. Al Saah was the kind of establishment that appealed to clients of different sections of the population, especially the middle class. The main course of the restaurant was chicken, which could be offered on bread for those who wanted to pay less or be served on dishes with various types of salads for the most discerning customers. But Al Saah was more than just a restaurant; it was the meeting point of most Al Mansour merchants, employees, and residents. In short, it was the most democratic environment on the planet earth where you could see the families mingling at the tables without worrying who is who.

On Monday, 7 April 2003, around 3:00 p.m., Abid Abdul Masih, his wife, Sanaa, and their three daughters, Lana, Miriam, and Lava, all under the age of ten, entered the restaurant greeting the owner who was behind the counter, "Hi, Mr Hamid, how are you doing?"

The girls jumped in Hamid's direction, shouting joyfully, "Hi, Uncle Hamid, where is the chicken?"

Hamid came out from behind the counter. He hugged and kissed the girls, saying, "Everything you want, Uncle Hamid has." Then he turned to Abid, answering, "Trying to keep alive, Abid. May Allah protect us in these difficult days."

"Yes, Hamid, only God can protect us in these tough days. I can't understand why all that has been happening," replied Abdel Masih.

"No one can, no one can."

Abdel Masih insisted, "But why? I need to know why."

"They are saying that it is to overthrow Saddam Hussein."

"All this for only one man, is that possible?"

Hamid gave Abdel Masih a look and warned him, "Take care, my friend, better to be careful."

Nodding his head unhappily, Abdel Masih asked, "Where is my friend?"

He was asking about Ahmed Manary, his long-time friend. They used to join the families for Monday dinner. Hamid answered, "I haven't seen Ahmed, but his family is at the table waiting for you and yours."

Sanaa and the kids were already there. Abdel Masih walked in the direction of the table, which was occupied by Salma, Ahmed's wife, their sons, Mohamed and Saif, and their daughter Shams. Abdel Masih greeted Salma and asked, "Where is Ahmed?"

"He is not feeling good. He is always sad and depressed. He preferred to stay home," Salma said.

"No one is happy," Abdel Masih said. "Who could be? But what can we do? We have children to take care of. I will go and bring him; you can start eating. We will be back soon."

He turned to Hamid and said, "Take care of the people there. I will bring Ahmed to eat with us."

Hamid retorted, "Go ahead, I will take care of everything." Abdel Masih left in a hurry.

Abdel Masih ran the two blocks to 14 Ramadan Street and headed to Ahmed's house on Badran Street. As he approached the door, he started yelling. "Ahmed, better open, you will go with me anyway."

Ahmed opened the door and tried to smile. "Oi, Abdel Masih, you shouldn't bother coming here. I am okay."

"But I am not," Abdel Masih said. "We can't miss our dinner. It is sacred, like your Friday worship and my Sunday mass."

"I see that there is no way to resist," Ahmed commented as he put on his jacket.

"No, no way. Come on before they eat all the chicken."

On the same day, life in the Central Command at the Green Zone was just ordinary, like every Friday, with fewer people working. However, at about 2:00 p.m., everything changed abruptly. An alarm began to sound among all the buildings using the highest emergency code. The order ran like a ray all over the corners of the camps, calling for 'attack formation.' In just minutes, the soldiers were organised in their divisions, armoured cars were ready in war formation, and helicopters were shredding the sky above their heads. The direction was given immediately: "The suburb of Al Mansour must be besieged; no one is allowed in or out." As they streamed from the compound, the troops were divided into two groups. The first took the right direction on 14 July Avenue to Damascus Street with the mission of surrounding the Al Mansour district from the east and north. The second group was directed left to Qadissaya Avenue to besiege the suburb from the west and south. Soon, the Al Mansour district was completely isolated from the world. Andrew received a phone call from Mr Adams

"Andrew, you are joining the troops heading to Al Mansur, take your camera, I will be there, get some shots, but be careful, see you later."

The two men, Ahmed and Abdel Masih, left and headed to the restaurant, but when they arrived at 14 Ramadan Street, the world had been changed. Tanks and armoured vehicles filled the street, and hundreds of soldiers were blocking the way yelling for everyone to keep far away. Before either of the two men realised what was happening, they were enveloped by the deafening roar of a huge airplane flying very low. Seconds later, a violent explosion threw the two men to the sidewalk. After a while, Ahmed was able to open his eyes. At first, it was difficult to see anything; a huge cloud of dust and smoke was obscuring everything. Ahmed struggled to get up and started looking for his friend. "Abdel Masih, Abdel Masih, where are you?" Minutes later, he heard Abdel Masih's voice, sounding strained and uneven.

"Ahmed, I am here." Ahmed rushed to the source of the voice, where he found Abdel Masih lying down in the middle of the street, wounded and covered with blood.

"Are you okay, my friend? What happened? Where are our people?" Ahmed asked. Helped by his friend, Abdel Masih rose with difficulty. The two men started to run in the direction of the restaurant to find their families. Soon, they stopped because there was nothing to look for—Al Mansour was gone. All that remained at the site of the restaurant was a mountain of flame and rubble next to a huge, bottomless crater, strewn with debris and smelling of burning flesh. The crowd that gathered after the explosion was struggling to get in to see what was left of their loved ones, but the soldiers were firm and tough, keeping everybody out of the place. The situation started to turn tense and dangerous. The anger of the people was turning to madness, and the hyperactive alertness of the soldiers was turning into aggression. The tanks and armoured vehicles moved to form a barrier between the people and the army. The area was isolated and submitted to a thorough search before the order for withdrawal was given and the troops started to move back to their bases. The place was emptied of soldiers and left to the population that remained in waiting.

The two men turned and looked in the opposite direction, but there was no restaurant in that direction either. There was no restaurant, there were no buildings, and there was nothing in any direction, just an immense empty space with a huge fireball in the middle. Reality was collapsing within them like inflamed embers.

"Sanaa, Salma, Seif, Lana."

"Salma, Mohamed. Mirian."

"Mirian, Lava, Seif."

"Hamid, Sanaa, Mirian."

Ahmed and Abdel Masih ran about screaming the names of their family and friends, looking everywhere, running in all directions involuntarily. A long time passed before they understood that everything in the neighbourhood had been obliterated, taking with it Sanaa, Salma, Lana, Mirian, Mohamed, Lava, Seif, Hamid, and a great many other people.

At Central Command, people felt a mixture of apprehension, fear, and uncertainty. Everybody was asking what was the goal of the mission and what had been the outcome? Soon, rumours began to circulate along the corridors about the goal of the raid. The gossip claimed that the incursion had been fomented by reports from U.S. and British intelligence. Both sources agreed that Saddam Hussein and his two sons, Uday and Qusay, would be meeting with important assistants in the Sa'ah restaurant, located on the square at the intersection between Al Mansour Street and Amirate Street. Immediately, the command decided to take the opportunity to eliminate the Iraqi president and gave the order to bomb the area and kill Saddam where he was. The orders were unambiguous; the place had to be pulverised, with no chance of anyone surviving.

The orders were executed exactly as had been specified: a B1 aircraft dropped two GBU-31 bunker-buster bombs shortly after 3:00 p.m., and to have no doubt about the completion of the mission, after a three-second interval, two more 2,000 lb. bombs were dropped. The target of enough firepower to uproot Saddam's family since his great-grandfather, the intersection between Al Mansour and Amirate, was obliterated; the restaurant, the square, and everything there was literally wiped off the map. However, the results were far from what was desired. Later on, it was revealed that the intelligence was wrong and that no fugitives from the deposed regime had been in the restaurant. The feelings of deep disappointment and frustration that resulted were overwhelming; the operation turned out to be a huge failure.

Andrew was shocked. It was the first time for him to really experience the war. He was there, and he saw it all before and after. He saw the building thrown into the air like a feather. He saw the floor disappear and multiple human beings shredded like pieces of paper. He was aghast, he turned to Adams questioning, "How could anyone commit such a grievous mistake? How could that be explained or accepted?"

Adams tried to calm him down "Calm, Andrew, cool down, that is the war and in war, there is no room for emotions, much less need for explanations."

But Andrew was uncomfortable, he felt that he needed to talk, he wanted to ask many questions, but he knew he was in war and in war, you don't ask, you don't think, you just act. He tried to keep his anguish to himself, but it was not easy. The agony took him back to the moment he received the news that Jonathan was dead. It still bled in his soul. *How did you die, beloved brother? Did death come for you the way I saw today?* The tears filled his eyes. Adams stands up and hugged him saying, "I understand your feeling, I did cover many wars, and all are the same, brutalism, killing and destruction, and I never found out why."

Andrew replied, handling Adams the negatives of the pictures he picked in Al Mansur district, "This is the point, why? Why did we need to go through that?"

On the edge of the huge crater that was all that remained after the explosion, Ahmed sat motionless. Gazing fixedly at nothing, he clutched a black banner asking for condolences for the death of all the members of his family: his wife Salma, fifty, his sons Mohammed, twenty-seven and Saif, twenty-four, and his daughter, Shams, twenty. Near Ahmed was his friend, Abdel Masih, also holding a black banner, asking, in the name of the Father, the Son and the Holy Spirit, for sympathy for the loss of his wife Sanaa, thirty, and his daughters Lana, Miriam and Lava, the eldest of whom had not yet turned ten years old.

Chapter 13

Another war was raging simultaneously in Kirkland, where Andrew's departure had left the house without sun, without joy, and without grace. His absence left Verona and Donald without motivation, with nowhere to go, and no reason to go anywhere. The feeling they shared now was completely different from the one they experienced when Jonathan left. Instead of relief, there was fire burning the heart, and in place of the comfort they enjoyed when Jonathan left, now they felt a pliers crushing their stomachs. Initially, they had only one way to deal with the situation: crying, crying, and crying. For days and days, tears were the answer to all their questions.

Where is he now?

Is he eating well?

Does he think about us?

Will he be back one day?

When the tears fell short of giving them answers, they started to ask each other, and soon the question turned into accusations and even impulses of aggression.

"You could have been less violent with the other one; you knew that Andrew loved him," Verona told Donald.

"Now it is my fault. And you, what did you do? You are as much to blame as me," Donald said.

"You put him out of the house; you started our disgrace."

"Our disgrace is losing Andrew, not him."

"And now, what we will do without our son? Do something to help."

"What do you want me to do? There is nothing that I can do."

Verona began to yell and cry. "Bring my son back to me. Bring my Andrew back. I can't live without him."

But they knew that Andrew would not be back, at least not as soon as they wished.

Their life was going from bad to worse, and of course, someone had to answer for what had happened, and for each of them, no doubt, the guilty party was the other. Donald found his escape in travelling. He resumed making trips, preferentially long ones. For Verona, her life was hell either way; with Donald home, her existence was a continuous struggle, fighting and feeling disgust, and when he travelled, her life was one of emptiness, loneliness, and endless sadness.

One month was all that Verona was able to bear. By March, she had reached her breaking point. She ran to the phone and called Meagan. "I beg you, tell me anything you know about Andrew. I need to know where he is. I want to talk to him. He needs to come back home."

Verona had to wait a long time for Meagan to answer, and she never expected, or wanted, this answer. "Andrew joined the army."

Verona screamed like a wounded animal. "No, Andrew, no, He is the only thing I have, God no."

She dropped the phone.

When Donald came home, he found Verona in a faint on the floor. When Verona came back to herself, she found Donald looming over her, trying desperately to wake her up.

"Verona, what happened? Tell me what happened to you?" Donald asked.

Verona murmured, almost inaudibly, "Andrew joined the army."

"Who told you that?"

"Meagan."

Donald's response was despairing. "Please, don't tell me that. I hate that girl. How could he do this to us? What will we do now?"

"I don't know, but I want my son back. You have to bring him back to me. Say you will, please, say you will."

"I miss him as much as you."

Early the morning of the second day since they heard the news, they headed to the army Enlistment Centre in downtown Seattle to plead for information about their son. The officers in the centre directed them to the personal affairs office. In the office, they were attended by Lieutenant Samuel Christianson. They cried, begged, and implored for help. They told the lieutenant that their son left the house in anger after an argument with his parents and they never saw him again, and now they had learned that he had joined the army. Lieutenant Christianson made a huge effort to calm them down a bit, and finally he got them to pay attention to him. "Please, listen carefully. I will check all the information you gave to me, and I will try to get the information that is available to the families of our soldiers. Just give me a couple days and I will get back to you."

They left their address and phone number and implored to him to act as fast as he could.

Twenty-four hours later, the phone rang in the McCoolens' house. Verona leaped to answer the phone, and it was, as she expected, Lieutenant Christianson.

"Hello, Mrs McCoolen?"

"Yes, it is me. Please tell me what you found out," Verona said.

"Of course, Mr Andrew McCoolen voluntarily joined the army on 10 February 2003. After his training period, he was deployed for a mission abroad. That is all that I can say for now."

Verona's wail knifed through the phone. Lieutenant Christianson paused for a minute, then he resumed. "If you wish to write a letter to him, we can deliver it to him in a few days."

By now, Verona had collapsed again. Donald took the phone from her and said, "Yes, we will do that. Where can we deliver the letter?"

"In my office, just call me and I'll be waiting for you."

"Thank you."

"Take care, Mr McCoolen."

It took Donald a long time to calm Verona down. She was hysterical, hyper-emotional, and uncontrollable. "We lost our son. We will never see him again."

Donald shouted, "No, Verona, don't ever say that, he will be back."

"No, he will not. It is the same story. The other one never came back."

"Why are you mixing things up? Forget about the other. Our son will be back. Let us try writing a letter."

After a lot of talk and a good deal of patience, he was able to get her attention. "Tell me, Verona, what we will tell him. I am ready to write." They started, stopped, started again. They agreed, disagreed, argued, and cried. It took three hours for them to finish the letter telling Andrew that since he left, their life had become very bad. They told him about their fights and their suffering, and they implored him to come back to them as soon as possible.

Verona called Lieutenant Christianson, who was kind enough to send somebody the very same day to pick up the letter.

Two weeks passed without any sign from Andrew. Verona called the lieutenant's office, and he came on the phone. "Hello, Mrs McCoolen. The letter was immediately forwarded to Andrew's unit, and I have the confirmation that the letter is already in his possession at this moment. You should receive a reply from him soon."

The answer arrived two days later, but not from the lieutenant. This time it was Meagan who called to inform Verona that Andrew had called her and asked her to tell them that he had received the letter, but he had no intention of coming back soon.

Verona was expecting exactly the answer she received, but even so, she was devastated. She had hoped that the authorities were having difficulty reaching him, or it was taking a long time to deliver their letter, anything, but that Andrew had received the letter and ignored their appeal—that was too much for her and for Donald.

"And now, what can we do?" Verona asked.

"I don't think there is anything we can do," Donald replied.

The days passed in a colourless blur, full of nothing and going nowhere. Donald and Verona tried to submerge their anguish in alcohol and loneliness. They isolated themselves from everyone and everything. They were like a small boat in the middle of the ocean, buffeted by the waves, tossed by the wind, unable to guess where they would end. They isolated themselves even from each other. It was common for them to spend days together without exchanging a single word, just drinking and crying. Verona was always alone, whether Donald was at home or on the road, just like Donald was always alone, whether at home or driving the roads across the country.

In the second week of May, small units started to patrol the streets of Baghdad, just about the time the insurgency began. Small groups of suspected guerrillas began to attack the occupying troops, especially in Baghdad, Fallujah, and Tikrit, in the so-called Sunni Triangle. The insurgents attacked the American troops with assault rifles and grenades, but their most important weapon was the improvised explosive device, IED, planted to ambush U.S. patrols and convoys. The army increased the patrols, added more soldiers, but failed to detain the escalating insurgency campaign. Conflicts between the occupying forces and the population reached a risky level, with crowd uprisings and small scuffles.

The tactics of the insurgents were getting better, with improved organisation and more effective attacks against the troops. The situation was demanding action and it came with 'Operation Peninsula Strike.' More than one thousand American soldiers using armoured vehicles, helicopters, and small boats set up roadblocks alongside the Tigris River near Ishaqi, Balad, and Al Duloiya. Rapidly, the operation led to the capture of almost four hundred Iraqis, but the real targets of the operation were never found among those captured. Operation Peninsula Strike was designed to capture the former Minister of Defence of Iraq, Major General Abul Ali Jasmin, and former head of the military academy, Brigadier General Abdullah Ali Jasmin. However, neither man was arrested during the operation.

The results obtained by Operation Peninsula Strike were far from what was hoped for. Subsequently, the operations of the insurgents escalated, and the ambushes against the troops came more frequently and seemed better prepared and more operational. Many other operations were launched to suppress the insurgency, likewise without success. During the summer, the number of attacks exceeded a dozen a day, inflicting many causalities among the troops. The American troops tried a policy of carrot and stick, executing some benevolent actions and promoting procedures to connect with the Iraqi population. Meanwhile, the military operations were harsh and increasingly retaliatory, leading to the detention of thousands of innocent civilians and other harmful acts, like chopping down palm trees and other vegetation to deprive the guerrillas of cover for ambushes, while at the same time depriving farmers of their livelihoods.

Increasingly, the population suffered from the chaotic condition of basic services, and people's anger likewise grew. Most locales had no water, no electricity, and other basic amenities. Soon, the anger was converted into fury and translated into bombing. On 19 August 2003, the violence reached unexpected levels with the bombing of the headquarters of the United Nations in the Canal Hotel, which had been hosting the UN Assistance Mission in Iraq. The result was horrific, with the death of the head of the mission, a very respected Brazilian ambassador and twenty-two other people, and more than one hundred were wounded. The effect of the Canal Hotel Bombing among the troops was very bad and left many unanswered questions. How did the insurgents get into the compound without being searched? Why had the UN mission, which had arrived just five days before to help the Iraqi people, been targeted? Things got worse ten days later when an explosive device blew up the Imam Ali shrine, killing dozens, including Shia leader Ayatollah Mohammed Baqir Al Hakim. Shadows of civil war began to appear in Iraq's heaven after the explosion was linked to Sunni groups.

The response of the troops came in the form of the Iron Hammer counteroffensive, which was launched in November; the number of patrols was increased with more soldiers. The patrols were protected by U.S. air power and artillery fire, and a better surveillance strategy was established. The effort produced immediate results; the rebels' attacks dropped significantly. The success was crowned by the capture of Saddam Hussein on a farm near Tikrit on 13 December.

Chapter 14

On 28 November 2003, Donald told Verona that "On 1 December, I will be making the last trip for this year. It might take a long time, but I will do my best to be back by the 20th."

"Okay, have a good trip," she answered carelessly.

On Monday, December 1, around 5:00 in the morning, Donald left Kirkland heading to Guadalajara in the central region of Jalisco in Mexico. He knew it would be a forty-five-hour trip, long and tiring, but he had no choice. It was the end of the year, and all his drivers were out delivering across the country. For Verona, the only thing left was to wait for him to come back, to wait before he went on another trip; that was her life now. What Verona didn't expect was that this trip would take much longer than that. Now, it was already Christmas day and Donald wasn't back yet, and what was more worrying, he wasn't answering his phone. Verona called Donald's aides at the company, and they were also worried. The last communication they had from their boss was on Monday, 15 December, when he told them that he was initiating the return trip. That was the same day Verona received her last call from Donald. On 26 December, Verona called the police.

"Officer Morales. How can I help you?"

"My name is Verona. My husband is missing. He should have returned one week ago, but he hasn't shown up."

The officer replied, "Please, ma'am, calm down and give me enough information to understand the situation."

"My husband's name is McCoolen, Donald McCoolen. He is a truck driver. He was on a business trip to Mexico, and he should have been back last week."

"When was your last contact with him?"

"On the fifteenth; he told me that he was starting the trip back."

"And then?"

"I have not heard from him since then."

"Forgive me, ma'am, but I need to ask: Are you sure he went to Mexico?"

"Yes, I am. I called him at the hotel several times."

"Okay, ma'am, please tell me the licence plate of his truck."

"GCC-3303."

"Okay, ma'am, I will run a check and I will call you back."

"Thank you."

One day later, Officer Morales called Verona. "Ma'am, your husband crossed the border on Friday, 5 December, through U.S. Customs and Border Protection in Nogales, Arizona. There is no registration for his return."

Now very concerned, Verona asked, "And now, what can I do if the police can't help?"

"I am sorry, ma'am, but it is another country. We can't do anything there. Maybe the embassy can help."

"Thank you," Verona said, and hung up.

Verona passed the first days of the New Year in fear, agony, and deep distress. It was now a full month since Donald left. She felt cold in her stomach and dark clouds started to fill her mind. Once more, Verona found herself on the phone with Meagan asking for help. "Meagan, forgive me, but I have nobody to talk to. I need your help again."

Meagan answered coldly, "What is it now, Mrs McCoolen?"

"It is Donald. He left one month ago for Mexico and never came home. His phone is dead, and the police can't help because they believe he is still there. I am afraid something bad happened to him."

Meagan was touched. "What do you want me to do?"

Verona replied, "I think Andrew needs to know. He needs to look for his father. I tried to call him, but, you know, he wouldn't take my calls."

"I am not sure if he will be able to do that, but I will contact him. I'll get back to you as soon as I can."

Meagan was able to reach Andrew on 4 January 2004. "Andrew, I know that the last thing you need is bad news, but I need to tell you something very frightening."

"What happened, Meagan?"

"It is your dad. He left for a trip to Mexico on 1 December, and never returned. I called Verona yesterday and learned that he crossed the border on the fifth, but there are no records of his return. That is what worries me."

Andrew asked, "Did they try to call him?"

"That is another worrying point; his phone is dead."

"That is bad, and of course he is not calling anyone."

"The last time your mom received a call from him was on the fifteenth."

Andrew took a few minutes to think, then he resumed the call. "Meagan, forgive me. I was thinking."

"That is okay. Sorry, but I needed to talk to you. I believe that something unusual has happened to Donald."

"I hope not. Anyway, I need to talk to my commander to see what I can do. I will call you tomorrow for sure."

Monday, 5 January 2004, early in the morning, Andrew informed Sergeant Campbell about his father's disappearance. Campbell contacted Colonel Walsh, who called both Campbell and Andrew to his office. Colonel Walsh took the matter seriously. "Look, Andrew. I worked many years in our facilities in Tucson, and I know how dangerous this area is, especially on the other side of the border. You should go immediately and find out what happened to your father."

Colonel Walsh looked at Sergeant Campbell and asked, "Is he excused to go, Sergeant?"

"Yes, Colonel, he is allowed to go."

Colonel Walsh returned to Andrew and said, "We have a service flying home tomorrow. Let me check if I can find a place for you." After some calls, Colonel Walsh told Andrew, "You are all set. Get ready to fly tomorrow. I will call the people in Tucson to help you. Contact Colonel Patricia Holms." He turned to Campbell and said, "Prepare his papers to fly with our mission tomorrow."

Campbell stood up and replied, "Yes Sir."

Andrew also stood up and added, "Thank you, Sir."

Early on the morning of 7 January, Andrew arrived at Washington Dulles International Airport. He bought a ticket to Sea-Tac Airport where Meagan was waiting for him. Their meeting was full of emotion, love, and tears. "God knows how I have missed you," Meagan said, tears in her eyes.

Andrew hugged her tightly and said, "You know, Meagan, hugging you, I feel like I am hugging both of you at the same time."

"Me too, I wish he was here now."

In the car, Meagan asked, "Where are we going?"

"Kirkland," Andrew said.

"Verona will be happy to see you."

"She is still my mother. I don't forgive her, but I can't hate her, either."

On the way, Meagan told him everything she knew about his father's disappearance and observed that he was very concerned. She asked, "You look like you fear something. Do you?"

"Something wrong happened, that's for sure. He would never stay all this time without contacting my mom or the office to learn about the business."

"What do you think we should do?"

"We need professional help; alone, we will lose too much time and we don't have time to lose. We don't even know where to start."

"What do you have in mind?"

"A private detective, I will talk to the police first, then I will hire someone to help."

When Verona opened the door and saw Andrew, she couldn't believe her eyes. She grabbed him, yelling and crying. "Andrew, my son and my life, is it you? Is it you? Really you? You are here. I have missed you so much."

Their encounter was very emotional, and they needed time to adjust to seeing each other again. Finally, Andrew suggested to his mother, "We need to go to the police station. On the way, you can tell me all the details I need to know."

At the police station, they were welcomed by Officer Morales, who answered all their questions. Finally, Andrew asked him if he could recommend a private detective. Morales said, "The police can't make a recommendation, but we can offer you a list of registered private detectives in the area and you can choose one of them."

The list showed the name, picture, and resume for each detective. Andrew pointed at one named Alicia Young, who was forty-one years old, and asked Morales, "Do you know her?"

"Yes, I do. She is a very bright woman. She had a long career as a police officer. You would be in good hands with her."

"Ok, let us go. We do not have time to lose. Thank you very much, Officer."

One hour later, they were at detective Alicia Young's office in Seattle. Her secretary asked if they had an appointment. Somewhat upset, Andrew answered, "No, we don't, but we need to talk to her. It is a matter of life or death. Please ask her if she can make some time just to learn about the case."

From their demeanours, the secretary could tell that their case was serious, and she needed only a few minutes to convince her boss to see them. They rushed inside the detective's office and immediately Andrew let her know everything about Donald's disappearance. Alicia expressed deep concern and said, "You are right; we have reason to be worried. It is now twenty days without contact. What do you intend to do?"

Andrew answered immediately, "We need your help."

"It will be two hundred a day and expenses," the detective said.

"Deal, when do we start?"

"Immediately; he may be at risk of death." She pointed at Andrew and said, "You will come with me. We will start from the last point he was seen, Guadalajara, then we will make our way back tracking his truck."

Alicia called her secretary, "Tania,"

As the secretary appeared in the office, Alicia resumed pointing to Andrew, "Try two tickets for me and him to Guadalajara International Airport for today, if not for the first hours tomorrow. Rent a car, a good one, with a driver, at the airport."

She turned to Andrew and added, "Go with her to give her your information and to sign the papers."

Alicia tried to get from Verona all the information that might help in the search, half an hour Tania and Andrew were beck with the flight guaranteed.

"Alicia, I was lucky, I got two tickets for today, the flight departs 09:15, and it is a nonstop flight. The car will be waiting there, I also arranged a room in the closest hotel to the airport, and you will have couple hours to sleep before starting the search," said Tania.

"Thank you, Tania, good job," replied Alicia, then turned to Andrew saying, "Are you ready, we don't have too much time."

Andrew answered, "My bag is in the car, any time."

"Ok, let us go."

During the five-hour flight to Guadalajara, Alicia asked Andrew to tell her all the story of his father disappearing, "Andrew, I am asking because all the details are important, any information could help us to understand what is happening, tell me everything about your dad, his family life and concerns."

Andrew told her about the sad life his parents were going through. "Look, Alicia, my parents' life started to be very depressive since I left home and joined the army, they never accept that, we were distant since then and I had very limited contact with them."

"Why that?"

"I had a brother that I loved too much, they forced him to leave home, he died in Afghanistan."

"It was only you and him, right?"

"Yes, and now I am all alone."

Alicia was touched, "No way to fix your relationship with your parents? I see you still love them."

"Sure, I do, but it is hard to forgive."

"It is a double torture, must be tough living with that."

Arriving in Guadalajara, the driver was waiting for them carrying a placard with their names, the driver introduce himself, "Soy Joseph Gomes, tu chofer." on the way Alicia let the driver know why they were in Mexico. Few minutes later they were in the hotel, Alicia asked the driver "Joseph, what time we can go to the police station to get information about our case?"

The driver answered, "Se suponía que debían trabajar las 24 horas, pero para encontrar personas de alto rango para ayudar serán las 08 en punto."

"Ok, then 07:30, I want you here, I want to stop first by the last place he was seen, then I go to the police."

"SI, señora."

On Thursday, 8 January, 07:45 Alicia and Andrew were at the 'Empresa hogar y oficina,' which was the last place Donald had been seen. The manager confirmed that Donald had delivered the goods and equipment on 14 December and he let them know that he would be going home early the second day. Alicia divided the road from Guadalajara to Tucson into sections, the first from Guadalajara to Guadalupe, the second from Guadalupe to Torreón, then to Chihuahua, and finally to El Paso or Tucson. Immediately after, Joseph drove Alicia and Andrew to the police station where they asked for help to discover if there had been any accident or arrests in the area during the period of December 15 to 25.

Officer Mario Gonzalez was assigned to help them. Gonzalez was thirty-four years old, active, and very interested in everything related to the United States. He started by asking about the prices, Hollywood stars, the mansions of Beverly Hills, and everything in America. Alicia had to stop him abruptly. "Officer, we are very worried about the life of Mr Donald McCoolen. Could you kindly check for us if there is any record involving him in the last month?"

Gonzalez apologised. "Forgive me, but I love the United States. One day, I will be a police officer there. Let me check…Here in Guadalajara, I don't see anything. Where else would you like to check?"

Alicia replied, "Mr McCoolen disappeared on the way between Guadalajara and the U.S. border. I divided the way in sections. Let's take a look at each; try one by one."

Gonzalez said, "You will have to be patient, that will take some time, but I will try to speed the process by the phone. What is your first section?"

"Guadalajara to Guadalupe."

Gonzalez called the police station in Guadalupe and questioned them about any accidents or arrests during the period mentioned by Alicia. He asked them to check the name of Donald McCoolen. Gonzalez stated that it was an emergency and recommended celerity. They promised to get back to him with the answer in two hours.

During that time, Gonzalez called the police in Torreón, Chihuahua, and El Paso. Soon they had the answers, but only the one from Torreón seemed important. The officer in Torreón informed them that he had a record of a truck accident close to the city of Leon Guzman, but they couldn't say more than that because the truck had been scoured by looters, and even the plates had been stolen. The Torreón police added that the driver was in the municipal hospital in serious condition.

Alicia turned to the driver questioning "How long Torreón is Joseph?"

"Son unas 10 horas conduciendo, poco más de una hora por aire."

Andrew questioned, "Are there airports close here and there?"

"Sí, los hay, lo que no puedo garantizar son vuelos," replied the driver.

"What you recommend?" Alicia asked.

"Puedo garantizar lo que estoy haciendo, es como al mediodía ahora, si empezamos ahora, estaremos allí como a las 10 pm."

Alicia looked to Andrew advising "We can't take any risk, we will go with Joseph, domestic flights here are not very trustworthy,"

Jumping in the car she added, "Let us go."

Joseph stopped by a mini supermarket and bought water and snacks. "It will be a long trip, we will stop only once in the middle, probably by the Zacatecas, so I got enough water and snacks to help until we stop to eat something," Joseph said and started driving.

Starting the trip, Joseph offered them an idea about the trip. "Son unos 700 Kilómetros, aquí usamos kilómetro, pero son alrededor de 450 millas en medida estadounidense, partes de la carretera son de peaje, y esas son buenas, otras partes no tan buenas, tenemos que ser pacientes. Haré lo mejor que pueda, si quieres dormir puedes hacerlo."

Both Alicia and Andrew were very tired, they slept very little during the night before, so they couldn't resist, soon they fell asleep.

Five hours later, Joseph called them, "Señora, señor, ahora estamos entrando a Fresnillo," As they woke up, he added, "aquí está el final de la carretera 23, nos incorporaremos a la 45 en dirección a la 49. En Fresnillo podemos encontrar un buen lugar para comer, si nos detenemos?"

They agreed immediately, ten minutes later, the car stopped at Casa Kalpa Steak & Grill, located on Avenida Huicot #223, Fresnillo. Forty-five minutes later, they were back on the road to Torreon. Arriving Torreón, they arranged hotel to sleep asking to be called at seven o'clock at the morning.

Friday, the two entered the police station in Torreon, anxious to learn more about the truck accident. Officer Derlis Sanchez was waiting for them. "Welcome. Officer Gonzalez from Guadalajara told me about the case. I hope that we can help." Immediately, Sanchez started to talk about the accident.

Alicia noted that Sanchez was having a hard time expressing himself in English and soon interrupted, "Oficer, se voce quer falar em espanhol. esta bem para nos."

Feeling relieved, officer Sanchez explained, "El accidente ocurrió el 15 de diciembre alrededor de las 22:00 horas, pero nos informaron solo un día después. Parece que el conductor perdió el control y el vehículo se estrelló contra el terraplén. Tardamos mucho en llegar a la camioneta y cuando llegamos nos quedamos impactados; todo había sido arrancado del camión, la licencia de conducir y todos sus documentos habían sido robados, y el conductor yacía entre la vida y la muerte."

Andrew could not hold back his tears, and Alicia held his hand. "Let us go to the hospital. We will see what can be done."

Sanchez offered to drive them there. Once in the hospital, they rushed to the room, where Andrew was shocked to find his father almost dead. Alicia hugged him and said, "Andrew, thank God, we found him, and he is still alive. We will move him to Seattle, and the doctors there will save his life."

The doctor explained to them that even though he was alive, he was in critical condition. He also let them know that the doctors had done all that could be done, but he also admitted that the hospital was simple, and their capability was limited. They immediately started the process of hiring air transportation to Seattle. The U.S. Consulate General in Guadalajara was very cooperative and helped them to get the transportation on Sunday, 11 January, which had seemed impossible on the weekend.

Sunday early morning, an ambulance transported Donald to Torreón International airport, where the private jet was waiting for him. Joseph drove Alicia and Andrew to the airport. Andrew thanked him for his effort and asked him joking, "Do you accept the tip in dollars? I don't have pesos."

Joseph replied, "No se preocupe, Sr Andrew, fue un placer ayudarlo, me alegro de que su papá siga vivo." Andrew gave him a good tip and thanked him again. At the airport, they all get in the plane and started the trip to Seattle.

Sunday evening, Donald was rushed to the emergency ward of Shoreline Clinics and Medical Centre in Seattle; Verona was already there waiting for them. After the initial examination, one of the doctors came out of the intensive care unit and told them, "The situation is very critical. He has been in a coma for twenty-five days now, and some procedures that should have been done weren't because the hospital couldn't afford the necessary equipment. He needs to go through surgery immediately. The bleeding in his brain increases the pressure and causes a loss of oxygenation. We need to fix that to see if we can reverse his condition."

Andrew asked anxiously, "Is it risky, Doctor?"

"Yes, it is. He might die during the surgery, but he would certainly die if we left him as he is. I need your okay to proceed."

Andrew looked to Verona questioningly, but she was lost, and he had to decide. "Do whatever is needed to save him, please."

"Fine, then you need to sign some papers. I will return to the surgery room."

Suddenly, all activity in the surgery room and vicinity became frenetic. Several doctors were summoned, aides and nurses, several devices and small carts with sterilised tools were moved inside the surgery room. Finally, surgery began at 10:00 p.m. Verona and Andrew waited in the hospital; later, Meagan arrived and joined them.

Andrew turned to Alicia to thank her "Thank you, Alicia, without your help we wouldn't be able to do it, early tomorrow I will stop by your office to make the payment."

Verona sat on a sofa close to the door of the surgery room and couldn't resist falling asleep.

Meagan and Andrew walked to the coffee shop and asked for coffee to help them stay awake. Meagan had a million questions for him, and he had a million things to tell her. Their talk was emotional; they spoke, they cried, they hugged each other, they recalled all their memories, and of course Jonathan was the main subject of the conversation most of the time. Andrew told Meagan, "You know, Meagan, I look at each old man I see in Iraq and ask myself, could that man be Jonathan's father? When I meet an old woman in the market or in a store, I ask myself, could she be his mother? Could she be the woman that gave me my brother and my best friend? It is torture for me, but I can't stop. I look for Jonathan in every face I meet there. Sometimes, I think I will meet him in the crowd, and he will hug me, wondering, 'What are you doing here, young brother?' I think I am losing my mind, Meagan."

"I understand. It is too much for you. Why don't you quit and come home?" Meagan asked.

"No, Meagan. I will never do that. I will go all the way carrying my pain and suffering. It is my fate."

At 6:00 p.m., they were called to speak to the doctor. "The surgery went well. It is now between him and God, but let me advise you, there was serious damage, and he is going to have to live with the outcomes of partial brain dysfunction." The doctor said.

Verona asked, "What can we do to help?"

The doctor replied, "Pray, pray as much as you can."

Andrew drove them home; they were all exhausted. Verona asked Andrew, "How long will you stay with us?"

"I am leaving on Thursday the 15th."

Meagan asked, "Why that soon? Why don't you stay and spend some time with your dad?"

"I am not on vacation, and I need to get back. A lot remains to be done there."

"Then let me say goodbye. I am going back to LA today. Let me know if you need anything."

Over the next three days, almost nothing changed. Donald remained in a deep state of unconsciousness, completely unresponsive. Verona and Andrew were there, in the same house, but they were as unresponsive to one another as Donald was to the world. Wednesday, Andrew went to the hospital to see his father. He asked the doctor, "Is there any hope?"

"Yes, there is hope. The damage was extensive but not to the point that it necessarily resulted in brain death. In two weeks, we will start the procedures to try to induce recuperation. If we succeed, it will be a very good sign."

"I need to get back. My furlough is very limited, and I can't stay longer than that."

"There is no need for you to stay," the doctor said. "It will be a slow and long process and will take months if we are lucky and are able to get him to respond. Take care of your life. We will take care of him here."

On Thursday, Andrew started his long trip back to Iraq. Arriving on Friday, 16 January, he reported to Sergeant Campbell, and soon was called to the colonel's office. Colonel Walsh asked him about his father, and it was clear that the information he received from Andrew caused him some worry. He suggested, "Andrew, if you want, I can move you to an administrative position, so it will be easier for you."

Andrew thanked him but refused the offer. "Thank you, Colonel. I like what I am doing. I will be okay."

Chapter 15

During 2004, Andrew had no down time. When he wasn't on patrols as a soldier, he was working with Adams as a photographer. When he wasn't chasing the enemy, he was running after the facts. The relation between Adams and Andrew was getting better and closer each day. Adams introduced him to Bassil Hamid Al Rayan, a young Iraqi journalist who was interested in writing a book about the war. Bassil met Adams during a news conference in the Central Command and told Adams about his project and requested his help. Adams welcomed the idea; in fact he badly needed the collaboration of an Arabic speaker who could reach people and uncover facts Adam couldn't. The partnership that developed between Adam and Bassil while covering the facts in Iraq was very useful for both of them, allowing since each man to be in the places that the other wouldn't be welcomed.

However, Andrew soon noticed that the relationship between Adams and Colonel Walsh was becoming uneasy. Walsh never accepted that Adams could be free to write articles and send them directly to the media, and he questioned whether he or another officer should look the writing over before it was published. Adams never accepted that and made it clear that what Colonel Walsh was proposing was a kind of censorship and that he, Adams, would never accept any kind of control or interference.

Adams also had the support of another Iraqi journalist, Belal Rahmani. Rahmani was a very well-respected journalist in Iraq. He had often denounced the Saddam government as an undemocratic dictatorship, and his harsh criticism earned him several periods of incarceration. When the troops arrived in Baghdad, the command treated Rahmani like an ally, but Rahmani's critical stance turned against the United States. He argued that the Saddam problem was an internal Iraqi affair and considered the war as an unjustifiable invasion. Adam had no problem with that. He believed that democracy can only be sustained by a diversity of peoples and ideas, but Colonel Walsh had great animosity for Belal, which he made no effort to hide.

Walsh's disapproval also involved Andrew. Many times, he claimed that many of the pictures Andrew took had security implications and shouldn't be released to the public, especially in the United States. However, the fact that the presence of a respected journalist, to run the media office had been established by Central Command, and that Adams had been selected by General Brenmann personally helped to soften the confrontation between Adams and Walsh.

Andrew also couldn't stop thinking about the situation of his father. The information he regularly received from Meagan was very alarming. The doctors needed almost forty-five days to take Donald out of the coma stage. After that he needed to stay for another long time in the intensive care unit. In May, when Donald was allowed to go home, he was still in bad shape; his brain injury had completely paralysed the right side of his body. Verona wrote a letter and asked Meagan to forward it to Andrew. She begged him for help and told him that his father was almost half dead in the bed. He was unable to move by himself and he had huge difficulty in talking and swallowing. Verona told Andrew that she was not able to manage the company and she wanted to know what he would like to do with it.

In July, Andrew received permission to fly home for ten days. He arrived in Kirkland on 14 July, and Verona drove him to see his father. He was overwhelmed; Donald tried to move in his son's direction to hug him, but he was unable to remain upright; Verona rushed to help him Andrew approached and hugged his father. Outside the room, Verona let Andrew know she had no way to run the company and she didn't know if the employees were doing well or not. Andrew told her that he would never leave what he was doing to run the company, and it would be better if they sold it and used the money to guarantee their retirement. Verona agreed and they started looking for a business broker. Verona suggested that he call Linda White, their real estate agent, and check if she could help.

Linda was shocked by the news about Donald's accident. "I will stop by your house to see Donald. Then we can talk," she said.

"Can we talk on Monday, 19 July?" Andrew asked. "I will be leaving soon so we don't have much time."

"Don't worry, we have a section in our office to deal only with business transactions. I will ask somebody to go with me to accelerate the process."

"Fine, Linda, thank you. See you on Monday."

On Monday, Linda visited Donald and Verona. She was accompanied by another broker, Shalla Dodge. They explained to Andrew that they would go through evaluation before hitting the market. Shalla asked about the number of trucks, the revenue, and the employees and requested all the documents of the company. She also requested the name of the accountant and asked for permission to contact him. Andrew left a phone number for Shalla so she could call him if she needed. On Thursday, 22 July 2004, Andrew returned to Baghdad.

On top of all of Andrew's personal complications, he returned to find another fight running under his nose in the office. The friction between Yusra and Sergeant Campbell, which had been bad since the beginning, was reaching alarming levels, and it was clear that the reasons went beyond the office. On 23 December 2004, Andrew had no choice but to intervene in the battle taking place in the room beside his own office. On that day, Andrew returned to the office after shooting some pictures with a patrol and when he entered the office, he heard people shouting in Sergeant Campbell's room. It was clear that something very bad was happening there. Andrew rushed into the room and he was shocked by what he saw. Yusra was crying frantically with her dress ripped down her chest. Even in her condition, she was restraining Amin, who was desperate to attack the sergeant. Sergeant Campbell, whose unsteady state testified that he had consumed lots of alcohol, was screaming and threatening both the Iraqi interpreters. It didn't take much imagination for Andrew to understand what had happened, and he knew that he had to find a definitive solution. He approached the sergeant and murmured in his ear, "Sir, may I take them to my office, so I can talk to them?"

Campbell moved his head signalling yes. Andrew moved closer to Amin and said, "Come with me; in my room we can talk better." Then he turned to Yusra and asked for her help. "Please, Yusra, help me. Let's go into my office; it will be better for all of us."

Yusra pushed Amin gently out of the room and the three of them moved into Andrew's office.

In the room, Yusra began raving. "He has harassed me since the very first day. He tried to force me to kiss him, and he ripped my clothes. If it hadn't been for Amin, I don't know what would have happened. I can't stay here anymore."

Calmly, Andrew said, "Yusra, I am sorry to tell you it is not you who decides who can stay where. I am aware of the problem and I believe you, but it isn't me either who decides. We have to solve this problem here."

Amin asked, "What solution do you suggest? He will never leave her in peace. He will never realise that he can take our land, but not our honour."

"Calm down, Amin. I am trying to help. If we take the problem up, we do not know what will come from there, and I doubt very much the command will back you up. In their view, you tried to attack an American soldier and that is an act of terrorism," Andrew said.

"Terrorism is what he was doing to her. He was trying to rape her in his office," Amin screamed.

"I believe that, but I am not sure they will."

Yusra looked at Amin and said, "He is right. I will never forget what you did for me but let us listen to him."

Andrew added, "I will suggest switching Yusra with Adnan. Yusra can come be my assistant and Adnan can take over her place there. Does that sound okay to you, Yusra?"

Yusra agreed immediately and begged Amin to accept the deal, but he resisted the plan with a great deal of resentment.

"How could we let it get this way?"

Andrew said, "That is the best solution we can get. What other solution do you suggest? Isn't saving her your priority?"

Though clearly unhappy, Amin agreed. "Okay, do what you think is best for her." Andrew asked them to stay in his room and went to Campbell's office.

With Campbell it wasn't that easy. The sergeant was furious, and he shouted, "Andrew, you can't trust those people's word. Don't forget who you are and who they are."

"Sergeant that is not the issue now, we have a woman who suffered an attempt to be raped, and it will not be good for anyone if the story comes out."

"Do you think that anyone will give a damn about this Iraqi bitch?"

"Sergeant, she is Iraqi, but not a bitch, and the command would hate to have trouble right here under their noses. Let us be reasonable."

"Which side are you on? Do you think I will forget this man advancing on me? He will have to pay for that, I swear he will."

Andrew became more serious, and said, "Sir, I am trying to avoid more troubles. I believe we shouldn't be questioning who advanced on whom now."

Still furious, the sergeant asked, "What do you want to do?"

"My proposal, Sir, is that you transfer her to my office and move Adnan to her place. If you agree, we can fix everything right here."

"I don't want this whore with me anymore. She can go to hell; I don't care."

"Okay, Sir, I will report that you ordered the transfer, thank you."

Andrew went back to his office to let Yusra and Amin know the conclusion. "Okay, it is done. The sergeant agreed."

He turned to Yusra and said, "Yusra, now go home, get some rest and try to forget this. From now on you will have no problem."

Yusra got up and asked Amin, "Are you leaving?"

Andrew interrupted. "No, Amin will stay; I need to talk to him."

Yusra left, and Andrew turned to Amin and said, "Amin, you will have to go back there. You have no choice. You will have to work under Sergeant Campbell's orders. Please don't get in trouble; Yusra will be okay now, and I hope you will be as well. Do I have your word on that?"

Now composed and serene, Amin said, "I will do my best, I promise."

On 17 November 2004, Meagan called Andrew. "Andrew, how are you?"

"Oi, Meagan, what a lovely surprise. I miss you a lot," he said.

"I miss you too. Tell me about yourself. Are you taking care of yourself?"

"I am okay. Please tell me about Dad and Mom."

"Your mom is okay, but your father is not doing very well. Verona had to hire a woman to help her take care of him. Do you have any idea about coming here soon?"

"I don't think there is any possibility during the next few months. Do you ask for any specific reason?"

"Yes. Really, I have two reasons. The first is that your father asks about you every time he opens his eyes. I asked the doctor if seeing you would make any difference. He said, morally, yes, but physically, nothing will help, the damage is irreversible. Sorry to have to tell you that."

"You don't have to apologise," he said, wiping his hand across his eyes. "I have been expecting that since the last time I saw him."

"Second, a buyer made a full offer for the company," Meagan added. "Shala, the broker examined the financial situation and says everything looks good. If you agree, she can open the escrow. Your mother told me that she has Donald's power of attorney, so she can sign for both of them, but she hopes you can come and help her with that."

"There is no way I can think about leaving right now. You can send me the proposal by army mail. I will send it back with my approval if it looks okay."

"I can do that for you."

"Please, Meagan, tell me more about my father."

"It is sad to see him this way. He is unable to take care of himself, and he has huge difficulty speaking and understanding."

"What do the doctors recommend that can help him?"

"I am sorry, Andrew. They have made it clear that little can be done. They recommended physiotherapy, but the most important thing is to take care of him."

Meagan heard Andrew sobbing, and she was touched. "I am sorry, Andrew, I didn't mean to make you sad. You know I don't have too much sympathy for them, but I feel very sad for them now."

Andrew was moved, and after a few seconds, he told Meagan, "Thank you for helping, Meagan. I will try to speed the papers when I receive them. I will call them right now."

Andrew called Verona. "Hi, Mom, how are things there?"

It took Verona a moment to control her emotions. "Andrew, is it you? How are you? Are you being careful?"

"Mom, I am okay. I called to hear about you and dad."

"He is very bad," Verona said. "He can barely move, and he can't take care of himself, but he is always asking for you."

"I am sad to hear that. I am disappointed in both of you, but I love you. Please tell him that I love him. I can't feel any differently. He is my father."

"I will. He will be happy to hear that. Are you coming soon?"

"No, I can't, but I told Meagan to send me the proposal for selling the company. I will send you a note if it is okay, so you can sign. Keep the money in a savings account and wait until I am home. If you have any trouble, call Meagan to help you."

"I will do that. Please call us when you can."

"I will. Take care."

It looked like normality was returning to the office. Yusra started working for Andrew. She was more agile and smarter than Adnan, and that was very good for Andrew, who badly needed someone to help him to process and print the pictures. She was also helpful in preparing and forwarding the reports; finally, she looked happy and seemed calm. On Tuesday, 15 March 2005, when Yusra arrived at Andrew's office, she discovered that he had prepared a big surprise for her. He had printed a very beautiful picture of her with the legend 'Happy Birthday Yusra.' Her face shone, and she looked even more beautiful than usual. After some hesitation, she laughed and said, "For me? What a surprise. I thought I had to die first before you would take my picture."

Andrew laughed deeply and said, "No please, stay alive and I will take all the pictures you want."

"Aren't you here to show your people how many enemies have been killed?"

Andrew was surprised by the comment. After a while, he said, "I am really sorry for that. I know how terrible the war is. My goal really is to let everyone know that war is evil."

"For whom?" Yusra asked, deeply saddened.

Moved, he took a moment to regain control of his emotions, then he said, "Believe me, Yusra, my soul is bleeding as much as yours. Maybe one day I can tell you, my story."

Yusra tried to alleviate the situation, saying, "Forgive me, Andrew. You are so nice to me; you remembered my birthday and I shouldn't be talking like this."

"No, Yusra, you shouldn't apologise. I understand your pain perfectly."

"I am sure you do, but now let me thank you for the beautiful picture. Will you sign it? Then when you become famous, I can make some money out of it"

Andrew laughed. "In my country, they would call you mercenary."

"What about you? When is your birthday?"

"4 November. If you want to give me a picture, you'd better start learning."

"You know, I was thinking to ask you to give me some directions on how to take better pictures, so I can be more helpful to you."

"I would love to; I will check my schedule and find some time for that."

"Thank you."

On Monday, 21 March 2005, Andrew called Yusra and asked her, "Yusra, I am thinking about taking some shots this afternoon in Al-Zawraa Park. Would you like to take the opportunity to learn a little more about photography?"

Yusra took a while to answer. "Yes, I will, I will go."

Andrew asked, "Is something wrong?"

"Nothing is wrong. We can go."

"But you don't look comfortable."

"Please, let us talk about that in the park."

At the park, Andrew explained to Yusra how to use the camera in the best way to take a good picture, he devoted good time explaining to her the Correlation between Shutter Speed and Aperture and how those elements together determine exposure. He handed her a small camera and said, "Feel free. Choose the scenes you like and create your pictures. Don't worry; today, you can make as many mistakes as you wish."

"It would better for you to be worried. Maybe my pictures will be nicer than yours."

Andrew laughed. "First, you need to take the cap off the camera. Otherwise, you will get nothing."

Two hours later, they sat and started eating a lunch Yusra had prepared. Andrew asked, "You promised me you would tell me why you took such a long time to accept my invitation. Will you do that now?"

"Sure. The fact is that I had three big problems: first, a girl here doesn't go to places with a man the way it used to be in other countries. Second, if this man is an American, things can quickly become difficult, third, if this man came to Baghdad on the top of a tank, then it is really much more complicated," Yusra explained.

"I understand perfectly, but then why did you accept?"

"Really, I don't know. It's just that I felt that you were so caring and sincere."

"I truly was, I mean, I truly am. Please believe me."

Going back to the pictures, they spent the rest of the afternoon working. At the end of the day, Andrew was impressed by Yusra's achievement. He said, "Yusra, you have improved a great deal. Now, I can't let you get any better; if I do, I might lose my job."

The first thing Yusra said to Andrew the following day was, "Thank you. You made me feel like a human being yesterday."

"Why is that?" Andrew asked, wrinkling his brow. "What do you mean?"

"I mean exactly what I said. For a long time, I haven't felt like a human being, but yesterday I remembered when my dad used to take us to Al Zawraa to play. That was a long time ago, good days that will never come back."

"Why not? Everything can be fixed."

"No, you are wrong, Andrew, you are wrong, there are many things that cannot be fixed. Some things, good or bad, when they happen, they are forever."

Andrew fell in a deep ocean of darkness and kept looking for nothing, murmuring, "Some things, good or bad, when they happen, they are forever, they are forever, and they are very bad, forever and very bad, forever and very bad."

Yusra felt deep sorrow for Andrews, she felt that she touched a very sore spot embedded deep in his memory, but that is still alive and bleeding. Immediately Yusra apologised. "Forgive me, Andrew, I didn't mean to hurt you, but I see that I did."

"Not you, Yusra, it wasn't you, but they did, they did."

"You want to talk about that?"

"Not now, please, not now. See you tomorrow."

On the way home, Yusra couldn't stop thinking in Andrew's question, "Why did you accept?" She knew her answer was vague and evasive even for herself, she knew that it was something more than photography, more than work obligation, or need to improve. It was something like feeling desire to fly high, to sink deep in the ocean or to touch the sky. But what was that that made her ignore the risk of being seen with a man in the park, and overall, American man. She tried all the ways to discover what that was, but she was running in circles, returning always to the very beginning, asking herself, what was that. Yusra was also undergoing other feeling she never experienced before, a kind of joy of being free like a bird, innocent like a flour and happy like a child.

Two days later, Andrew asked Yusra, "Do you still want to learn photography?"

She felt her heart beat faster, tried to disguise it by asking, "It seems you want to lose your job."

Andrew laughed and said, "Sort of, but if it was for you, it would be worth it."

Yusra was touched. "You have always been a gentleman. Thank you."

"Is Friday good for you?"

"No, not Friday, on Friday, the park will be loaded. Let's do it on Monday."

However, Yusra and Andrew couldn't fulfil their promise because the next day, Thursday, 24 March 2005, they received shocking news: Amin had disappeared. In fact, he had not been seen since Tuesday the 22nd, but weirdly, Sergeant Campbell didn't report his absence until Thursday, and even more oddly, the communication stated that Amin had deserted and joined the Iraqi guerrillas. Yusra was struck in her soul by the news. She rushed to Andrew's office. "I don't believe a single word of this report. Where is Amin now?"

Andrew was also distressed. Something didn't add up. *Why did Sergeant Campbell take so long to report? And why had Amin left his belongings behind?* "Calm down, Yusra. We will find him." Andrew said.

"That will never happen. Thousands have disappeared and none were ever found." Yusra replied with great anger.

"We will find out what happened."

"I will tell you what happened: they took him to Abu Ghraib, with the thousands of innocent victims that have been physically and sexually abused, that have been tortured, raped, and murdered."

"We don't know what really happened. Please calm down."

But Yusra was uncontrollable. She screamed, "We didn't know what was happening in Abu Gharib until we saw the pictures, and we don't know what is happening now in other, similar places."

"I am sure that action will be taken. The president asserted that those were isolated incidents and that he wasn't aware of those shocking facts."

"Please, Andrew, don't treat me as if I am a stupid person. I have a college degree, and I am well informed. Many humanitarian organisations announced that the president was aware of the situation, and they believe that he endorsed these kinds of acts."

Andrew was stunned. "What are you telling me, Yusra? Is that true?"

Yusra ended the discussion. "You said that you will find out about Amin. Why don't you find out about that too?"

She left in tears.

Neither Andrew nor anybody else discovered any information about Amin; he had disappeared into thin air. Oddly, no one bothered with that except Andrew and Yusra.

Andrew tried to get information from Adams. They had spent a long time working together and had become good friends. "Adams, I wonder what happened to Amin? Do you believe that he fled and joined the guerrillas?"

"No, I don't," Adams said. "I talked to Belal about that, and you know that Belal has trusted sources among the guerrillas. He assured me that they had never heard of him. But this is the kind of subject you can't get mixed up with. We are already in trouble, and we don't want to stir up anymore."

"You mean with Colonel Walsh?"

"Yes. He is very unhappy with us. He has tried to interfere many times, but I have been able to stop him."

"What is he claiming?"

"He is unhappy with some of my articles, he doesn't like some of your pictures, and he hates everything about Belal. Is that enough for you? He wants us to work under his supervision, one thing that I promptly refused."

After a few minutes of silence, Adams continued. "Up to now, we have had the support of General Brenmann, but I am not sure how long we can count on that."

"We aren't doing anything wrong; we are telling the truth. Isn't that our duty?"

"Which truth are you talking about? Each person has his own truth, and only the strong people make their truth prevail. So, you especially have got to be careful. In our world of today, you are not allowed, even, to have a truth, you are a low-ranking soldier, and it is easy for you to get hurt."

On Monday, 25 April 2005, Yusra told Andrew, "It is more than one month now, and we have found out nothing about Amin. His wife and kids keep asking me about him, and I don't know what to say."

"Yes, Yusra, and you keep asking me about him every day, and I don't know what to say. I am shocked and stunned. Sometimes I go to the park and I sit there alone for hours thinking and trying to understand, but I always end exactly where I started."

"I am afraid we will never understand," Yusra added.

Having nothing to say, Andrew left.

Andrew was sitting in the park diving deeply into his thoughts and uncertainties, suddenly, he heard someone asking, "Do you accept company?"

Initially, he thought that he went far in his sadness and disillusion, and that was just imagination, but the voice insisted, "Do I have your permission?"

When Andrew turned to verify who is talking, he had a pleasant surprise.

"Yusra, is it you?" Smiling, Yusra answered.

"I was sure you would be here."

"How nice of you to come, I am tired of thinking alone."

Yusra sat close to him and asked, "What is bothering you?"

"My head is just like a volcano before eruption. I am dealing with too many issues, and all of them are profound, sad, and complicated."

"Would you share your agony with me?"

"No, Yusra. I know that you carry on your shoulders as much weight as I do, and I know how much you suffer in silence. Instead, I wish you would tell me something about you, your family, and your life. I know nothing about you."

"What do you want to know?"

"Tell me about your family, your life, and the people you live with, and you love."

Yusra stared faraway for a while, then asked, "It is a long and sad story, are you sure you want to listen?"

Andrew replied, "Sure I do, please let me know about you."

Yusra took a deep breath and started, "My father is a licensed pharmacist. He started working in the drugstore owned by my grandpa. After getting his licence, he opened his own. When he was twenty-three, he married my mother; she was his cousin and used to live in Kuwait. My grandfather came from a big family that used to live in Basra in the south. When the British split Kuwait, part of my family lived across the border, many families were divided. Both parts of our family decided to preserve the bonds and tried to maintain the family connected, marriage was the most important link to keep the family together and connected."

Yusra rested for a couple minutes then restarted. "So, in January 1982, my grandfather and my father travelled to Kuwait and returned with my mother, who was already married to my father. One year and a half later, the result was me."

"Not bad," Andrew said.

"What? How dare you!" Yusra screamed at him.

They laughed, and Andrew tried to explain what he said. "I mean, it is good. As a matter of fact, it is a very good result. They did a wonderful job."

Yusra's face started to redden. "Thank you. We were four kids, me, two brothers and one sister."

"Why *were*?" Andrew asked.

"Because we are three now; I lost my brother Kazem."

"I am sorry to hear that. What happened?"

Yusra took a moment to collect herself, then started. "Kazem was my youngest brother. He was born on 3 December 1988, and was diagnosed shortly after birth with cystic fibrosis, which causes inflammation and scarring in many organs of the body, leading to permanent damage, especially in the lungs, but also the pancreas, liver, kidneys, and intestines."

Yusra was crying more than speaking, and Andrew tried to console her. "Yusra, I am sorry. I didn't mean to put you through this suffering again."

"That wasn't the suffering; the real suffering came after," Yusra answered.

She paused briefly, then resumed. "Initially, we were able to control the disease. The doctors kept him on one or more antibiotics at all times, even when healthy, to suppress any possible infection. They told us that antibiotics are necessary, especially whenever pneumonia is suspected or when lung function is seen to be in decline. At times, he needed to be hospitalised, but at that time all the medications were available, and we were able to keep him in good shape. However, at the end of 1990, we were surprised by the invasion of Kuwait and the Gulf war. After that, our real suffering started."

"What do you mean?" Andrew asked.

"The sanctions made everything difficult. As time passed, finding food or medicine became exceedingly difficult. The doors were being closed one after the other, and every alternative that was found to supply the people with their needs was immediately blocked. By 1998, the antibiotics we needed for my brother disappeared completely, and we had no alternatives. In despair, my father crossed illegally into Kuwait over the border near Basra and asked our relatives there for help. They arranged the medication he asked for in a quantity sufficient to aid my brother for a long time, but when he was trying to cross the border back to Iraq, he was caught and the medication was confiscated, my father was held in jail for three months.”

“Why did they confiscate the medication?”

“They alleged that it could be used for military purposes. By the time he was released, three months later, Kazem had died.”

At this moment, Yusra completely lost control and stammered inconsolably, “I was fifteen years old. My brother died in my arms pleading for some air to save his life, for something to help him to breathe. He was just a kid who wanted to live. Why, why?”

Andrew was also in tears. For a long time, the silence spoke for them. The word ‘why’ flew back and forth from her head to his and returned without an answer. They kept thinking, asking, and enquiring without a single word until it was dark, and they had to leave.

The week passed quickly and suddenly it was Monday. It was the afternoon, and they were both at the park.

“Yusra, thank you for coming, I was afraid you would never come again.”

“I shouldn’t, but I needed to come just as much as you.”

“Why?”

“I don’t know. Please, don’t keep asking me questions I don’t know how to answer.” After few minutes she resumed, “Something in you makes me feel secure, something in you makes me happy, something in me tells me to come.”

“It is the same with me Yusra, it is not Monday, it is not the park, and it is not the pictures, it is you, Yusra. That is the truth and you can’t imagine how happy that makes me.”

They spent the afternoon talking, avoiding all subjects that could disturb them. They had a nice time.

Since that day, with the flowers all around in the park, yet surrounded by the feeling of fear and apprehension, the sun brightening on Baghdad sky, even shattered by the war, and the good feelings flowing between, Yusra and Andrew induced them to make the commitment to meet in the park every Monday afternoon.

On Monday afternoon, everything was always perfect. The sun was bright, but never scorching. The wind was gentle, delicate, and refreshing. The park was more colourful, beautiful, and dazzling.

On Monday afternoon, everything was always perfect. The flowers flashed the most beautiful colours, the birds sang the most romantic songs, and the trees extended their shadows to cover people's souls.

On Monday afternoon, everything was always perfect. There were no patrols, no fighting, and no war. Kinder feelings overcame hatred, hearts spoke louder than weapons, and something good, deep, and sweet was growing within people's souls. They were getting closer and feeling better off each day. Their happiness lasted for months.

Chapter 16

It was Monday, 15 August 2005, and they were at the park for their weekly dose of joy and happiness.

"I wish the week had more than one Monday," Andrew said.

"I wish all the days of the week were Monday," Yusra replied.

"Do you like poetry?" Andrew asked.

"I do love poems, romances, songs; the word is my passion."

"Then I guess you write, correct?"

"Sometimes, writing is my way to talk to myself and to listen to my soul."

"Is that already a poem?"

Yusra laughed. "And you? When will you let me see some of your writing?"

"You look sure that I do write."

"The way you act, the way you see the world, the way you are, tells me that."

"You're right. I used to put my thoughts on paper. I had a single reader, who used to listen and comment on my poetry. Now, I do not have that person anymore." "

Why do you say that, Andrew?"

"Please, Yusra, do not ask me that, at least not now."

"Would you accept another listener?"

"Yes, Yusra. As a matter of fact, I brought a poem to read to you." Andrew started reading:

Is it you?
Is it a bright star walking like a woman?
Is it the beauty being human?
Is it the light? Is it the night?
Is it the dream coming true?
Filling the hope with a thousand colours
Healing the wound, we thought it never would

Bringing back the sweetest smile
Planting a tree
In the middle of the desert
Is it the rain, coming again?
To cool the heat in my heart
Drops of pearls, like the tears
In the child's little eye
Is it a bird, diving deep?
In the endless sky
Is it my heart, flying far? Looking for you everywhere,
Is it the way, going away?
Taking you far, bringing you back
Driving me mad
Between hope and despair
Is it the sun heating my heart?
And shining in my soul
Is it the joy filling your eyes?
Deep and blue
Is it the reason to be? The way to go
Is it the hope breaking through?
Is it love? Is it you?

For a long time, the silence reigned among them. Finally, Yusra asked, "When did you write this poem?"

"This week, I finished it just yesterday." After some time, he said, "Forgive me, Yusra. I wrote it for you."

Yusra needed some time before she could speak. "For me, it is very beautiful, it is marvellous. Do I deserve all that?"

"Every single word, it is more than a poem; it is a picture. Your picture created by words."

"That reminds me one of our greatest poets, Nizar Kabany. One of his best poems is entitled 'Drawing by Words,' which is the name for one of his collections."

Andrew held Yusra's hand, and he felt her shaking from her hair to the bottom of her feet, but she left her hand slipped in his. The universe stopped moving for the day to stay continually, the sun stationed behind the clouds for the afternoon to never end, the time kept at a standstill waiting for them. It seemed as though eternity had covered them forever.

Monday, 22nd was the most anticipated day in the lives of Yusra and Andrew. Though they were working together, seeing each other every day, they started to count the seconds on Tuesday, 16. On the 22nd, they were in the park eating the lunch Yusra had brought.

"I am already exploiting you, getting my Monday lunch for free," Andrew said.

"Don't worry," Yusra said. "I have no intention of paying you for the photography lessons."

"So, you need to enhance the lunch; I deserve more as a professor."

Yusra laughed and said, "You deserve the best; I promise to do better next time."

The afternoon was a piece of heaven, the park became a spot of paradise, and the planet stopped circling the sun. The universe wore its warmest shades, the sky displayed its prettiest blue, and the clouds appeared in their most romantic shapes. Yusra and Andrew were like two birds flying in an endless sky, unrestricted by time, limits, or shadows. Everything was set for them, everything was cheering for them, everything around became a love boat, with them inside, gliding in the sea of eternity. Unwillingly, they observed that time had passed, and they had to leave.

On Tuesday, 23 August, Andrew was called to Colonel Walsh's office. The officer approached him and said, "Andrew, I am afraid I have bad news for you. It is from home."

Andrew replied, "Is it my dad?"

"Yes. He passed away yesterday. I am sorry for your loss."

Andrew tried to restrain his emotions, but he wasn't able to; he broke into sobs. "Sorry, Colonel," he stammered.

Walsh hugged him and said, "Don't worry. I have arranged a place for you on the flight home today. You have a few hours to pack your bag and take the shuttle to the airport."

"When should I come back?"

"It is a short trip. The return flight leaves DC on Friday, so you will be back on Saturday, 27."

"Thank you, Colonel."

Andrew left quickly. He returned to his office, where he told Yusra about his father. She hugged him and whispered in his ear, "I'll be waiting for you."

And that was all he needed to carry with him on his flight.

Arriving at Sea-Tac Airport on the afternoon of Wednesday, 24 August, Andrew found Meagan waiting for him. They hugged each other and Andrew asked, "What happened?"

"Your dad never really recovered," she told him. "His condition worsened drastically on 15 August, and he soon went into a coma and needed life support. On 21, Sunday, the doctors informed your mother that he had experienced irreversible brain death and recommended the withdrawal of life support, which she authorised on Monday, the 22nd."

Andrew was saddened to hear about his father's suffering. Though he would never forgive him for what he had done to Jonathan, he was never able to stop loving him as his father. Meagan noticed Andrew's anguish and immediately wondered why. Holding his hand, she said, "This story is already over, and it is time to move on."

Andrew said, "I don't think so. There is another chapter to be written in Iraq."

"Did you get any information about Jonathan's family?"

"Not yet. I have not had any chance, but I will. I need to do that."

"Please be careful. I am not sure you should touch this subject there."

At this moment, they arrived at the McCoolen home. Verona stood outside the door waiting for them. She hugged Andrew and sobbed on his shoulder. After a while, she said, "Donald is gone, Andrew. Now, I am alone. Now, I have no one."

Andrew hugged her and tried to give her some relief. "Don't worry, Mom, there are many people to take care of you. When will the service take place?"

"Friday at 10:00."

"The same day I am scheduled to return."

"That soon? Can't you stay a little longer?"

"Sorry, but I can't. I'll go with Meagan to the funeral home to see that everything is taken care of."

On the way, Meagan asked Andrew, "Why are you going back so soon?"

"The situation there is not very good. We are being attacked almost daily, and I need to get back."

"This is what worries me the most. Please, be careful. My wounds still bleed, and there is no space for more."

"I am trying, but you worry me the same way."

"Why?"

"Three years have passed now and you have almost no life, no fun, and no happiness. This is not good at all."

Heaving a sigh, Meagan asked, "What do you think I should do?"

"Find somebody, be happy. You are a beautiful woman, and you can't spend the rest of your life alone."

"I still love Jonathan the same way I always did. Sometimes, I imagine him coming through the door with his fascinating smile, calling my name."

Again, she cried quietly. Andrew hugged her and said, "Meagan, you know how much I and my brother loved each other. He was my brother, my best friend, and the light that used to guide my life. Then suddenly, Jonathan was gone. We will never accept that, but we need to find a way to keep going."

Meagan tried to regain control over her emotions and agreed, "Yes, we should try, at least try."

"You should find somebody to help you heal. It is much harder to do alone."

Meagan surprised Andrew by asking, "And you, when will you find someone to give you some comfort?"

His answer was no less surprising, "I already found her."

"Wow, tell me everything. Where, when, who? Tell me all at once."

Andrew was happy to take her out of the darkness and said, "Calm down. I'll tell you everything. She is a wonderful person. She works with me in the office, and once I saw her, something told me she would be the woman of my life."

"Who she is and how did this happen?"

"She is an Iraqi woman; her name is Yusra, and she works with me in the media office."

Somehow, Meagan was shocked. She spent a few minutes trying to understand, then she asked, "How could that happen? I mean, in the middle of a war; how is that even possible?"

Andrew said, "It happened because our feelings are real and sincere; it happened because love just happens. When it comes to love, there is no how, no why, or by what manner. I did not decide to love her; I just felt the love for her taking over my heart, filling all the spaces, and becoming my way of life. I didn't care about the colour of her eyes because the colour of her soul was fascinating. I didn't care about her accent because she was saying that she loves me."

"Andrew, I am worried about you."

"You shouldn't. I feel like I have come back to life now. For the first time since I lost my brother, I feel the desire to live. I want to be happy again. She helped me to discover that I still have a heart and I still can love and be loved."

Andrew opened his wallet, took out a picture, and handed it to Meagan. "Let me introduce her to you."

Meagan looked at the picture and observed, "She is really very beautiful. I am happy for you. What do you intend to do?"

"Once the war is over, I will bring her here. We will get married and have kids, and the first boy will be named Khaled Jonathan."

"It is good to see you happy again, but please be careful. I couldn't bear to see you depressed again."

On Friday, 26 August 2005, at 10:00 a.m., the funeral service for Donald McCoolen was conducted. The ceremony took one hour to allow Andrew to reach his flight to DC on time. Verona insisted on going to the airport to say goodbye to her son. Meagan offered to take her back home. At the airport, Andrew asked Meagan to stay in contact with Verona, at least until he had come home, and she promised to do so.

On Monday, 29 August, Andrew and Yusra were in the park again, among the flowers and the birds. Andrew brought with him a small battery recorder, and Yusra brought some Arabic music tapes.

Andrew told Yusra, "I brought some special music for you."

"Which one?"

"Listen," he said, and loaded the tape in the machine and started the music.

"Unforgettable, that's what you are; Unforgettable though near or far."

When the song ended, Yusra's eyes glistened. Misreading her mood, Andrew asked, "What is wrong, Yusra? Didn't you like the music?"

Yusra answered, "Nat and Natalie Cole that is really unforgettable. It is not the music; it is about us. I am worried and frightened."

"Why?" Andrew asked.

"Where are we going? What future can we expect?"

Andrew, shocked, drew closer to her and said, "Why are you saying that, Yusra? We love each other, isn't that true?"

"What will we do with our love? Can we forget who we are? Can we ignore the war destroying everything around us?"

"We are two people in love hoping to live together forever. I would never hurt you, Yusra."

"It doesn't matter what the name is, Yusra or anyone else, she's the target, and it doesn't matter who's on the other side, Andrew or anyone else; he's the sniper."

Feeling Yusra slipping away from him, Andrew said, "We are not doing anything wrong."

"But of course, we are. For your people, what you are doing is treason, and for my people, what I am doing is sin."

Andrew insisted, "I would never betray my country. And you, what wrong are you committing?"

"Of course, we have. You came here to kill not to love, and I am supposed to fill my heart with hatred for you, not passion."

After a pause, Yusra spoke again, "Our way forward is blocked; we have nowhere to go. I think about that all the time, we do not have any chance."

"How can you say that? I would never accept that. I love you, and this is the only fact in my life."

"There is another fact we can't ignore: we are enemies. We can't change that."

Andrew replied, "We can't change our hearts, either."

"My people will never accept you."

"And my heart will never accept anyone but you."

Again, silence reigned for a while. Yusra looked at him with eyes full of tears and said, "We are trying something dangerous, unsafe, and risky. And it is also impossible."

"There must be a way to go, there must be a place to be."

"Not for us. Will you tell your people that you love an Iraqi, Arabic, and Muslim woman, with the cloud of hate for all that is Iraqi, Arabic, and Muslim covering America?"

Without waiting for his answer, Yusra added, "Will I be able to tell my people that I love an American combatant, with our rivers running with blood instead of water?"

His heart in turmoil, Andrew mumbled, "I can't lose you; I can't go through that again. I have had enough. God, please no. It is too much for me."

"What are you saying, Andrew?" Yusra asked. "What does that mean?"

Struggling with his pain and emotions, Andrew tried to answer. "I have had the kind of pain that no one could support. At that time, I wanted to die. I wish I could have; I wish I could have."

Taking hold of his hand, Yusra asked, "Tell me what made you suffer so much? Talk to me; my heart and my soul are all open to embrace your pain."

Andrew, hunched over to shield his gut, started talking. "I had a brother, a kind and generous person. We used to love each other as much as we could. He was killed in the Afghanistan war."

"How? Why? Your parents must be stricken. They lost one in one war and now the other is going through another one."

"No, they are not. That is what hurt me most in the story, and the most shameful part as well."

Yusra pulled back to get a better look at Andrew. "What does that mean, Andrew? I am getting confused."

"When I was born, Jonathan, my brother, was five years old. As I grew up, I noticed that my parents were very bad with him; they were always angry, impatient, and distant toward him. Everything good was for me and nothing for him—the best schools, the best toys, and especially the care and love was all for me; nothing, absolutely nothing, was for him.

"Of course," Andrew continued, "I couldn't understand why they acted that way. He was such a good person, kind and polite." Andrew paused to bow his head and take a deep breath, then he resumed. "Despite that, we developed a very close and deep relationship. He was my friend, my idol, and my protector. I used to share my things with him, and when I was in high school, he bought me my first camera and encouraged me to study photography.

"The break finally came when the Twin Towers were attacked on 9/11/2001. My parents turned on my brother and treated him like he was somehow guilty for what had happened. At that moment, I could not believe what I saw, but they threw him out of the house and told him they didn't want to see him again. Jonathan joined the army and died in Afghanistan defending America."

Andrew needed a few minutes and a lot of affection from Yusra to resume the story. "The big surprise and disappointment came later. During a discussion with my dad about Jonathan, he shouted that Jonathan never was my brother. I started searching in Jonathan's belongings and I found the page of an old newspaper with the picture of an Iraqi couple and some notes in my brother's handwriting, calling them 'Baba' and 'Mama.' A wider search led me to the terrifying discovery that he was an Iraqi child who had been lost in the marketplace in Seattle and my dad found him and kept him for himself to be his kid, because he thought that he would never be able to have a natural child."

Yusra was stunned. "What are you telling me, Andrew?"

Trembling and with eyes full of tears, Andrew said, "That is the truth, Yusra. I discovered that his father was a doctor working at the University of Washington as a visiting professor. He was forced to leave two weeks after the disappearance of the child, and never had any information about him."

"Did you learn the identity of those people?"

"Yes, I did. I have all the information about them."

"Have you thought about looking for them?"

"I think about them all the time. You can't imagine how much I loved and still love Jonathan, and no one gave me as much love as he did. Only God knows how much I miss him. When I discovered what my parents had done, I left them. That was when I joined the army."

"And now, Andrew, what will you do?"

"I really don't know. I wish to meet the parents of my brother, but what will I tell them? Would I tell them that their kid was kidnapped and forced to change his name and his mind? Should I tell them that their kid had the hell of a life being rejected and disdained by the people who were supposed to care for him? Can I tell them that their son had already gone, and that they would not be able to say goodbye to him or give him a hug? Do I have the right to ask them for forgiveness for all of that?"

At this point, Yusra was in tears, and Andrew was no less moved; they had to stop. They needed time to digest what Andrew had just said and to think what to do. Wiping her eyes, Yusra suggested, "That is enough for today. We need time to assimilate what we just learned."

Andrew agreed. "It is also late, and we need to go. Thank you for listening."

After they stood, Andrew held Yusra's hands and said, "Please, Yusra, I am deeply ashamed about what my parents did; they did the same to me, because once I discovered the truth, I was ripped from my parents the same way he was. Please, forgive me."

Chapter 17

On Wednesday, 14 September 2005, Yusra entered Andrew's office and said, "I will be finishing the report with Belal. Once it is done, I will leave it on your table to be reviewed."

"Yusra, I brought some information about my brother for you. Please check with Belal if he has any knowledge about this matter, but please ask him to be very discreet. We can't let this get out." He handed her an envelope containing many pictures and pieces of newspaper.

"I will be glad to do that. I was thinking the same thing. Do not worry, I will do my best."

On Monday, 19 September, early in the morning, Yusra stopped Andrew as he passed her desk and said, "We need to talk. I have a lot to tell you."

"Come to my office," he replied.

In the office, Yusra said, "I questioned Belal about your brother. He went through all the papers you gave me and told me that he remembers the case. He was just beginning as a reporter, with *Al Thawra* newspaper, which gives him the chance to be very close to the sources of information."

She stopped briefly and added, "I do believe it is better to talk to him by yourself; he can show you the part of the story that you know nothing about."

"Is he willing to talk to me about that?" Andrew asked.

"Any time you want. He is waiting for you now, if you wish."

"Let us go then. I am anxious to know everything about Jonathan."

Belal received them very warmly and immediately started talking. "Andrew, Yusra told me about the little kid that disappeared in the States, but I wish to hear the story from you to be sure we are talking about the same person."

Andrew started, "Jonathan, or Khaled…"

At that point, he choked up and found it hard to speak.

"Take your time," Belal said. "I can understand how difficult this must be for you."

Andrew resumed. "Whatever the name was, he was my brother. I loved him, and I miss him every day. He was kidnapped from the market place in the city of Seattle in May 1981. We grew up as real brothers, we loved each other and for sure our relationship was the best thing in our lives. Our parents were very cruel to him, and in 2001, they demanded that he leave home. At that time, he was a brilliant graduate student at the University of Washington, and he was engaged to a beautiful and nice girl, Meagan. He left all that behind and joined the army. He was killed in the battle of Tora Bora."

Belal said, "Yes, from the first part of your story, I can see that it is the same history I was thinking of. I was very close to the case; the journalist named to work on the case selected me to help him. The case became a national concern in Iraq because the university exerted huge pressure on the media to keep the case alive. Dr Omar Al-Dahany was an imminent professor and he generated the solidarity of everybody, but unfortunately, time passed, and the case became cold, though not for the Al-Dahany family, as I know there was a lot of suffering there."

"Do you have any information how they are now?" Andrew asked.

"Not really, but I can get the information easily. I just need to visit the university and talk to my friends there."

"Would you do that for me? I need to know; I owe that to my brother."

"Okay, just give me a couple days. I will see what I can do."

Early on the morning of Monday, 26 September, Andrew and Yusra met Belal in his office. "I am afraid I don't have good news for you," Belal said.

"Tell us what you found out, please," Andrew asked.

"Okay. I visited the university, but I couldn't find much information there. The first obstacle was the war; the university is officially closed and classes are cancelled. A very few professors have shown up at their laboratories trying to save their research but have faced huge difficulties. Also, the fact that it was twenty-five years ago and almost all the people from that time have left the university. The real help I got was from Dr Rashid Basheer Bustani, the former dean of the school where Professor Omar Al-Dahany used to work. Dr Bustani is eighty years old now, retired. He lives in Kazmia, close to the Tigris River, where I visited him.

"Professor Bustani welcomed me and asked why I am interested in Al-Dahany's life. I told him that I have some information about the kidnapped child and I wish to share it with the family, hoping that may bring them some closure.

I saw one tear dropping from the eye of the old man, then he said, which I recorded and translated to you, have a look." Andrews started reading the deposition of Professor Bustani:

It looks like this family was selected by destiny to experience all the suffering and pain of all its generation. Dr Omar passed away in April 1984. The young man could no longer support the fact that he had lost his son. He lost his son, and we lost one of the best talents the university ever had. He was a brilliant researcher and a great professor, but he couldn't cope with his loss; no one would. After that, we tried to help his family, but it was difficult. The family fell apart at once, and we lost contact. Maybe Professor Maha Al-Tighany can help you little more. She was his assistant, and she took over the lab after his death.

Andrew needed to take a pause, Belal was saddened and Yusra has her eyes full of tears. They were all disturbed by his news. Yusra was sniffling, while Andrew was lost in thoughts of his brother. He could not understand why some people had to suffer so much, paying for the mistakes that others made. He asked Belal, "Did you get in contact with the mother? Is she still alive?"

Belal said, "First, I need to discover where Dr Tighany lives. Hopefully, from her I can discover a little more about the family. I was told that she was the one who had stayed in touch with the family. I am working on that."

In the afternoon, Andrew approached Yusra and said, "Yusra, it is Monday, the day we used to meet. Could we meet in the park? I miss you so much."

Yusra looked deeply into his eyes. "And you think I do not? I miss you every single moment. I think about you during the day, I dream with you every night. You have changed my life and given it a new meaning. I rush to the office early just to see you a little longer. I leave late to enjoy being with you for a few extra minutes. Don't you see that? But we can't, we just can't," she said and began to cry.

"We can't give up. We need to talk," Andrew said.

"About what, about love or about war? Talk about us or talk about Amin, Khaled, or Al-Dahany? Can't you see how many barriers there are between us? It is kidnapping, it is death, it is blood, and it is war, too many oceans to cross without boat. How can we ignore all that?"

Andrew insisted, "No one will kill our love. There is no weapon capable of killing the love in the heart. We will never allow that."

Yusra continued to argue. "We who? We what? We are nothing; we don't exist. Would you like to know who we are? Just listen to the poem that earned Belal a highlighted place on Colonel Walsh's blacklist."

"What poem? Please, Yusra, tell me about it."

"If you want to know more about that, then we really should go to the park. Here is very risky."

Later on, in the park, Yusra brought out a print of the poem. She said to Andrew, "Listen to the poem. It will tell you who really we are, or at least, how we are been seen." Yusra started to recite the poem with eyes dripping tears:

We are not on the map
We are not on the page
We are not on the road
Going anywhere,
We are not here, we are not there
We just don't exist
We can't, we won't,
We have gone,
We are done
And if we want, we don't
Just because we can't
No how, no why, we just don't

* * *

We are the shadow of nothing
The history that no one count
And no one even cares about
The secret, in the box, deep in the river
"The day the fish come out"
"The man who never was"
No name, no hope, no place
No way, no colour, and no face

We just are not, or something close
The small stone in the giant shoes
We are bothering the five o'clock tea
The baseball game they want to see
The monster dream coming through
The great assault they want to do

* * *

No future has been left for us,
And, also, no past
No place to be, not even the last
No right to dream, with the lovely one
No right to feel the heat of the sun
It is the big Lie you must believe
The autumn grey, but no fallen leaves
We are the black missing the white
The every wrong without the right
The deepest dark that never light

* * *

That is the way they want
The way we have to be, we must
The way they colour the face
The face must get the paint
The way they decide to tear the soul
The soul has to be cut,
they draw the picture, and you must fit
We are, I mean we were
And now we are not

After a long time, Andrew was able to ask, "When did Belal write this poem?"

"In February 2003, when the invasion became imminent and we felt that we had no choice. He published this poem in a small newspaper. Soon after, a

168

society called *Writers for Resistance* published the poem and distributed it everywhere. After the invasion, the poem became an anthem of the resistance for the people here. Soon, the poem was seen as a blow against the invasion. That is why Colonel Walsh hated Belal so much, but Belal was saved by Mr Adams."

On 30 September, Belal called Andrew. "I have some more news. Would you like to know?"

"Of course, we will be in your office in fifteen minutes."

Andrew told Yusra, "It looks like Belal has made progress. Would you like to hear it?"

She got up immediately and, in a few minutes, they were in his office. "Hi, Belal, please tell us what you have got."

Belal needed some time to start. He seemed to be groping for the right words. Finally, he began, speaking haltingly. "This was the hardest mission I have ever had as a journalist. It was like digging up graves, and this is something profane and unholy for us. I had to go back twenty-four years and ask about a story that no one wanted to talk about. I was lucky to meet Dr Maha Al-Tighany. All the information that I collected came to confirm Dr Bustani's words, *'It looks like this family was selected by destiny to experience the suffering and pain of all its generation.'* She told me that Kareem, Omar's father, passed away one year after Omar's death. He used to visit his grave every day. One day he didn't return. When Dina, his granddaughter and Khaled's sister, went to check on him, he was dead. He was buried in the same grave with Omar, but they respected his wish to keep a space between them for Khaled. It was heart-breaking.

"Rafik and Ghada wanted to move Rania and Dina to Basra to be with them, but Rania rejected that promptly. 'No, I can't go anywhere. I need to stay here to take care of Omar. I have to be here to welcome Khaled when he comes back.' They soon realised that she would not go anywhere."

Belal took a moment to breathe, while Andrew and Yusra waited. After a while, Yusra asked, "How are they doing now?"

Belal answered, "Really, I don't know. Dr Al-Tighany told me that she lost contact with them ten years ago, but she gave me their address."

"What do you intend to do?" Andrew asked.

"I need to know the security situation in the district where they live. The address I got is in Al Ameria District, a popular area, so it is a very risky place. Of course, I am thinking of visiting them. I am planning on that."

"You think we will be able to go with you?" Andrew asked.

"I am not sure. Walking in the streets of Baghdad with an American is not a good idea these days."

Andrew added, "I need to talk to her. I need to ask for her forgiveness. I need to tell her that her son was a good man and a good brother."

"Do you think that will give her relief or drip acid on her ulcerated heart?"

"What can I do?" Andrew blurted. "I need to do something."

"Nothing can be done," Yusra said. "Some things, good or bad, when they happen, they are forever."

After a few minutes, Belal added, "Let me collect more information, then we can see what we should do."

"Thank you, Belal, for helping, it would be very difficult to make any progress without you," Andrew said before leaving with Yusra.

On 4 October, Belal called Andrew. "Are you determined to talk to the Al-Dahany family, I mean, what remains of them?"

"Of course, I do. Have you had any contact with them?" Andrew said.

"Not yet. They live in the same apartment they have lived in since they came back from the United States. It is only Rania and Dina; I asked my wife to contact Dina and to tell her that I am writing an article about her father's legacy at the university, and I would like to talk to her. My wife told me that she was very polite and said we can go any time."

Expressing all his anxiety and stress, Andrew said, "I am ready any time. Can we go today?"

"Not today, I need some time to make the arrangements. Don't forget that it will be an operation condemned by both sides, Iraqi and American."

"That is right," Yusra agreed. "If we got caught by the Iraqis with an American, there will be hell to pay, and if you get caught by the Americans with two Iraqis, the outcome will be the same. We must be very careful."

She turned to Belal and asked, "When do you think we will be able to do it?"
"I believe we can do it on 10 October in the afternoon," Belal said.

"Okay, that is fine. I will be ready," Andrew commented.

Chapter 18

Monday, 10 October, 2005 at 2:00 p.m., Andrew was waiting for Belal to start the most difficult trip of his life. He had prepared for this journey as much as he could. He was anxious, stressed, and scared. He was about to visit the house where Jonathan was born and where he took his first steps. He was about to meet Jonathan's mother and sister. He asked himself a thousand times what he should say to them, and if he should apologise for the crime committed twenty-four years ago. Should he tell them that his father had kidnapped their kid and ripped him from his family and his life?

Andrew's head was like a volcano ready to blow. He had gone through many pictures of Jonathan to take with him, but he wasn't sure if that was the right thing to do. *Would seeing these bring relief or suffering for them? Would that help heal their wounded hearts? Would that cool their lacerated souls? Seeing their son graduating from high school and college without being there to give him a hug, wouldn't that be a fire burning the already scorched heart? How could he explain to them that Jonathan or Khaled had struggled to have the love of people who were not his parents, while his real parents here were ready to give their lives to give him a hug?*

Andrew was in bad shape; he was sad, ashamed, and scared. *Should he introduce himself as Khaled's brother? And how could he explain that? Should he tell them that his father had stolen an innocent child from the marketplace, and while they were ripping the skies calling for their son, Donald, the father of the person who was talking to them, was running with him to his house in Everett? Should he tell them that he missed Jonathan, Khaled, as much as them? And should he expect them to believe that?* Then Andrew noticed that he was crying like a child who had lost his parents.

Yusra was shocked when she entered the office and saw him crying. She sat close to him and asked, "Are you distressed because of the meeting?"

"It is too much for me. What can I tell and what shouldn't I?" Andrew replied.

"I have been thinking about that all the time. What makes the situation disgraceful is that he is not here anymore, so they will have to go through all this anguish again and in the end, they will discover that he is gone. Such pain is unbearable."

At that moment, Belal entered the office, and it was not difficult for him to sense the cloud of sadness that was filling the room. He commented, "I can understand what is happening. I too am deeply touched."

He looked at Andrew and said, "It is up to you. If you want to quit, we can."

"I can't quit. I can feel my brother asking me to do this. I need to meet them. They are the people who really belong to him. They have the right to know what happened to him."

Yusra rose and said, "Okay, then let us go."

Andrew reacted immediately. "Not you, Yusra. It will be only me and Belal. It is very risky for you."

"I need to go to give you support," she argued. "You are strongly affected emotionally, and I would like to be by your side."

Andrew insisted, "Thank you, Yusra, but please stay out of this adventure. I can't be the cause of any harm to you."

Belal interrupted, "He is right. It is a dangerous mission; better to stay out of it."

Yusra tried to insist, but Andrew begged her to stay. "Yusra, if anything goes wrong, we need you free to help. It is my responsibility, and I will face it. Please stay here for us." Finally, Yusra agreed and they left.

At noon, they left in Belal's car from the Green Zone, Belal advised Andrew, "Be prepared; it won't be an easy job."

Belal entered the Qadisiya Highway, but soon he turned right into Jordan Avenue. After a while, he turned left on Rabie Street heading to Sefarat Street. He told Andrew, "We are almost there. After we cross the highway, it is the third street on the right, no. 52."

They crossed the highway and turned on the third street on the right, but they had to stop immediately; the street was blocked by military armoured cars and armed soldiers. Belal turned to Andrew and whispered, "This is what I was afraid of."

Andrew retorted, "How they did discover where we are going?"

"It was Bassil. I always suspected his role there. I never swallowed his story of writing a book about the war."

"Are you sure?"

"I caught him once trying to overhear my conversation on the phone, and I also suspected that he was inspecting my notes on my desk, but I never thought he would dare to do that."

By this time, the soldiers were already close to the car, yelling, "Get out of the car. Put your hands where we can see them."

Once Belal and Andrew were out of the car, they were ordered to lie on the ground facing down. They tried to ask what was happening, but they were not allowed to speak. In seconds, they were handcuffed and ordered to lie without moving. Andrew and Belal were arrested and transferred to Central Command in the Sheraton Hotel.

The news soon reached the media office and drove Yusra crazy. She rushed to the phone and called Adams.

Adams was shocked when Yusra told him what had happened, "Why didn't Andrew tell me any of this?" Minutes later, Adams was in Yusra's office asking, "Tell me everything, I want the full story."

Yusra was in a bad state, Adams tried to comfort her, "Yusra, I know how hard it is for you, but you must hold on to tell me what happened."

Between tears, Yusra told him the story of Jonathan and Andrew's suffering with everything that happened.

Three days later, Colonel Walsh and Mr Adams were called to General Brenmann's office to discuss Andrew and Belal's situation. The meeting was set for Monday, 17 October. On Friday, 14 October, Adams called Colonel Walsh. "Hi, Walsh, I think it would be good for everybody if we talk before meeting the general."

Walsh agreed. "Sure, we can do that. Can you stop by my office this afternoon?"

"I will. Is four o'clock good for you?"

"Perfect, I'll be waiting for you."

At 4:00, Adams entered Walsh's office. "Thank you for having me here, Colonel."

"You are welcome, Mr Adams. I also felt that we need to talk about this matter."

Adams started. "Let us begin by agreeing that no big mistake was committed, nothing that can bring concerns about our safety."

"In civilian life, you can use this classification, small and big violation, but in the military that doesn't work, Adams. A violation in military jargon has only one face and it carry always the same size that is the big one."

"Don't you think that those two families have already suffered enough? Do you think it is fair to punish them for trying to heal?"

The expression on Colonel Walsh's face changed; he looked touched and said, "I agree. There has been too much suffering. I learned from the reports how the life of the Iraqi family was destroyed, and I was informed how our soldier was hurt by the loss of his brother."

Adams commented, "Andrew was trying to give the family of his brother some closure. He had the best of intentions."

"He should have talked to us. He should have asked for our help, not the Iraqi guy's support. You know I never trusted Belal."

"Would you support him?"

"I understand it would be difficult. It is war, it is a serious disciplinary violation, and not the only one."

Adams grasped immediately what Walsh wanted to say. "Are you talking about Yusra?"

"Yes. We have the reports about that as well."

"Did you find anything compromising?"

"Not really, just the romance."

"That is something right, not wrong, Colonel."

"In Shakespeare's world, Mr Adams, you would be very right, not in the middle of an American war in the Middle East."

Adams, deeply worried, said, "If that became public, the girl could be killed by her people."

Colonel Walsh agreed. "True, it is a serious violation for them."

Both men thought for a brief time, then Adams asked, "Colonel, what do you have in mind?"

"First of all, Belal must be pulled out of the media office. We cannot allow a local citizen to act this way under our nose. Second, the romance must be ended for good."

"Colonel, if I agree to let Belal go for good, would you take Yusra off the hook?"

"Then Andrew must be moved from Central Command; he should be transferred to a base outside of Baghdad."

"I do believe we have a deal. Thank you, Colonel."

"Thank you, Adams."

On Monday, General Brenmann started the meeting by asking, "Colonel, what did you find out in your investigation?"

Colonel Walsh reported, "Sir, starting with Private First-Class Andrew Gaston McCoolen. He enlisted on 10 February 2003. On March 4, he was transferred to Kuwait. On 20 March, he joined the troops when the war started. He belongs to a middle-class family; his father owns a small transportation company; his mother is a stay-at-home mom. Nothing was found against military conduct.

"The Iraqi party is Belal Rahmani, journalist. He was a strong critic of Saddam and spent many times in jail for that, but after we started our operations in Iraq, he turned his batteries against us. Immediately after receiving a communication about the suspected operation, they were planning, we put them under severe surveillance; every word was recorded, and every movement was captured on video. The tapes and videos were examined thoroughly by two independent commissions; nothing criminal was found, there was no evidence of foul play; they never talked politics; they never exchanged any written or photographic material."

General Brenmann asked, "What was the nature of the operation?"

"The story that they gave during the investigation was confirmed by our intelligence. They were trying to contact an Iraqi family that lost a son in Seattle in 1981."

The general showed more interest and requested more information. "Tell me more details, Colonel."

"Dr Omar Al-Dahany was a visiting professor at the University of Washington. On 9 May 1981, he lost his three-year-old son, Khaled, at the Pike Place Market in Seattle. The boy was never found, and the case went cold. Now, we know that the kid was kidnapped by the McCoolens. His name was changed to Jonathan, and he was registered as an adopted child from Brazil. On 25 September 2001, Jonathan joined the army and took part heroically in our operations in Afghanistan. He died in Operation Anaconda in Tora Bora."

General Brenmann remained thoughtful for a couple of minutes, then said, "Then our private was looking for the family of his virtual brother."

"All the reports, sir, indicate that they were good brothers and close friends," Colonel Walsh said.

The General asked, "What do you think, Adams?"

"I don't see anything wrong, General."

Colonel Walsh said, "Adams may not see anything wrong, but I do see something wrong. We are here for war, General, and we can't allow this kind of weakness."

Adams replied firmly, "It is strength, not weakness, Colonel. The real strength is to be really human above everything else."

"Not during war, Mr Adams," the Colonel argued. "This soldier was correct and never mixed his duty with his personal interest, but you can't guarantee what others might do."

The general looked sharply at both of them and said, "And now? We must make a decision."

Adams insisted, "If nothing wrong happened, why must we make a decision?"

"We are at war, Adams," the general repeated. "How can we maintain order and discipline among the troops if we allow this kind of behaviour? We have got to take action and it must look harsh, even if it is not. I will decide what to do later. Thank you."

On Wednesday, 19 October, Colonel Walsh and Adams were called again to the general's office to receive his decision: "Andrew McCoolen, transfer to Haditha; Yusra Rashid Kaidany, back to Sergeant Campbell's office; Belal is dismissed from Mr Adam's office."

Colonel Walsh asked for permission to speak. "Allow me to express my thoughts, General. Yusra can't be back in Campbell's office; they had problems working together."

Adams also objected. "If I lose Belal, I will need someone to help me. Sir, why don't you let Yusra join my office to do the job Belal was doing?"

General Brenman asked Colonel Walsh, "Is that okay with you, Walsh?"

"No objections, General."

"Ok, then send Yusra to the media office."

On the same night, Andrew was released from the command in Baghdad and ordered to join a convoy going to Haditha, one hundred and sixty miles northwest of Baghdad.

All the way to Haditha, Andrew was thinking about his brother. *Didn't Jonathan deserve to let his family know what happened to him after he was lost? Didn't Jonathan deserve to tell his parents that he tried, even as a child, to send them a message of love and a cry for help on a small piece of paper showing their pictures? Didn't Jonathan deserve that his family knows that he was brave and that he died for what he believed was right?* The answer for all those questions looked like no, no, and no. Andrew remembered Dr Bustani's words: *It looks like this family was selected by destiny to experience the suffering of all its generation.* Involuntarily, he found himself completing, "*It looks like Jonathan was selected to carry his part of suffering to the grave.*"

In Haditha, Andrew was assigned to a room with three other privates, Jesse Bennett from Virginia, Shawn Foster from North Dakota, and Randy Wood from South Dakota. He was welcomed by his roommates, who knew that he had been transferred against his will and tried to make life easier for him, but it wasn't easy. Andrew was in a kind of fugue state; he was incommunicative, stupefied, and stunned. He would receive his orders, comply with, and execute them in an almost robotic manner. He gave the impression that he wasn't living; he was just going through the motions. He was thinking all the time about the mission that had been aborted one step from the end. He couldn't shake the feeling that he would meet his brother in Seattle and that he owed him an explanation.

Andrew also was thinking all the time about Yusra. His love for her was real, deep, and sincere, as much as his suffering. Yusra was his love, his happiness, and his dream for the future. Yusra was his daily dose of joy just by seeing her. His week used to start on Monday and to end on Monday; the days between just served to fill the space, and now he had no Monday, he had nothing to see and nothing to wait for. Time for Andrew in Haditha was the worst possible; he was far from everything he loved, he was far from photography, the art he loved and chose to make his life, he was far from Adams and Belal, the two friends he had met in the middle of the war, and he was far from Yusra, the love he couldn't resist and that defeated all the barriers, ignored language, ethnicity, religion and that was stronger than bullets and spoke louder than cannons. Andrew was alone, isolated, and unhappy. It was impossible for him to cope with the loss of Yusra. Life without her was empty, static, and meaningless, the nights long and lonely, the days hard and violent.

Within a few days, Andrew had learned that life in Haditha was much more agitated than in Baghdad. The level of guerilla activity in the region was very intense and aggressive, and so was the troops' response. Andrew was warned by his roommates to be very careful and never leave the compound alone. He had the opportunity to confirm that by himself. The guerilla attacks and ambushes were more frequent and elaborate, and consequently the number of causalities was higher than in Baghdad.

On 10 November, he received a surprising visit. He was summoned to the office of Captain Paul Woodrich, commander of 3/1 Kilo Company, 3rd Platoon. Arriving there, he was surprised by the presence of Mr Adams. It was a joyful moment for Andrew. He hugged Adams and thanked him for coming. Captain Paul left the office, saying, "Since the talk will be about photography, I am going out. I'll be back soon."

Once the captain was gone, Adams pulled an envelope from his pocket and gave it to Andrew, saying, "This is a letter from Yusra. Keep it to read later. I don't know if you will be able to answer. Maybe, on my next visit, I can help."

When Andrew asked about Yusra, Adams said, "I am sorry to tell you, but she is not happy. She looks like a wilting flower. I am sad for you and for her. The worst thing is that nothing can be done. Maybe now it is impossible, but in the future, we can try with Brenmann."

A few minutes later, Woodrich came back, Adams left, and Andrew ran back to his room and started reading:

Andrew

It is now 21 days without seeing you, without talking to you or listening to your voice. It is now 21 days without appreciating your smile or feeling the joy in your eyes. It is now 21 days without "Hi, Yusra, good to see you."

"But you saw me yesterday."

"It is good to see you every day."

That was our good morning every day, that was what we dreamed every night for tomorrow, and now we are living without good morning, without tomorrow and without hope, joy, or inspiration.

One day I told you that we are having all the odds and hindrances against us, and that our love is impossible, and now I am learning every minute that what is impossible is living without you. I miss your smile shining into my day, and I miss your words warming my heart. I miss your love giving me a reason to live, a cause to keep going, and a purpose to continue fighting for what I believe in. It is now 21 days without night, dream, or tomorrow, 21 days of a life that is worthless, because life is meaningless when you awake and don't know what to do with your day, since there is no day without you.

It is now 21 days since you left, since my world stopped moving, since my days stopped on that Friday you left, and since Saturday never arrived, because without you there is no Saturday, there is no world and there is no life. I know now how much I love you, and that our love is huge, real, and overwhelming. I do not care where you were born; I do care about the depth of your feelings. I do not care what the tint of your eyes is; I do care about the colour of your soul. I don't care which language you speak; I do care that you say that you love me in any language you know. I love you and I do not care from where you came; I do care that you are going with me.

Andrew, I spent all my life watching my brother suffering from his illness, from his isolation, from his weaknesses. I saw him, in his last days, lying in bed, with eyes fixed on the door, desperate to see his father coming through carrying his remedy, and I saw my brother begging for a pinch of air to stay alive. But the medicine never arrived, and he couldn't have his nip of air and he died, just because he was born here.

Andrew, I spent more than half of my life going through suffering, pain, and agony. I watched people starving for a tiny portion of food, and I saw people dying from lack of food. I watched people pleading for medicine to relieve their pain, and I saw people dying because they never found medicine. I grew up learning to accept the little and to nurture the fear. I spent more than half of my life cultivating the feeling that we do not deserve more than what was given to us, which was, and still, nothing.

I spent more than half of my life missing the smiles on the faces around me, and looking for hope, promise, or dreams. Then I discovered after years of exhaustive searching that we have no right at all, just because we were born here. So, I understood that we were struck off the list of humanity, and if I had been born here, all that I have to do is to keep waiting to die here.

Suddenly, one day you entered the Sergeant's office. No one will believe it, but I can swear, I saw you on top of a white horse. You came in like a ray of the sun, picked me up on the horse and floated in the air to your place. Too bad the distance was so short. It wasn't only in the sergeant's office that you entered, you entered into my life, into my heart, and into my soul, and you entered into my dreams, my hopes and my way of life. Since that day, life has never been the same. Since that day, the waters started to run in the rivers strong and undulating. Since that day, the heat began to fill the ray of the sun, warming the heart and the spirit. Since that day I suddenly discovered that I still have a soul, that I have feeling and that I have the right to love. I even dreamed to be loved.

Since that day, living for me was to see you in the morning, to stay with you all day, and to dream of you all the night. Since that day, living for me was to love you, even knowing that our path was replete with spikes, hurdles, and barriers. I knew that our way was full of fear, fire, and danger, but I decided to go forward, because without you I wouldn't have any life at all. My life was, is, and always will be loving you. And now, I am alone, my day is empty and senseless, my night is long and tearful. Suddenly, I found myself cut off from my yesterday, ripped from my tomorrow, jailed in my day without hope or expectations. I used to ask myself, could I have been born to suffer, watching my brother dying for a pinch of air, watching my father struggling to find food to feed his family, and watching my mother crying for not finding a remedy for her chronic pain? Now I wonder if I was born to suffer your absence after giving colour to my life and helping me discover something I did not now before—happiness?

And now, I am without you, without the colour, without the light, and without knowing what I am living for. Should I wait for you? Could I dream of seeing you again? Could that be the end? Still, I am able to say that I love you more than anything else, including my own life. I love you and I will love you while my heart is beating, while the blood in my veins is running, and while my soul still remains. Please, Andrew, never forget that.

It is not just about missing someone
It is the same feeling that everything else is gone
The brightness of the stars, the blue of the sky
The road under the feet in the middle of the run
It is about you, and you are the only one

* * *

It is not just about loving you or not
It is about living and without you I don't
It is about expecting you coming
Feeling you leaving
Having tomorrow to wait for
And yesterday to remember
It is about life, and life without you I can't

* * *

It is not just about getting together anyway
It is about having the sun
Shining in my soul every day
Seeing the blue deep in the ocean
Feeling the green in the field
The sweetness of the smile of a child
It is about me, And for me
You are the only way

I love you
Yusra

Chapter 19

Andrew's transfer to Haditha completely changed Yusra's life. She had no happiness, she had no inspiration, she had no life, and what was worst, she had no peace. Anbar Province was the most violent and aggressive district against the American troops in all Iraq. The news about the struggle in 2005 was scary and alarming. By the time Andrew was sent to Haditha, the violence of the confrontations between American troops and insurgents had reached alarming levels.

The year 2005 began in Anbar already bleeding. The Second Battle of Fallujah, which had been officially declared ended on 23 December 2004, was still running in all its burning and brutal effects. The battle was the most violent and heaviest confrontation and urban combat U.S. Marines and army soldiers had been involved in since the Vietnam War.

The problem was aggravated because the Commanding General of the Multi-National Force in Iraq and the Iraqi government had conflicting ideas about the nature of the situation in Anbar and the strategy for the confrontation. The commanding general considered that the real problem was pro-insurgent foreign fighters coming across the Syrian border and believed that the Marines should take over the job of clearing and securing the Western Euphrates River Valley. In contrast, the Iraqi government assumed that the biggest problem facing Iraq was the car bombing in the area, which was why the Iraqi partner wanted to concentrate on Baghdad's neighbourhoods where the vehicles were assembled.

At any rate, it was clear that any solution for the problems in the Western Euphrates River Valley must start in Fallujah. During the first months of the campaign, the army relinquished command of the Anbar governorate to the Marines. The city started to fall under the influence of insurgents, which led to an increase of violence against the American presence. The outcome was the complete withdrawal of troops from the city, a decision that was never absorbed by the high command of the troops in Iraq. Soon, on 3 April 2004, the 1st Marine

Expeditionary Force received a written command from the Joint Task Force, ordering offensive operations against Fallujah.

The so-called First Battle of Fallujah, planned to curb violence in the city, started on 4 April 2004. The Marine Expeditionary Force launched a major assault, with 2,000 troops, in an attempt to retake the city. After innumerable rounds of air bombardments targeting suspected insurgent positions, the Marines started their move to take over the city. Scout snipers were positioned as a fundamental element of the strategy, averaging thirty-one kills apiece during the battle. The resistance in Fallujah was beyond the expectation of the Marines; however, the rebels in Fallujah held on and the fight was brutal, street by street. The troops needed three days of fierce combat to gain control over a small part of the city.

The high command also confronted a huge problem when members of the Iraqi Governing Council (IGC), the provisional government of Iraq, which was formed on 13 July 2003, protested against the operation, arguing that the American attacks were killing civilians, not insurgents. Soon, the protests were so vehement that they considered these operations by the Americans unacceptable and illegal. On 1 May 2004, the United States withdrew its forces from Fallujah, admitting that the result was an operational failure. The bitter results of the Fallujah operation generated the Second Battle of Fallujah in November that year.

As was expected, after the withdrawal of the troops from Fallujah in May, insurgent strength and control began to grow to such an extent that by September 2004, the city was completely dominated by insurgents. This situation could not be tolerated by the command, especially by the Marines. The bitter results of April's battle were straining the souls of the occupying forces, and the call for new confrontation was growing lauder. On 24 September, the coalition formed by American, Iraqi, and English troops started preparations for the Second Battle of Fallujah.

When the Second Battle of Fallujah was planned, the shadows of the first battle were everywhere, in the mind of the command, in the preparation of the soldiers, and in the tactics employed during the battle. The high command decided to apply the shock and awe doctrine, in other words, crushing power and stunning displays of fire and human force that did not allow the enemy any chance to be aware of the battlefield and extinguish its will to fight. For the Second Battle of Fallujah, the U.S.-led coalition totalled about 13,500 combatants, supported by 3rd Marine Aircraft, Navy, and Air Force and U.S. Army field artillery battalions, as well as sniper elements. The number of insurgents in Fallujah oscillated between 1,000 and 3,000. It was known that some guerrillas, fighters, and their leaders fled the city before the attack.

The coalition's move on 8 November was preceded by intense shelling and air strikes that hammered the city heavily and repeatedly, forcing about 300,000 civilians to abandon the city. The troops faced fierce resistance and had to deal with concealed sniper positions and booby traps. The urban fight was brutal, and the coalition needed several days of street fighting to secure the central area of the city. The battle continued against pockets of resistance installed by the insurgents, extending the battle for several more weeks.

Military operations ended formally on 23 December 2004, with the declaration of the coalition victory, but by all accounts, it was a victory that no one was ready to celebrate. The insurgents in Fallujah were largely destroyed, but at a very high cost in lives. The fight in Fallujah proved to be the bloodiest confrontation of the war in Iraq involving American troops. About 110 coalition forces were killed and nearly 600 wounded in the battle, approximately 3,000 insurgents were killed or captured, and a huge number of civilians, considered to be in the thousands, were killed.

The wounds left after the Second Battle of Fallujah continued to spout blood and hatred all over the country. The rebels, who supposedly were mostly wrecked by the attack, changed tactics and multiplied the small-scale strikes across Iraq, and that was the colour that tainted the face of 2005. By the spring of 2005, the number of incursions was extremely high, and the results were troubling. The modus operandi of the relationship between the troops and rebels in Anbar was characterised by attacks planned by the troops and retaliation from the insurgents using IEDs and car bombs. Operation Matador, on 7 May, which intended to eradicate the rebels from the city of Ubaydi, ended short of its goals because the insurgents apparently fled the city before the attack and returned to it afterwards.

The high command then began a series of operations in Anbar with names like New Market, Sword, Hunter, Zoba, Spear, River Gate, and Iron Fist. The fiercest combat occurred in August during Operation Quick Strike conducted by the Marines in Haditha. The result of the operation was tragic; in two days of combat, twenty Marines were killed, six snipers were ambushed, and fourteen Marines lost their lives on 3 August when their vehicle hit a mine outside of

Haditha. By October, more Americans had been killed in Anbar than anywhere else in Iraq.

In this turmoil, Andrew was introduced to the facts of everyday life in Anbar, especially around Fallujah and Haditha, explosions, deaths, raids, and IEDs, which were also echoed in Yusra's heart. Every day, she received the information and reported it to Adams. Many times, tears hindered her from reading the report or completing the information. At the end of October, Adams asked her if she would prefer to be relocated to another department, but she promptly refused, saying, "I am suffering terribly by the news that comes from there, but I would die if I didn't know about Andrew."

On Friday, 18 November 2005, about 2:00 p.m., Yusra got the huge break she was waiting for.

Mr Adams called her to his office. "Yusra," he told her, "we are going to Haditha tomorrow. General Brenmann needs a report about the situation in the Anbar area, especially Haditha and Fallujah. We will be having breakfast with the troops at oh seven hundred. Can you be here at oh four hundred?"

"I will do my best; I will be here," she said.

"Okay, try not to be late. It is a military action, so timing is vital. I will ask the driver to pick you up at oh three fifteen. Is that good for you?"

"Yes, it is. I will be waiting for him. Thank you, Mr Adams."

Yusra couldn't believe, will she be able to see Andrew, will they be able to talk, is that true. It was too much for her to believe, it was too much happiness for her to bare, she wanted to dance, to sing, and to do anything to tell the world how much joy she was feeling. Navigating in her contentment, she went back to the very first moment she saw Andrew, the first time they went to Al-Zawraa Park. Yusra shivered when she reached the moment he touched her hand, and went all red when she remembered that she liked it, suddenly she caught herself asking, *will he be able to do that again*? Yusra wasn't able to sleep for just one second, she was anxious, she was tens and she worried. She was fearful that something changes or something odd happens, she kept looking at the clock each fifteen minutes, then each five minutes and then she kept her eyes stuck on the clock all the time.

At exactly 3:15 on Saturday morning, 19 November 2005, Yusra was at the door of her house watching the driver arriving exactly on time. "Miss Kaidany, are you ready?"

"Yes, I am," Yusra answered and jumped in the car.

They arrived at the gate of the Green Zone eight minutes before 4:00 a.m. To their surprise, they were stopped at the gate by the guards because they did not have permission to enter the zone at night. One officer approached the car and questioned the driver. "Do you have special authorisation to cross the gate before oh six hundred?"

The driver stated that he hadn't. Yusra, in despair, asked the officer, "What can we do now?"

The officer asked for the identification card of both and said, "I need to locate the officer in command and request permission."

It wasn't easy to find the officer in command and to get the permission. It took about twelve minutes, time enough for Yusra to see Adams leaving on the other side of the gate. Yusra stayed where she was for a while without knowing what to do. She needed to go to Haditha. It would be her chance to see Andrew and to know about him. She couldn't just stay waiting; she needed to see him. She knew it wouldn't be easy, plus she remembered Adams warning her against meeting Andrew in Haditha. "It would not be very wise."

But she didn't care, she wouldn't miss this chance for any reason. "The hell with all the wisdom of the world, what is wise in the way that we are living now? What is wise in killing each other? I need to see Andrew, to be sure he is okay. That is the only wise thing for me now."

Yusra didn't know if she was talking to herself, the walls, or no one at all. She didn't know if she was speaking or if she was delusional, but she didn't care. All that she wanted at that moment was to know about Andrew, to meet Andrew, to see Andrew. Yusra turned to the driver and asked, "I need to go to Haditha. Can you take me to Haditha?"

The soldier answered immediately, "Sorry, I can't do that. I can't go out of Baghdad."

In tears, Yusra begged him, "I need to go there. Please, help me."

The soldier was touched and said, "I can drive you to the control point on the 97, close to the airport. There you can find a ride. That is all that I can do."

Yusra accepted immediately. "Fine, take me there, please."

The driver added, "Then give me a couple minutes to get the permission to leave now."

Minutes later, the driver came back with permission. Yusra was in misery inside the car. Soon, they were going along July 14th Avenue heading to

Damascus Street. Forty minutes later, they spotted the control point. The driver stopped the car and said, "Sorry, Ms Kaidany, I can't be seen there."

Yusra jumped out of the car and said, "That is good for me. Thank you."

She walked in the direction of the point carefully. Soon, one of the soldiers asked her to stop and to identify herself. When Yusra presented her documentation, the soldier asked her, "What are you doing here at this time?"

Yusra answered, "As you can see, I work for the media office. My superior is already on his way to Haditha. He will be waiting for me there."

The soldier checked in the office and came back to confirm, "Yes, Mr Philippe William Adams left the control twenty-three minutes ago. Now, how can I help you?"

Yusra pointed to a white taxi stopped for check and said, "If this car is going to Haditha, I can get a ride with them."

The soldier said, "It is better you talk to them."

Yusra walked to the car, which was occupied by four people, the driver and three young men.

She gets closer to the driver asking. "Good morning, are you going to Haditha?"

The driver confirmed, "Yes, mam, those young men will join the school there."

"Please, allow me to join you, I need urgently to go to Haditha, there are people waiting for me there, I can pay for the ride."

"No, mam, you are most welcome, you don't have to pay nothing, their parents already paid."

The driver asked the young man in the passenger seat to move to the back seat of the car and invited Yusra, "Please, mam, get in the car."

Yusra told the officer and left the control point heading to Haditha.

It was 7:00 a.m. when Adams arrived at the Marine base in Haditha. He was received by Captain Paul Woodrich, who wished him good luck on his mission, and offered a rapid overview of the situation in the area. "Mr Adams, you are most welcome in Haditha. The situation here is very hostile; clashes between our troops and the insurgents are very frequent, with significant loss of lives on both sides. We are here to protect the Haditha dam. If this structure were demolished, we would have a huge energy problem. This region is a stronghold of the Sunnis; almost ninety percent of the people here are against the coalition forces. That makes this area one of the fiercest places against the troops since the beginning of the war."

The talk was abruptly interrupted by an enormous explosion, the two men were almost pulled out of their chairs; one of Captain Woodrich aides entered the office to report, "Sir, the 3rd Battalion, 1ˢᵗ Marines (3/1) resupply convoy was hit on the way to the base."

Captain Woodrich ordered, "Get a car for us immediately."

Arriving at the place of the explosion, they confronted a terrifying scene.

A squad from 3/1 Kilo Company, 3rd Platoon, which was on a resupply convoy, had been targeted by an IED, composed of 155mm artillery shells and explosive-filled propane tanks. The Humvee was smashed by the explosion, and the driver was killed instantly. The two other soldiers in the car were thrown out of the vehicle with severe wounds. The scene met by Adams and Woodrich was horrendous. Blood was everywhere, there were wounded soldiers, damaged vehicles, and some still-burning fire points. Close to the shattered Humvee, they saw Lt. Patrick R. Thomaz and Sergeant David Murphy, who had been in command of the squad. Mr Adams also saw that Andrew was close to them taking shots of the scene.

Out of the darkness, they saw a white car coming on the road in their direction. Sergeant Murphy moved in the direction of the car and ordered the driver to stop, then he ordered all the passengers to get out of the car. They were four men and a woman. Andrew who was close to the car was stunned, he couldn't believe in what he was seeing, *is it Yusra? Is that possible? Could be Yusra? Yes, it is Yusra, must be her, no one is like her, the world has only one Yusra. God produces only one Yusra. Yusra you are here, you came for me.* Andrew was pulled out of his thoughts by the terrifying sound of a blast of bullets

Without a single word, sergeant Murphy gunned all the passengers of the car down. A huge scream ripped the sky.

"Não, God não, Yusra não."

Adams immediately recognised the voice; it was Andrew, who began running in the direction of the white car. The sergeant, moving his gun in the direction of Andrew, ordered him, "Private, back to position."

But Lt Thomaz ordered firmly, "Stop, Sergeant."

At the side of the car, Andrew bent down and embraced Yusra, sobbing uncontrollably. The pain was unbearable and excruciating; the bullets in her body were burning in his soul and his heart. She blinked her eyes and looked at him, trying to smile. Andrew screamed, "Yusra, please don't die, I love you, I need you, I can't live without you, please God, don't hurt me again, I have suffered enough, please don't leave me alone."

With great difficulty, she managed to say, "I will never leave you. Just wait for me. I will be back, I will be a butterfly, and you will be my flower. I will be a drop of water, and you will be the river. Even if I go, I will be yours forever." Slowly, Yusra closed her eyes. The scream coming from Andrew's soul ripped the sky.

"No, Yusra, no, please don't go."

Lt. Thomaz ordered two soldiers to arrest Andrew and hold him in his car. Then he turned to Sergeant Murphy and pointed to three houses on the other side of the road.

"Take those houses," he ordered.

The sergeant immediately gathered his squad and gave instructions to 'shoot first and ask questions later.' The first house was cleared by the Marines the way they had been trained to do it. First, they tossed in frags and then sprayed the houses with a machine gun. After that, the soldiers entered the house; everybody was down. The same strategy was followed in the second and third houses, bringing the killings to twenty-four Iraqis, including women, children, and an amputee man in a wheelchair. Mission concluded, the sergeant and his squad reported back to the lieutenant.

"Mission completed; houses are clean, sir," said Sargent Murphy.

"Send the bodies to public hospital."

The bodies of the Iraqis were loaded in two American Humvees and transported to the local hospital in Haditha.

Back at the base, the turmoil was immense. People were running back and forth. The high command of the base called an immediate meeting. The discussion quickly turned contentious, producing at the end a kind of report that were later transferred to the headquarters Marine base, in the northern corner of Ramadi. On 20 November, the Marines issued a press release from Camp Blue Diamond in Ramadi reporting the deaths of a U.S. Marine and fifteen civilians due to the explosion of a roadside bomb and an attack by Iraqi insurgents. The report of the Marines was disputed by human rights organisations and the American media.

Chapter 20

On 15 December, Adams was back in Haditha to learn about Andrew. When questioned, Captain Woodrich said, "Mr Adams, we are about to decide that now, but unfortunately, it looks like it will end in a Court Martial."

"But why?" Adams asked. "The situation can be decided administratively without a court-martial punishment, I mean through Article 15 of the Uniform Code of Military Justice, non-judicial punishment—NJP."

"Not with the case report offered by Sergeant Murphy."

"What is in the report?"

"Insubordination, Fraternisation with Iraqi, Officer Misconduct, not to mention the violation of 158 U.S. Code § 3591(c, d)."

Stunned, Adams asked, "What the hell is that?"

"Intentionally participated in an act, contemplating that the life of a participant in the offence, and the victim could die as a direct result of the act; or intentionally and specifically engaged in an act knowing that the act created a grave risk of death to a person."

Adams asked, "Which person? It was only him in the line of fire."

"The person was him, and he is still a military personal."

Adams was feeling deeply saddened and angry by the situation in the same time. After a couple minutes, he asked, "Captain, when do you think that we will know the decision?"

"I don't believe that we will have this information this year. It is not a high priority matter, maybe by March next year."

"My I have permission to see him?" Adams asked.

"I will send somebody to drive you there," Woodrich said

In the room, the two men sat looking at each other without speaking for a long time. They had feelings, they had emotions, they had sadness, despondency, and tears, but they had no words. With great difficulty, Adams gathered enough strength to say, "Andrew, we are not done yet. You know that I will fight for you with all my power. I will not stand by watching life hurt you once more."

Andrew was far away; he wasn't in the room, he wasn't in the base, and he wasn't in Iraq. Andrew wasn't in the world anymore; he was just passing through, like a cloud floating over the earth unaware what is happening below. Adams tried again. "Andrew, I will do my best to help. I will not leave you alone. We still have space to work in."

Finally, Andrew moved his head and whispered, almost voicelessly, "There is nothing to be done, Mr Adams. It is all finished; I am already gone."

"No, you are not. You are still young and have a life to live."

"I have nothing. Half of my life went with Jonathan, and the other half left with Yusra. What can life be for me now?"

"Andrew, you can't lose hope. Things can be fixed."

"One day she said, 'Some things, good or bad, when they happen, they are forever. Nothing can be done, it is forever,' Mr Adams."

Adams paused, then he told Andrew, "I have another message for you from Belal, he is very devastated by what had happened, he put his feeling in a new poem and ask me to deliver it to you; he knows you like poetry."

Adams took the paper from his pocket and offered it to him. Andrew opened the paper and started reading.

Just Terrorists

While we are enjoying our meritorious rest
While we are delighted with the beauty of the sunset
While we are saying nothing and doing enthusiastically, the same thing,
a little terrorist in Baghdad is being killed.

* * *

While we are driving our fancy cars
With tanks stuffed with oil from the Middle East
While we are smoking our Cuban cigars
Watching our favourite game with passion and heat
Another little terrorist in Kabul is being killed

* * *

While we are enjoying the last Hollywood motion picture
Drinking cooks and dreaming with big mac
Lying on the beach, excited by the ocean
Playing with the water, going forward, coming back
More little terrorists in Palestine are being killed
Thousands of little terrorists somewhere are being killed
Millions of terrorists everywhere have been killed
Sleeping, dreaming, playing, or praying
Pure like the sun, beautiful like flowers
Doesn't matter
Caesar said they are all terrorists, and they have to be killed.

Andrew replied, while passing something to him. "I also have a message for you: pictures of terrorists being killed."

Looking at what Andrew had put in his hand, he hissed, "The memory card of the camera, how did you get this?"

"I pulled it out of the camera before it was confiscated."

"And what do you want me to do with it?"

"You are a journalist; do your job."

"Can you imagine how much this can hurt you?"

"More than what has already been done? Please let the world say goodbye to her."

Adams wondered, "You mean Yusra? Were you able to get her picture?"

Andrew answered through tears. "I must have gotten a pic of her. I was taking pictures when the sergeant stopped the car and ordered the passengers out, I realised that it was Yusra. Suddenly, he started shooting, that was when I stopped, but, at that time, she was falling to the ground."

Andrew lost completely the control of his emotions. Adams was devastated, he tried to give some support to Andrew, but it was difficult, he was as touched as Andrew.

After a while, Adam said, "I should tell you that my newspaper started an investigation about Haditha. Should I add the pictures to the case? Please think thoroughly before you give your okay."

"Mr Adams, what is left for me to think about? Sometimes the worst thing in life is to live. Someone has to talk for those who can't talk for their self."

"It is terrible to see you feeling this way. I hope to see you soon."

In March 2006, Adams launched his bombshell. That was when *Moment Magazine* published his article with the results of its investigation into what he called the 'Haditha Killings.' The article was shocking and disturbing. Adams stated that all the versions offered by the Marines were false, denying that there was any kind of interaction or military action in this case, but, for him, it was merely shooting people. The article reported that, in retaliation for the death of one soldier when a Marine convoy hit a roadside bomb earlier that day, the First Marine Division killed twenty-four unarmed civilians in Haditha, Iraq, on 19 November 2005. The report mentioned that one of the victims was a seventy-six-year-old amputee in a wheelchair, while other victims included children and women. Adams harshly criticised the attempt to disguise the atrocity as ordinary and unavoidable results.

The effect of the publicity was immediate and effective. Since the facts stated in the article conflicted with the official report issued by the troops, a criminal investigation was initiated on 9 March by the Navy. On 19 March, it was formally admitted that the Marines killed fifteen civilians. At that time, several official investigations began to determine the responsibility of the commanders under the U.S. War Crimes Act. The Iraqi government started its own investigation. The first reports about the results of the investigations appeared on 2 June, revealing that twenty-four unarmed Iraqis were killed by twelve members of Kilo Company. The investigation also blamed the rules of engagement established by the Bush administration, which encouraged the indiscriminate carnage of civilians, carelessly called, 'collateral damage.'

Finally, in December 2006, the American army, based on the investigation related to the Haditha incident, filed charges against eight of its members. The charges included unpremeditated murder, negligent homicide, assault, and false statements. Charges of unpremeditated murder of twelve persons were filed against the squad leader, who had to respond to the killing of six individuals during combat engagement. Commanders were also charged with dereliction of duty, obstruction of justice, and making a false statement.

Another storm burst when the Haditha incident became public on 9 March 2006. This time, it was inside the Marine base in Haditha. All the members of the high chain of command were enraged by the article, especially by the picture that occupied the central position of the article and was featured on the first page of the magazine. The picture showed the white car with doors opened, the sergeant with his gun in hand and five bodies on the ground. The photo was shockingly revealing. There was no difficulty guessing to whom the credit should go, and the decision was issued rapidly: "Court Martial for Cpl Andrew McCoolen, Charges: Insubordination, Fraternisation with Iraqi, Officer Misconduct, violation of 158 U.S. Code § 3591(c, d) and release of reserved information to external source," pointing as hard evidence the photo of the car, Sergeant Murphy and the victims lying on the ground.

On the second day, the general court martial received the Court Martial Data Sheet with its fifty-eight items completed. The trial was set for 13 March 2006. Andrew dismissed the free military attorney and refused to hire a civilian lawyer; the military judge ordered the presence of a military attorney as a defendant counsellor. Deliberations began on the fourteenth. The government offered evidence and the testimony of witnesses to corroborate a long list of accusations against Andrew, including release of reserved information, creating a grave risk of death to a person, Insubordination, Fraternisation, and Officer Misconduct. The panel deliberated for two hours. Meanwhile, the military judge addressed Andrew. "Once the members are back from the deliberations, the trial will terminate if you are acquitted of all accusations. Alternatively, if you are convicted of any offence, the court will determine your sentence. You still have the opportunity to present evidence in extenuation and mitigation of the offences of which you have been found guilty, that is, anything about the offence(s) or yourself you think the court should consider in settling your sentence. Do you understand these rights that you have?"

As he had done during the trial, Andrew remained silent, and he asked the counsellor to do the same.

On 25 March 2006, the verdict was published: According to U.S. Code; Title 10, Armed Forces; Subtitle A. General Military Law; Part II. Personnel.

Chapter 42. Uniform Code of Military Justice; Subchapter VIII. Sentences; Section 856. Art. 56. Sentencing. And considering the offences punishable under sections 880 & 881 of this title, the court determines:

1. Dishonourable discharge of the defendant, after serving the time imposed.
2. The court-martial imposes upon the defendant the sentence of confinement for six years and ten months, without eligibility for parole.

3. The prisoner must be transferred immediately to the United States Disciplinary Barracks on Fort Leavenworth, Kansas.

On 18 April, Meagan received a letter from Andrew.

Dear Meagan,

I am writing from the United States. I didn't tell you about my flight because you wouldn't have been able to see me. A special car from Leavenworth Penitentiary was waiting instead. I was sentenced to six years and ten months of incarceration, without eligibility for parole. I was accused of releasing a picture of some people that were killed in Haditha, I was send to Iraq to photograph the war and was convicted of photographing the war. Please don't be sad, don't cry, and don't have any doubt about my character. I never did anything wrong; I never betrayed my country, and I always honoured the memory of my brother who died defending America. I always regretted Jonathan's death, and now I wish I had the same destiny.

You might be anxious to know about Yusra, I am sorry to tell you that she is dead; she was shot in Haditha. She was in the car with the other people that appear in the picture released and that earned me a prison sentence. I was there, I saw her die, and I couldn't do anything to help her, I wasn't able to save her life, to tell the killer that Yusra never was enemy, and never did anything to harm anybody. I had no chance to tell her killer that Yusra was peaceful, pure, and beautiful. Meagan, I lost Yusra for no cause and no reason, all the certitude I have is that I lost Yusra, that she is gone and forever, she is gone and with her, I lost what had remained with me after I lost Jonathan.

And now I am struggling trying to understand why? Why Jonathan had to die, why Yusra had to die, and why I still here feeling their absence like a fireball burning my heart and my soul.

Please tell Verona and take care of her.

Thank you, Andrew

Meagan was shocked. She tried desperately to reach Andrew on the phone, but it was impossible. The answer she always received was to be patient and to wait until he called her. She called Fort Leavenworth without success.

Meanwhile, she contacted Verona. "Verona, do you know anything about Andrew?"

Verona answered worriedly, "Why? What happened? Is he okay?"

Meagan replied, "I don't know. I received a terrible letter saying he is in prison."

Verona screamed, "What? When was that? Tell me what happened."

"I really don't know very much. I just received a letter, and he didn't give any details. I am trying to reach him, but it is really difficult."

"I will call the army; they will have to give me an explanation."

Verona called the same office that helped her when Andrew enlisted. She told them that she had lost contact with her son and begged them for help. Two hours later, an officer called her. "Ma'am, Mr McCoolen, Andrew is serving his time at the United States Disciplinary Barracks at Fort Leavenworth, Kansas."

That was enough to drive Verona crazy. Involuntarily, she called Meagan. "Meagan, what did he do? Why is he in prison? I need to know."

Meagan was also living the same agony, and it was only on 11 May, that she was able to reach Andrew in Fort Leavenworth. "Andrew, how are you? You can't imagine the agony we are living."

"Actually, I can. How are you, Meagan? How is mom?"

"She is in bad shape; we all are. Tell me what happened."

"I was considered guilty of military offences and sentenced to time in prison, afterword, I will be discharged from the army."

"Can we come to visit you?"

"No, Meagan. It is a long way for very little time. Please tell mom to wait for me. I don't want to be seen in prison. Thank you, Meagan." The call ended with both in tears.

On 25 January 2013, the last day of the jail time, early at the morning, Andrew was called from his prison cell and ordered to wear his military uniform, he was guided to the director office where two military officers were waiting for him. The highly ranked officer introduced himself, "Private Andrew, my name is Lieutenant Jamie Wiggin, I am here to proceed your dishonourable discharge from the army of the United States."

After reading the sentence, Lieutenant Wiggin concluded, "According to the order given by general court martial on 25 March 2006, based on the charges of or reprehensible behaviour against the military conduct, you are dishonourably discharged from the army of the United States with the forfeit all of benefits you would receive from your military service."

After the ceremony, Andrew was returned to his cell and advised to collect his belonging and be prepared to be released. On the afternoon Andrew was released, waiting for him were the cold, Adams, and a huge emptiness. Adams hugged him affectionately and said, "Now that this matter is definitely closed."

"What do you mean?" Andrew asked.

"The last two episodes were yesterday with Sergeant Murphy's sentencing and today with your release."

Amid Andrew's silence, Adams continued, "He got a rank reduction and pay cut, but no jail time. All the others were acquitted."

In the face of Andrew's silence, Adams asked, "What do you intend to do with your life now?"

"I really don't know; I need time to get my life back," replied Andrew.

"I can find a place for you as a photographer on the magazine."

"Thank you, Adams, it was a picture that sent me to prison for seven years. I need to find my own way. See you."

Adams wasn't able to hold back tears as he watched Andrew going away.

The End